BETRAYAL

1

It was another dismal Sunday morning for Shannon
Dobberty, the same old hangover filled with the usual guilt
and annoyance at how her life was panning out these days.
She was fast approaching 30 years old and still doing the
same stupid things as a decade previously. Only then,
being young and immature, she felt she could justify her
actions to some extent. Now it was different. She was
older and should be wiser. She wished she had behaved a
little better the night before, shown some maturity but
instead she had merrily consumed a carryout at home
before proceeding to the bar and knocking back a mixture
of drink including a cocktail or two. She was sure it was a
Bloody Mary that she had, but there was a Tequila or two
at some point also! Of course, it was meant to be a quiet,
civil evening in the house, a few drinks, a little music. She
laughed to herself as early afternoon yesterday she had
been considering a DVD of some description, perhaps a
chick flick or a comedy, but after polishing off a couple of
large glasses of white wine, one thing had lead to another
and before she knew it, she was in the pub carrying on with
the rest of the gang. She had no-one to blame but herself.
Once the drink was in, the wit was out and she cursed
herself for her lack of will power. The cocktail at the end
had been her downfall not to mention the cigarettes she
had insisted on having once she had seen a few others
indulge in her old habit. It seemed she had no problem
going without the nicotine during the week but come the
weekend and associated booze, she just couldn't resist a
wee draw. It wasn't that she was crazy about smoking but
whenever she spotted a couple of the others heading
outside, well, it just felt that the Nicotine was calling her
name. As soon as she had pulled on that first cigarette, for
some reason, the effect of the drink seemed to multiply.

Even the thought of smoking now was making her feel sick, she could still taste it in her mouth and smell it on her clothes. She felt like she could throw up, her stomach was heaving and suddenly she felt sweaty and ill. And so, there she was after puffing down on that stinking cigarette, dancing crazily around the sawdust-floored bar like some mad lunatic. She squirmed as she recalled doing her ancient party trick, acceptable when you are twenty, but perhaps not quite the done thing for a twenty-nine-year-old, trying to snare a proper, decent man. What normal minded bloke would regard her as a potential permanent partner when she was bending her joints for all to see, like she was in the middle of some Pilates class? She hadn't even realised she was double jointed until whilst watching some silly TV show one night, she had decided to try and copy the moves of one of the so-called celebrities who reckoned she was the country's finest ballerina. As this young girl performed her act to some atrocious soundtrack, Shannon decided she would give it a go and when she managed it, she couldn't resist the temptation to perform it again and again in front of whoever might be paying attention. And Shannon wanted attention. She craved it. She hated that she was so needy, but she felt she just couldn't help herself, the same way as she couldn't help getting completely hammered. Of course, it hadn't always been that way although she had always enjoyed a party and a few drinks but in the last while things had changed, she felt lost and no longer recognised herself. When she was drunk, she didn't care about anything or anyone, it gave her confidence. No inhibitions, no reservations, she was Shannon, an exhibitionist! She knew it wasn't real confidence but that didn't matter. It could have been worse, she supposed. At least she hadn't done anything stupid like saunter off with some half wit and head back to God knows where for a night of passion. That wasn't her style by any means, it never had been, but she recognised the need now to cut down on the booze otherwise at some point there would undoubtedly be consequences. Weirdly when she was in that inebriated state, she didn't give a hoot about consequences, she thought she was invincible!

Enough was enough, she thought, as she lazily crawled out of bed and waded into the bathroom for a shower. The room was a mess, clothes scattered everywhere, makeup smeared on her pillow, shoes lying the length and breadth of the room from last night, when she was trying to work out what to wear. No point worrying about that now, she decided as she stepped over what looked like a bit of food. Oh god, what on earth was on that plate? She didn't know whether she was going to puke or just collapse in a heap, but she didn't fancy either option. Perhaps a spell in the shower would wake her up and she would feel better afterwards.

2

Flicking on the bathroom light, she sauntered over to the mirror and peered at the reflection that greeted her. It was not good, a sorry sight for sure. She cursed herself for not removing her make up the night before, although was somewhat consoled that her new Clinique foundation was perfect, as though it had just been freshly applied. Her eyes told a different story however, with the black mascara and eyeliner forming their own little river of darkness down her pale, tired face. She knew she looked alright for her age; quite young looking with her dark blue eyes and jet-black hair, but the aging process had begun its journey, she assessed miserably, as she carefully examined the faint lines around the sides of her eyes. Crow's feet – the first sign of aging, she thought. She cleansed her face, before quickly peeling off last night's clothes which she tossed on the floor. They stank of booze and stale smoke. It was disgusting. She stepped under the shower, and immediately held her head upwards to the water as if waiting for a miracle that would see her feeling right as rain with immediate effect. Then she began scrubbing her skin vigorously with her beloved body brush and her special molten brown shower gel. She was meticulous about body brushing because whilst she didn't have much cellulite, she was determined to take every preventative measure she could. She had read that body brushing; particularly dry body brushing was great for the circulation and for breaking up the fatty deposits that caused cellulite. Probably a load of ole crap, she thought. Another gimmick to make women like her think that she could honestly prevent it by purchasing all these silly, expensive creams. I mean, what really was the difference in all the lotions anyway. Her mum always used Simple soap and she had perfect skin but then her Aunt used Clarins and really, she couldn't tell any difference except in price. Well, if Simple was good enough for her mum Simple was good enough for her. She really ought to stop buying those silly magazines because they just highlighted all the issues she wanted to ignore. The same articles were covered weekly by various magazines only in different ways. There were always photographs of so-called celebrities plastered all over the front covers and throughout the pages inside, looking impossibly fit and gorgeous. Of course, there were those that had work done (70% she was sure), a helping hand courtesy of the surgeon himself, but she would never resort to those measures, not that she could afford them anyway. Maybe if she won the lottery it would be a different story. Chance though would be a fine thing for she had never won anything in her entire life. She knew herself that she shouldn't be influenced by the pictures in the glossies, but it fascinated her how good some of these celebrities looked and now with her 30th birthday looming, she was determined to start looking after herself a little better. It was time to exert a tad more discipline, certainly in terms of her diet. She needed to cut down on her chocolate intake for a start, but above all else, the demon drink and the greasy carry outs which consumed her weekends. Having shampooed and conditioned her hair she grabbed a large, fluffy towel from the rail and wrapped herself in it before stepping on to the scales to check her weight. She always did this, morning and night and whilst it was daft and obsessive, she couldn't help herself. Funny how some girls she knew never weighed themselves, preferring to assess their weight by the fit of their clothes. But no, that wasn't for her. She monitored it religiously. That way she could rein it in if she thought she had put on a few pounds. It seemed this morning that despite the huge meal she had eaten and the copious amounts of alcohol she had knocked back, there was no change. It occurred to her then that she had been violently sick. It was no wonder her stomach was churning. She felt terrible. Her head was pounding like a drum, her throat felt red raw and worst of all, she was having difficulty remembering how the hell she had got home, except that somehow she had actually managed it, so that was comforting if nothing else, she thought. A loud rap on the bathroom door startled her as she clutched the towel around her tightly.

'Shannon, you okay in there?' she heard.

'Yes, coming now Mel,' she quickly replied, recognising the chirpy voice of her flatmate. She unlocked the door and re-entered the bedroom, relieved to see Mel, who hopefully could fill in a few gaps from the previous night. Obviously, Mel must have seen her home safely and she was extremely grateful for that. She wondered if Mel's boyfriend Tom had stayed over and felt embarrassed that she had no memory of leaving the club or coming home. However, she was much too ill to focus any energy on her drunken actions now or on who may or may not have witnessed them.

She wandered over to her closet and picked out her favourite replay jeans and a white top as Mel stood, arms folded, watching her intently. Shannon looked at her and laughed, 'What's up with you?' she asked, an uncertain smile starting to form.

'What's up with me, Shan? What's up with you and why is a certain Mr Mc Glynn lying sprawled out on your sofa again? What is going on with you two? I thought you were just friends but there he is, as ever, stuck to your sofa like a loving blister. For goodness sake, you have even given him his own key. Sure, he might as well move in.'

Shannon sighed. Pete was her best friend; she loved him to pieces – as a mate, nothing more and nothing less and she was quite certain he felt the same. He had never said anything to indicate anything otherwise although occasionally she had noticed him look at her in an odd sort of way, like there was something he might have wanted to say, but he never did. She had met him when she was a young girl at the local youth club where she had grown up. She had lived for those weekly Friday evenings when they sometimes talked shyly to each other. He was good looking with his dark eyes and floppy hair and was popular with the girls, who all fancied him. He never seemed bothered though; preferring to keep to himself whilst ignoring their silly giggles. He found them mainly irritating and immature. He never participated in any of the activities that took place at the club, he just seemed to hang around, on his own. When her dad had gained a Principalship in a well renowned all boys' school in the city, she was devastated. Of course, she was only eleven years old, but the family relocated, and she was heartbroken. Her parents had no idea of course why she was so upset, and she knew better than to tell them as they would only ask questions and want to know all about the subject of her distress. There was nothing to tell anyway. She was an eleven-year-old, 'in fantasy world', a great but completely unrealistic imagination, she felt that she was his princess, buying her sweets and coke and chatting to her, whilst avoiding and showing no interest in anyone else. He always had loads of pocket money and she remembered saving her own for two weeks just to be able to buy him something back. When the time came for the big move to the city they had awkwardly bid each other goodbye with promises to keep in touch with the odd letter here and there but eventually the contact petered out and it was several years before she heard from him again in an unexpected message via face book. It was funny and weird but nice to see his name pop up after so long. She was thrilled and quickly accepted his message request and after just a few weeks of exchanging news, they arranged to meet up and when they did get together in a little internet café in the city centre they clicked from the start, but it was apparent to her that the romantic notions she had possessed as a child were no

8

more. At one time in those early days when they had reconnected, he had admitted a desire to bring their companionship to another level, but she had insisted that it would be pointless to potentially ruin a good friendship and that was the end of that. It was a bit awkward and mildly uncomfortable, but he had brought it up after they had been in the pub a few hours, so she wasn't quite sure if he meant it entirely. It was never brought up again and she was positive that he was just as glad about that as she was. Still, she was very fond of him and whilst he was a very attractive bloke with his broad shoulders and stocky build, she never thought of him as boyfriend material. Sure, he had the dark hair and eyes that were typical of her 'type' and they had enjoyed the odd innocent encounter, again after consumption of quite a lot of alcohol, but she didn't see him as a permanent fixture in her life, at least not in that way, and she was quite certain that whatever he had felt in the past he was long over it now.

'Ah Mel, it is what it is, I have known him for years. We grew up together, lost touch for a while and re-connected. To be honest, it is great that he is here in the city now. I think I would be lost without him. He has been so good and so supportive since Mum died and he was there through all the rest as well,' she explained, although deep down she felt annoyed that she was having to justify her friendship with him. Just because he was a man!!

'I know he was Shannon, sometimes I just think that you and him... that you would be good together,' Mel answered.

'No, that would not work. Anyway, Mel, tell me, how was I last night? Did I do anything stupid? Did I make a fool of myself or upset anyone? Did you bring me home? Where is Tom?' she asked, swiftly changing the subject.

'You were fine Shan, obviously pretty drunk, but so far as I know, you did not fall over or start any rows. You were a happy drunk, as the saying goes. I left early though with Tom for he had to work first thing this morning. He left me home and then headed back to his place. Pete promised that he would see you back safe and sound,' she stated. Shannon grimaced as she wandered into the living room praying that nothing had happened between them the night before. She honestly had zero recollection. At the very most she might have kissed him, but she would never have gone any further, otherwise he wouldn't be here on the sofa and she wouldn't have woken up in her own bed fully dressed. She would just have to play it by ear and hope that it was all innocent. She had kissed him before, admittedly he was a good kisser too, but for some reason, she just looked on him as a brother, it was so very strange, he was handsome and smart, but the spark was not there, not for her anyhow. He always told her how fond of her he was and she him, but they both knew deep down that they were better as mates and that was how it was. When Steve had walked out, Pete had provided a shoulder to cry on and had proved a huge support. Sometimes she joked that he was her very own personal bodyguard, as he was always close by and ready to snarl at anyone who said or did anything to upset her. She trusted him implicitly hence her reason with providing him with his own key to the flat. She thought it would be handy for her if she locked herself out. It was just a sensible and wise thing to do. At the same time, she reasoned that it would show him how much he was trusted and appreciated. She even had Sky Sports installed for him as he was mad about his football, so this meant that he could drop by and watch a game whenever he wanted. She had ordered him to come and go as he pleased and whilst certainly, he had been stunned by the offer, he was also undoubtedly pleased by the gesture and assured her so, at every opportunity. He had suffered the loss of his own parents several years before so there was a certain understanding and empathy between them, although they did not really talk about the events that had wiped out both his parents in one swoop. In fact, whilst Shannon openly talked about her mother Pete said very little about his parents, and Shannon did not push, for it was obviously much too raw.

3

'Morning Pete,' Shannon said sheepishly, popping her head around the door. The room was stifling, and she could detect a whiff of chips in the air. It was making her nauseous. She sauntered over to the curtains and pulled them apart gently, observing immediately the black clouds in the sky, looming above menacingly and no doubt on the point of unleashing a sea of rain. At the same time, she spotted a few towels swaying gently on the clothesline. Too bad, she thought, they could stay there, she was much too sick to sort that out. She closed the curtains again and switched on a lamp before turning her attention to her guest, who annoyingly displayed no signs of any kind of hangover.

'Hi Shan, how is the head this morning?' he said, slowly moving himself into an upright position, so he could see her properly.

Pete looked good, gosh he was ripped, she thought, feeling almost disappointed when he reached for his t-shirt and pulled it over his head. As much as she didn't fancy him, she appreciated that physique. Who wouldn't? He looked up at her and smiled, but beneath the smile she could tell she was about to be lectured in some form. She always knew where she stood with him. His mood was so consistent, and he always said it as it was. He was never bad tempered or grouchy, although on occasion, he would reprimand her over her drinking and subsequent party tricks. He absolutely hated when she did her party piece. He thought she was giving off the wrong impression, degrading herself and that it was inappropriate. She didn't mind him giving off though. She knew he was just concerned. He always looked out for her even when she didn't deserve it. She sensed a lecture was on its way this morning.

'I am alright Pete, thumping headache though! I feel dreadful, 'she confessed.

'How did we get home? I can't remember anything past midnight.'

'You were fine Shan, till you had a shot or two, lethal they are! If you just stuck to the one drink all night instead of mixing everything, you would be fine. And then you did that gammy leg trick which gained the attention of every red-blooded male in the bar. Thank God you were wearing your jeans. You really turn into a right exhibitionist sometimes, you know. Anyway, towards closing time I managed to drag you outside and hailed a taxi. You were doing the usual, singing and making up poems, and of course, everything rhymed. I don't know how you manage to make up something that rhymes perfectly and makes sense, when you are in that state. You had the taxi driver in stitches although when the hiccups started, I thought I noticed him accelerate. He was probably waiting on you to throw up in the back seat. Anyway, we came back here, via the Chinese of course. You know me, can't resist a curry chip at the end of a night. When we got back to the house, I sat up for a while and watched TV and you hit the sack, after spilling the contents of your stomach in the outside bin. Ugh, honestly Shannon, there is nothing to you. You really should take it a bit easier. There is just no stopping you sometimes. I take it you are suffering for it now?'

'I know Pete, I'm sorry, I really am,' she mumbled, feeling utterly ashamed. She knew the effect shots had on her. She just couldn't handle them.

'Never mind, it was a good night's crack and it is a new day. Have you any plans?'

Pete asked, realising that he had probably been too critical and that she was by now feeling bad enough without him making her feel worse.

'Yes, I was thinking of heading into town for an hour or two for some retail therapy but I could meet you later for a flick, if you fancy?' she replied hopefully, glad that the talk was over as she couldn't bear to think about it anymore.

'No can do Shan, I have a date tonight all thanks to you, and she is hot, very hot,' he smiled.

'Ha ha, pull the other one McGlynn, why would I fix you up when I can't even fix myself up?' she cried.

'Well, fix me up you did, Pete replied, and with that he jumped off the sofa and threw on his coat and scarf. 'I am meeting her this afternoon, so I am off home to get a shave and spruce myself up.'

'Hang on a second Pete. Who is she? Did I really fix you up?' she enquired, curiously.

'That's for me to know and you to find out,' he laughed, planting a quick peck on her cheek before heading off out the front door and down the street, looking very pleased with himself as he whistled some tune or other.

Shannon smiled after him before heading straight for the kitchen. She needed a very strong coffee, she thought, preferably black. Mel already had the kettle on the boil and the cups out as she rushed around clearing up the mess from the night before. Thankfully it wasn't too bad, just a few empty bottles lying around and the remnants of the takeaway that Pete had scoffed.

'He's off on a date tonight, said I fixed him up, but he didn't tell me who she was, just ran off chuckling to himself,' she told Mel.

Mel looked at her with raised eyebrows. She really didn't understand the friendship they had and found it very peculiar. She considered the pair perfect for each other. As far as she was concerned, they should just get on with it, get married, have children and live happily ever after, or alternatively at least try a date or two to see if they were compatible that way. She really felt compelled to bang their heads together and make them see sense but there was little point.

'It's you he wants Shannon. It always has been and it always will be. I don't understand how you can't see it. You're both as bad as each other, not seeing what's plain and obvious to everyone else. One day you are going to realise that for yourself and I hope when that day comes that you're not too late, I really do.'

Shannon burst out laughing, the usual response Mel noted sourly, sipping her coffee slowly.

'What about you Mel, how are you and Tom getting on? Any sign of wedding bells? I have never been a bridesmaid you know. You need to get a move on, so I get the chance to wear a really pretty dress?' she teased.

Noting that her friend had quickly changed the subject, Mel replied, 'you will be waiting a while yet, Shannon. We're in no rush to walk down the aisle just yet, but one day we will for sure, we have discussed it and it will happen, but not any time soon. And yes, when that day comes, you will be my Chief Bridesmaid. Perhaps you will even be my Maid of Honour. Who knows, with my record of organising I could be your bridesmaid long before that,' she laughed.

Shannon chuckled. She was well aware of Mel's organisational skills or lack of them. She would make a beautiful bride one day. She was so petite and pretty with her pale, perfect skin and elfin-like features. They had known each other forever but they were totally different in character. Mel was quietly spoken and more serious than Shannon but when they were together, they giggled and laughed like teenagers.

She was the sister Shannon never had and whilst they had their occasional ups and downs, they were few and far between. They always made up quickly as they couldn't stay angry with one another for any length of time.

'Mel, I am heading into town for an hour or two. Do you want to come?' Shannon asked.

'I wish I could darling but I have to go home for Sunday dinner, Mum is cooking a lovely big roast with all the trimmings and I dare not show up or there will be all hell to pay, especially as I missed last week. You know how precious she is about these things!'

Shannon knew this to be true for family dinners were mandatory for the Blacks and you declined at your own peril. All the same, it must be nice, she thought, to be part of a large clan like that, all meeting up in the family home for the traditional Sunday roast. She missed that. Ever since her mother had died and her father had taken up with Gemma who wasn't that much older than herself, she didn't have the same inclination to go to the family home. It wasn't that she didn't like Gemma, she was very pleasant and she seemed to make her dad happy, but it just wasn't the same. Gemma always welcomed her and there were no bad feelings between the pair, but Shannon just found it hard to comprehend that her fifty-five-year-old dad was now remarried to a girl only about five years her senior. How her father had managed to win her affections she didn't quite comprehend because Gemma was very attractive, very outgoing and not lacking in the confidence department. In fact, she had been engaged to another guy when she had met Shannon's dad Gerry, but he was soon ditched and before anyone could blink an eye, they were making it official in the local registry office. Now Gemma was living in the family home and doing all sorts of modernisations which Shannon wished she would leave be, at least for another year or two. She could understand that Gemma would wish to put her own stamp on the place but nevertheless it was painful to watch. Gemma loved interior design and the place now looked like a show house, very minimal and tasteful for sure, but Shannon liked how it was before. Her mum always had a clutter of ornaments, books, and photographs lying around but they had mostly gone now. The breakables had been carefully wrapped and hordes of books and photographs had been relocated to the loft. Shannon could go through them in her own time. Gone too was the carpet which had only been laid a month or two before her mum's premature departure. Her mum had spent hours choosing that carpet and for weeks before they had been tormented by all the different samples lying in various rooms of the house as she tried to make up her mind which one she liked best. Eventually, she opted for a beautifully, luxurious dark grey one but Gemma had it lifted and replaced with a dark, solid wooden floor, which she felt would be easier to clean. Shannon wasn't so sure about that. A dark floor usually showed up all the dust but apparently because Gemma was slightly asthmatic, zshe preferred to see the dirt whereas with carpets she had explained, the dust was hidden. A new, cream coloured kitchen had been fitted and a wall knocked down between the sitting room and study to create a larger living space. A conservatory was built at the back of the kitchen leading out to the beautiful garden where the whole family had spent many happy hours when she was a child. Thank God she had not changed the garden. Shannon had been thinking lately that she should start visiting more often, she had stayed away initially because she found it so gut wrenching without her mum there, but maybe it was time to look to the future. Who knows, maybe she and Gemma would bond; it was certainly not out of the question. She would never replace her mother but realistically Shannon knew that was the farthest thought from her mind.

Besides she had made her father's life more bearable and that was worth its weight in gold. He had been heartbroken by her mum's death, but it had been difficult because he had kept all his emotions locked up inside. He didn't want to upset Shannon by offloading his grief but that had backfired because Shannon had tried to diminish hers by having wild nights out and being reckless. Despite all the interior changes, Gemma had gained Shannon's respect

17

because she had been kind and considerate of her feelings and had told her from the offset that she could take anything personal or meaningful that she wanted from the family home and that nothing would be thrown out without her consultation and approval. But the only thing that Shannon really wanted was her mum and that was no longer an option. How she missed her!

Her mum had died as the result of a terrible car accident, a tragic and unnecessary ending to a life which should have continued for so many more years. Shannon remembered the afternoon it happened as vividly as yesterday. They had just eaten a lovely meal together, the three of them. As usual, her mum had been bustling around the kitchen, singing some little tune or other; CD player on at quite a loud volume. Her mum loved Paloma Faith, Rhianna and Gaga. She had even seen Lady Gaga in concert. Once the dishes had been loaded in the machine, she announced she was off to the shops to catch a few bargains in the Monsoon sale which one of her friends had told her about earlier that afternoon. Her mum loved shopping. They teasingly nicknamed her Shopaholic around the house. She loved her fashion and particularly her handbags and shoes. She had asked Shannon to go with her, but her daughter had refused stating that she was much too snug on the sofa with her blanket wrapped around her to venture out in the cold and wet. How she regretted that decision now. Perhaps, it would have turned out differently. She would never know. It had been raining heavily all day and it was gloomy and dark out. Shannon recalled her father trying to dissuade his mum from going, but her mum was insistent. Sure, what harm could a little rain do, she had said. But there was more than a little rain and unfortunately, her mum hadn't spotted a large pool of water on the road and she skidded. The car must have bounced over the ditch because it was found upside down in a field. A dead badger had been found close to the scene of the accident and it was thought that her mother might have swerved to avoid it and in doing so, lost control of her motor. Had the road been dry, she may have escaped with cuts and bruises but that wasn't to be. Perhaps if she had been discovered earlier, she may have stood a chance but unfortunately that wasn't the case and by the time she was found an hour or so later, she had already suffered massive internal bleeding. A passing motorist had witnessed the whole drama and rushed to her aid whilst frantically phoning emergency services. The ambulance which arrived within minutes promptly whisked her off to hospital, but she was already deeply unconscious. Her husband had been asked for consent to switch off the life support machine and they had stood together and watched as the end came. Shannon had been totally distraught but even now two years later, it didn't seem to get any easier. Many people who came to the wake and subsequent funeral told her she would get over it in time, but Shannon would never get over it. It was excruciating when people said that, and so many did but she tried to be reasonable, it would be easy to lose her temper and shout at them for being so stupid. She had to understand that folk just didn't know what to say and didn't understand. How could they? Every day, she tried to block it out as much as she could because the pain was too dreadful to bear. There had been no time to say goodbye and she missed her more than ever. Not only that, but the circumstances of her death were violent and tragic, sudden and heart-breaking. Her mum had been her best friend and confidante. They talked about everything. Of course, she was extremely close to her dad, but she just couldn't talk to him the same way or discuss the same things that her and her mum spoke about. He would be extremely worried and upset right now if he knew how much she was drinking, she thought guiltily.

'Are you okay?' Mel asked quietly. 'You're in a world of your own there,' she added.

'Yeah Mel, I'm fine, I was just thinking about my mum. Sometimes I feel incredibly lost, it's a lonely world without her in it and I know I am not helping myself, but I am going to try and change. I don't want to keep going out and getting drunk like that, half the time I can't even remember the next day. I want to do other things aside from going to bars and clubs on the weekends. I want more, Mel, I deserve more and this drinking, well, it's fun at the time but the next day I just feel depressed and lonely. I guess when you were talking about going for Sunday dinner, it just brought it home to me that Sunday dinners at Dobbertys ended two years ago. I'm sorry Mel, I don't mean to sound miserable or melodramatic, just feeling sorry for myself, as I normally do when I'm hung-over. Sunday is the hardest day of the week when you are single! It is a day for families and couples but when you are on your own, it is lonesome. I suppose I just don't like Sundays; it signifies the end of the weekend and the return to work, work and more work. However, I am going out to the shops now and when I return, I am going to think seriously about my life. I need to work out what I want and how to go forward, because I can't carry on like this or I'll end up on the Jeremy Kyle show or heaven forbid, in rehab and God knows what that would do to my dad.'

The two friends hugged, and Mel said nothing. There was nothing could be said, she knew Shannon missed her mum terribly and that no words could comfort her when she was feeling this way. All she could do was listen and be there. She couldn't imagine life without her mother for as much as she was overpowering at times and somewhat bossy and controlling, Mel loved her unconditionally for she was the kindest and the best mother in the world. Poor, poor Shannon, she had been through so many traumas in recent years, losing her mum in the most horrendous circumstances not to mention the disastrous break up with

Steve who had gone off to London with that awful Anita just three months before her mum's death.

4

Mel had liked Anita to start with, she had been part of their inner circle and none of them had thought for a second that she would get it together with Steve. In fact, they were always bickering and there was a tension in the air when they were in the same room. Anita had never warmed to Steve and the feeling appeared mutual. There was never any indication that there was anything other than pure loathing between the pair, so it was a shock to everyone when they got together. Steve had simply just upped and left without so much as leaving a note. There were no subsequent letters or phone calls. It was as if he had disappeared off the face of the planet, gone in a shadow of mystery, shattering Shannon's heart in the process, crushing her dreams and hopes for the future, a future she was sure was meant to be shared with him. Some time later, after a total lack of communication from Anita, they had discovered that the two of them had headed to London together. Poor Shannon had been utterly devastated by this revelation and barely had she time to recover emotionally from that; she had lost her dear mother in that horrible accident. All Mel could do was support her as much as possible, but she was finding it increasingly difficult what with Shannon's binge drinking every weekend. There was no stop button with her. She knew no limit as regards alcohol and lately she appeared to be drinking even more and when she reached that state, she was capable of anything. It was deeply worrying. She always grew so stubborn and there was no getting through to her which would be easily handled if they were at home but not so easy when they were in a pub. Shannon had a habit of taking off without telling anyone where she was going. One night she had left the pub in an awful state and started to walk home. Having realised that she had gone Mel ordered a taxi and when finally, she spotted her friend she had asked the driver to stop for her, but Shannon had stated she was fine and was enjoying the night air. She refused point blank to get into the taxi and Mel had no choice but to get out and walk the remaining distance home with her. She remembered how angry she had been that night, really annoyed that Shannon could be so blasé. It was as if at times her friend had no self-worth or self-love. It was almost as if she was inviting something distasteful to happen and when they had finally reached home, they had had a blazing row after which Shannon had burst into tears and ran to her bedroom slamming the door behind her. Of course, in the morning, she had apologised over and over and promised repeatedly that it would never happy again and she had stuck to it but still sometimes she was her own worst enemy and Mel was really concerned. She had moved in originally, on what was meant to be a temporary basis after Mrs Dobberty died, but almost two years later she was still there - and with things heating up with Tom she knew that sooner or later she would have to move out. She had no idea how she was even going to begin to broach this subject. It was immediately after the funeral that Mel had asked Shannon about moving in for a while. She had insisted that the other girl would be doing her a favour, that she really needed her independence, but the reality was very different. She wanted to ensure that Shannon was okay and the best way to keep an eye on her was to keep as close as possible. Of course, Shannon had naturally been thrilled by the offer and agreed instantly. The thought of returning to the flat had filled her with pure dread but with Mel around things were sure to be a little easier. In an ideal world, Mel would have remained at the family home and put some money aside for her future, but it was more important now to do the right thing by her friend. She truly felt that Shannon had been through such an awful trauma that she needed all the support she could get. She did not begrudge her decision but felt that now the time had come for them to go their separate ways. She would talk it over with her own mum later and see what she thought she should do. Her mum was good like that, always seemed to have a solution. She was very practical and Mel, who openly admitted to being indecisive, needed that practicality.

'I'm off now Shan, you know what my mum is like, I can't be late,' she stated, giving her a quick hug. Shannon returned the embrace warmly before thanking her again and walking out slowly to the front door where she stood and waved her off. At least the weather was good, she thought. There had been so much rain lately, a little sun would just lift the mood. Shutting the door behind her, she trudged across the hall to her lovely, spacious and extremely messy bedroom. How she loved this room! It was painted cream, the bed linen was cream with red embroidering, and the carpet was so soft she just loved walking on it barefoot. She adored her soft, leather headboard complemented by the leather chaise longue laid next to the double window adorned by expensive red and cream suede curtains which she had made especially. She switched on the flat screen T.V. selecting the MTV music channel before perching herself on her prized velvet stool in front of the large, silver framed mirror. She carefully applied her moisturiser following up with a light coat of foundation. She didn't bother about powder, she never did. She loved her makeup though and her make up bag contained all sorts of brands. Part of her couldn't be bothered with the war paint today as she was tired and hungover but nevertheless needs must, she thought to herself, as she smudged a little brown eyeliner beneath her lids and finished off with a coat of Rimmel's extra super lash mascara. She rubbed some cream pink blusher on her cheek bones and dabbed a natural lip gloss to her perfect v-shaped lips. She remembered the tip, 'Eyes or lips' and smiled. She preferred to go heavy on her eye makeup with less on the lips. Nothing worse than red lipstick as it could make even the whitest of teeth look yellow or end up on the teeth, the ultimate beauty malfunction as far as she was concerned. Sometimes she would interview candidates in her work and she never knew whether to tell them that their teeth had lipstick smeared on them. She always bit her tongue but often felt like passing over a tissue so they could wipe them clean. She thought of Pete and wondered who he was seeing later. He was being quite secretive, she thought. He must like this girl whoever she was because she couldn't recall him having gone on a date in a long time. She was glad though because he was a sweetheart and he deserved the best. She knew Mel thought they were made for each other but that was quite simply out of the question. She really was totally off track with that notion. He was her chum and that was enough. He had been there for her through thick and thin, just like Mel. He had listened time and time again to her whole sad sorry story, he had held her in his arms whilst she cried rivers of sheer grief and frustration, he never gave advice, but he held her tight and provided support repeatedly. He had dragged her out for long strolls in the countryside, for mountain walks, coffees in quaint cafes that she had never visited or thought existed and fish and chips in little harbour towns. He had taken her to the cinema, introduced her to friends or acquaintances as he described them, he had brought her to grief support groups, and he had eventually persuaded her to start living again. He had helped her with her confidence and self-belief which had taken such a battering when Steve had walked out. When her mother had died, he had been amazing, encouraging her to talk about it, that grief should not be stored but released in order that healing could begin. And she had released her grief over and over, night after night, for months after her mother's death. He had accompanied her to the graveside on many occasions and just sat by her side as she had poured her heart out

25

over her loss. Shannon liked going to the grave. She felt close to her mum there and Pete had understood that. It was strange though that for all his compassion towards her he still rarely mentioned his own loss. Quite often after a night's drinking she would curl in a ball in the corner of a room and break down. Sometimes she would run off and disappear for a few moments and he would race around until he had found her sitting alone somewhere, thinking, glancing through watery, blurred eyes at nothing, her thoughts on some memory. Often, she had nightmares and flashbacks, as she imagined the image of her mum in that smashed up, broken car. She had not gone to the scene of the accident; her mother had been escorted to the nearest hospital by ambulance before she even knew what had happened. Still the thought of her mum in the car, hurt and alone, was really at times far too much to bear. Typically, he would scold her for taking off and she would confess to just needing a few moments of peace to talk to her mum. She was quite aware of how this sounded but it was true, as far as she was concerned, just because her mother had died, it didn't mean she couldn't talk to her. So, as mad as it might sound, that's how she coped and that was okay with her. She knew that she was being irresponsible when she took herself off but when she had consumed alcohol any fear always disappeared out the window. She no longer cared and felt no fear. There was no doubt that he had been her rock since the breakup and without him she didn't know how she would have coped. He had been stunned when Steve had taken off with Anita, furious even and had said repeatedly he could kill him for treating her like that. She was glad that he had moved back to the city not too far from her, as he was great company and having come out of her breakup, friends were few and far between. She had become so engrossed in Steve that she had not made as much of an effort in terms of her friendships. That was to her cost when they broke up as she realised that bar one or two, she did not have the same social network as before. Certainly, some friends had drifted, not wanting to take sides or get involved. Others had turned up at her mother's wake, but they were at a loss for words and she had been in no fit state to talk never mind hear the words of sympathy being showered on her. Besides when the relationship ended, she had decided not to actively pursue mutual friends as she really did not want to hear anything about Steve or what he was getting up to. She sighed deeply to herself before jumping up off her stool and pulling out her favourite brown handbag from the bottom of her slide robe.

Lifting her wallet, mobile phone and car keys, she headed outside to her mini, her present to herself the Christmas prior. It was bright yellow and she had purchased it second hand, but she took great care of it and it always looked immaculately clean and new. It took her twenty minutes to reach town as the traffic seemed somewhat busier than usual for a Sunday. After parking in the multi-storey car park at Castle Court, she headed towards the main shopping area which was relatively quiet. Her first stop was Boots where she lifted some new moisturiser to try, a little make up and some other odds and ends before making her way to Eason's and purchasing a few magazines opting for Healthy Living and Running. Start as you mean to continue, she thought. She used all her willpower to ignore her favourite glossies displaying their usual glamorous covers. She smiled at the captions because quite often she found that what was printed on the cover was far from the truth, the inside story was always different from what was insinuated on the outside.

That done, she headed for Top Shop, her favourite store and splashed out on a pair of black denim flares and a pretty, silk cream top before hitting the House of Frazer at the Victoria Centre and picking up a pair of Fly Boots which were expensive, but she had to have them. They were a tan brown colour with a decent three-inch wedge heel, but she could walk in them easily and they fit like a glove. It was about an hour later when she noticed him. It had to be him! She would know that voice anywhere and it pleased and sickened her simultaneously. She didn't want to believe it was him as it had been over two years now but there was no mistaking that familiar drawl. She stood transfixed, rooted to the ground, she desperately wanted to flee but she couldn't. Her stomach was doing somersaults and she swallowed hard, trying desperately to settle her nerves. She felt as if her whole face was suddenly twitching and her eyes dropped a large, unwelcome tear. She quickly retrieved a tissue from her bag and dried it away but all the while she did not move, not a single inch. She couldn't. She suddenly felt queasy as a feeling of utter panic engulfed her whole being. He had not clocked her yet and she could quite easily disappear amongst the racks of clothes but for some reason her legs would not budge. They were stuck to the floor like superglue and she realised she could hardly breathe. If this was what a panic attack was, then this had to be a full-scale onslaught as she felt completely helpless, she could hear her heart thumping in her chest and still she could not budge. She watched and waited for him to turn around, breathing deeply and trying to keep very, very calm. She did not want to cause a scene, especially here, but she would be very interested in his reaction. He was thanking the cashier now as they shared a joke about something, and as he moved away from the till he looked carefully at his receipt before pocketing it. He had not changed in the slightest, still devastatingly handsome although somewhat scruffy and unshaven, which was unusual. He didn't seem as slim built now, in fact, he looked as if he had been working out, body building possibly. He had undoubtedly bulked up from the last time she saw him. His white t-shirt was tight and fitted, his arms muscular and the slight paunch of before was gone. He looked casual but healthy. When he finally glanced up, she was mesmerised by the look on his rugged, handsome face, for there was no mistaking his joy and delight. He rushed straight to her, enveloping her in a massive hug which she fought desperately to avoid.

She was completely taken aback but she was not naive, this was the love of her life and he had left her for her 'supposed' friend and fled the country without so much as a goodbye. She didn't want to be nasty to him, but she couldn't pretend that nothing had happened. He stood back now, his strong hands resting gently on her shoulders as he peered at her closely with his deep brown eyes, drinking her in as if to memorise every fine detail of her exquisite face. She didn't want to look at him. It was so difficult. He still made her melt and she could feel her heart pounding ninety to the dozen. She could not hang around either, she had to leave quickly, she knew that look and it frightened her. She knew she had never managed to remove the memories of how things were between them before he took off, but she felt that she had made headway. She didn't expect it to be like this or for all the old feelings to come flooding back. She edged back and looked at him curiously, wishing that her hands would stop trembling and that at least she could give the impression of being unfazed. She was struggling to hold it together, struggling to not cry, to keep the tears away, but it was only a matter of seconds before her body would betray her. It was all too much.

'It's nice to see you, I think, but anyway .... I have loads to do, so I'll be off, I guess,' she stuttered, coolly, and somewhat more curtly than she had intended. Now that he was standing just in front of her, she felt as though her heart was breaking all over again. Time, it would seem had not healed her emotions as much as she had assumed and she was almost afraid to speak any more in case he recognised that she was no more than a quivering wreck.

'Will you be seeing me?' he demanded. 'I owe you an explanation; I want to tell you why I left and what happened. You deserve to know,' he insisted.

'No Steve, I deserved your explanation two years ago,' she answered, with sarcasm.

'But Shannon, you don't understand, it wasn't just as simple as it seemed, please hear me out or at least let me contact you. I'm back in Belfast, have been for a while and I have been hoping to run into you,' he urged.

'Look Steve, I really have to go, I don't want to hear your explanation. You upped and left, and I picked up the pieces bit by bit and now you're history. I am over it, I am over you and really I don't want to know your reasons, because believe me, no reason justifies what you did.'

'Just five minutes please? We could go for a coffee,' he pleaded.

'Too late,' she answered, and with that she managed a weak smile before striding off as confidently as she could muster for her legs were trembling so much that she feared she would keel over right in front of him. She knew he was watching her as she walked away, but she strolled ahead not once looking back. Part of her wished he would chase after her, but he didn't. So, he was home, was he? Seemed he thought he could just waltz back into her life and start over where he had left off. Well, too bad, she thought. Suddenly she felt sick to the stomach, a mixture of nerves and the drink from the night before. She raced to the toilets and barely made it to a cubicle where she immediately threw up. When she emerged several minutes later, she washed her hands and wiped her mouth and face before re-applying a dash of blusher to her pale white skin. Her hands were still shaking and she decided to call it a day and go straight home. It had been too much for her and she had had quite enough for one day. The notion of shopping which had tempted her into town in the first place had disappeared as soon as she had clapped eyes on him. Who did he think he was anyway? Standing there, with those dark eyes, grinning like a Cheshire cat, like everything was alright, like they could just talk things over and all would be forgotten. He had ruthlessly abandoned her and to all intent and purpose he may as well have died the day he walked out, for the grief she had suffered had been unbearable and then her mother, her poor mother.....How she hated him, loved him, absolutely despised him and wanted to hate him for loving him and still loving him even though he had been a total and utter disappointment.

She could not deny the attraction or the devastating effect he still had on her but looks weren't everything. Her mother had drummed that in since she was no age. A person's character was far more important, she used to say, and he had proved without a shadow of a doubt, that he was severely lacking in that department. She wouldn't tell anyone about her ordeal because in truth, she didn't want to talk about it. She felt that the more you talked about something the more you thought about it and she did not want to think about it. He was not worth it. No, she wanted to focus on getting her life back on track and today's encounter had reinforced that longing even more. She wanted to cut down on her partying and drinking and she certainly didn't want him seeing her around in bars performing her gammy leg trick. She knew that getting hopelessly drunk like that demonstrated a lack of control in one's life. No, as much as seeing him had played havoc with her emotions, she would not give him the satisfaction of seeing her act the fool. True, she had always been somewhat of a party animal and probably that had been part of the initial attraction, but she was older now, not ancient by any means, but perhaps it was time for her to grow up and take some responsibility.

5

Later whilst soaking in the bath she wondered what had happened between him and Anita. They must have split up for he was behaving like a singleton, but he needn't think that he could worm his way back into her life. He had hurt her far too much. Why was he back anyway? Did he regret what he had done? It seemed possible but what explanation could justify him walking out on their two-year relationship with no warning, no signs and no contact whatsoever in all that time. Everything had seemed fine; in fact, if anything they had been happier than ever, settled and contented and very much in love, or so she thought. How wrong could she have been?

She recalled that the week prior to his sudden departure, he had been behaving a little different, erratically even, but he had been just as attentive to her and therefore, she had not been overly concerned. She remembered he had been out at a bar one night and had returned extremely upset. But when she had asked him what was wrong, he had refused to discuss it and she had not persisted, figuring he would talk to her when he was ready. For months afterwards, she wondered had he met Anita that night. Had he been unfaithful? But he had been so in love with her it seemed strange that he could be so fickle. Had he cheated before or was Anita the first? Why take off with her and to London above all places? It was so very strange. He had seemed over the moon to run into her this afternoon. At one point it looked like he was going to kiss her. Or had she misread the situation? Had she got it totally wrong? Should she have hung around for his explanation? Accepted his offer of coffee? No way, that was crazy, she thought. There was no good reason, there was no way back. He was weak and disloyal. He was a cheat, worthless, no good and he had a nerve, a cheek to think that she would listen to his excuses. He had caused her months of anguish and what really tormented her to this day was that for those three months prior to her mum's terrible death all she had talked about to her was him. She had cried and ranted and raved, and her poor mother had been demented. Shannon had gone off her food and lost a stone in the space of a few weeks. Her face had looked pale and gaunt and she had moped around the house in her dressing gown, not bothering to go out the door. At least she had seen more of her mother than ever during that time, but it filled her with guilt that she had been so depressed. But then again, how was she to know that God would steal her mum away and change things as they were forever? Had she known that their time together was coming to an end she would have acted in a different way altogether but there didn't seem much point going over that now. Besides her mum would have wanted to know what was going on. She tried everything she could to bring Shannon out of her den of doom but to no avail. She had managed to drag her to a bar one night where they shared a couple of cocktails and a few laughs. Her mum had been so vivacious, so much fun. They looked alike too, shared the same temper, her dad often joked. Her mum would know exactly what to do now, she felt. She was sure she was still very much around; sometimes she felt she could feel her presence and when thoughts came into her head she wondered if they were her own or if somehow her mum was planting them there. I wonder what she would say to me right now, she thought, picking up her faithful body brush and scrubbing her skin until it was almost red raw. She winced for a second, suddenly noticing the whopper of a bruise on her shin, another bruise she couldn't remember and another reminder of why she had to alter her ways. The funny thing was that her mum had liked Steve, she had warmed to him from that first meeting, but Steve had that impact on people. Everyone liked him! Everyone liked her mum too! It was inevitable that the pair would get on. So, there would be a fair chance that her mum would welcome a reconciliation and therefore influence Shannon to agree to a meeting. However, her mum had been none too impressed when he had buggered off so she would also advise caution. It was hard to tell!

'Come on Mum, help me through this, I know you are there and I need you. I need to sort out my life, become the daughter you would be proud of. Just give me some sort of sign, anything,' she thought. God damn it, why did other people always talk about signs from the dead, shadows and water trickling and weird, unexplained coincidences? Maybe that would be too much for her, she supposed. Maybe it would freak her out, it probably would disturb her, but she just wanted her mum to talk back, sensibly, give her advice.

'You're a big girl now Shannon Dobberty, I am right by you, quit the drinking, join the gym, get fit, make no hasty decisions, take one day at a time,' her conscience answered.

'But Mum, it is all one huge mess,' she whispered!

'It is as much a mess as you allow it to be,' she heard.

She lay there for a long while deep in her own thoughts, until she realised the bath water had started to cool and suddenly shivering, she slowly climbed out, wrapping herself in her mum's favourite fluffy, white dressing gown. After her mother had died her dad had told her to help herself to whatever she wanted but aside from some precious jewellery she had opted for the familiar robe she was so accustomed to seeing her mum wear. She loved it and when she wore it, she felt snug and safe. She was tired out now as it had been an eventful day following her mad escapades at the pub combined with the shock of seeing him again, but still she refused to dwell on it any longer. Ignoring the rumbles of her stomach, she sat down on her bed and applied her body moisturiser followed by a light coat of false tan on her legs, arms and chest. She didn't much care for false tan because too many girls were smothered in the stuff and it could look really awful, especially when poorly applied hence her reason for using a light version with utmost care paid to her knees and ankles and especially and above all, her neck. Oh, how many times had she noticed a perfectly tanned face perched on a tango orange, streaky neck? Totally shameful, that was a cardinal sin without a doubt. She didn't even know why she bothered at all, such a mess of bedclothes and towels and then sitting around waiting for it to dry like a coat of paint. But she just felt like some false tan, maybe inwardly she wanted to feel better, or to feel she looked better, or maybe she thought she would look more attractive to her ex if she ran into him again, although on reflection, that was just a joke. He wasn't into fake beauty, be it eyelashes or tans, or whatever else. He preferred the natural look, but she did not. She added an extra coat there and then, almost in defiance of what he would like. Mel would be back shortly after her day at home, but she wanted to be alone with her own thoughts and after setting her alarm clock she climbed into bed and fell fast asleep.

6

She woke up next morning before the alarm and was surprised at how fitfully she had slept. She still felt tired of course but she was glad that she had a good seven hours or so, especially after what had materialised yesterday. She was lucky to have managed to sleep at all. It was important now to somehow put Steve to the back of her mind, after all she had a job to do and that job she needed to keep. She didn't have time for distractions, and certainly not one of this magnitude. After a quick shower she threw on her suit, painted her face, and headed for the office. She was starving but chose to skip breakfast. She couldn't think about food - it was always the same when she got upset. The thought of eating simply made her feel ill. So much for being over him, yesterday had proved that she never was and probably never would be. It didn't take long to get to work and she was first in. She quickly boiled the kettle and made herself a large mug of coffee before logging on to her computer and checking her to do list for the day. She had never envisaged that she would work in a recruitment agency, but she enjoyed it and it was busy. She had gone into the agency a year previously, searching for employment but when the manager offered her a position within the agency itself, she had jumped at the chance. She was a people person and this job required lots of customer and client contact. She particularly liked this time of day because it was peaceful and quiet and she could get lots done before the mayhem commenced. By the time the other consultants arrived she had already completed lots of paperwork and prepared her notes for her pre-scheduled meetings that day. She had three client visits and anticipated a smooth day's work. First on the agenda was a visit to a manufacturing company who were searching for a new PA to the Managing Director. They were a regular client that had been using their services for years, so no hard selling was required. She simply took their job order and advised them that she had several suitable candidates on her books, she explained the terms of business and fees before proceeding to the next firm, an accounting practice which was extremely well renowned. This was a first visit and she was determined to make a good impression. First visits were very important and the competition from rival agencies was fierce, so she read up on the company beforehand and had a variety of CVS ready in her little black briefcase. If she could win the business, it would be lucrative and would boost her sales for the month. The more business she won, the heftier her commission and extra income would help her along nicely. Things were relatively quiet on the business front and if she could manage to satisfy this client and win new business, it would make working life easier for a couple of weeks. At the end of the day she had targets to achieve and as far as she had gathered, she would only ever be as good as last month's figures. If she had a bad month, sympathy would not be in abundance by any means. Plus, there was always the hope for repeat business, so it was necessary to ask the right questions and gauge as much information as possible regarding staffing requirements.

On arrival at reception, she was escorted to a rather plush waiting area, all very modern in its décor with some fabulous abstract paintings and several company magazines and brochures laid strategically on an ornate table. She declined the coffee she was offered stating that she was trying to decrease her caffeine intake in favour of a healthier lifestyle. She added that she wanted to start trying herbal teas but when the receptionist offered her a green tea, she politely declined that too. What a load of utter bull, she thought, as soon as she had said it. Everyone knew that green tea was disgusting, alright so it boosted the metabolism (allegedly) but it wasn't worth the vile taste in your mouth when you were sipping it. Oh, why could she not just sit and be quiet and say nothing. She always said more than was necessary particularly when she was nervous, not that the receptionist seemed to notice, as she ran around her work area, opening and closing filing cabinets and answering the telephone in between. Did that phone ever stop ringing? She reckoned she would have thrown it out the window by now.

'Miss Dolan will see you now,' the receptionist suddenly announced, before ushering her into the Manager's office. Shannon stared inside and gaped in disbelief. This just cannot be happening, she thought. Not Anita! How bloody unfortunate! First him and now her, in the space of twenty-four hours. Was God playing some sort of joke? Okay, so she had skipped Mass for a month or two but surely, she didn't deserve this for penance. As she stood by the door, all sorts of crazy thoughts were racing through her entangled mind. What should she do? Should she go? But she couldn't, could she? How had she missed such a critical piece of information, as the manager's name? It just showed how much this whole business of meeting him was affecting her. This was absurd. It had never twigged for a second that it was the same person! She lifted the job order she had printed off in the office and scanned it for something she had missed. Sure enough there it was, Miss A Dolan, typewritten clearly in bold, black letters. Never for one second had she suspected or even contemplated that it could be the same person. This must be a joke, she thought.

'My goodness, if it isn't...Shannon Dobberty. How are you?' cried Anita, stepping towards her, enthusiastically, hand stretched out to take hers. She appeared just as surprised!

'Anita, I wasn't expecting....,' she stuttered, shaking her hand, limply.

'But of course, you weren't,' Anita agreed, 'but here I am and here are you.'

'May I sit down?' Shannon asked, pulling out a chair and falling into it, before Anita had time to answer.

'Come on, get it together girl, deal with it,' her conscience reminded her.

Suddenly sitting up straight, she produced the job order and began to talk.

'You are looking for a new receptionist I believe?' she asked, curtly.

She was gobsmacked, but she must not show it, not under any circumstances. She must be professional, do her job and get out of here, as swiftly as possible. She could feel her head spinning. It all felt too much. And the way Anita was behaving, as if nothing had happened. What kind of a bitch was she? Didn't she realise the impact of her actions? And she was being so nice? Her mind was a whirl of thoughts which made no sense until suddenly Anita's voice brought her back to earth with a thud and she desperately tried to regain her concentration and focus on what she had to do.

'Are you okay Shannon? Would you like a glass of water?' she offered.

'No thank you; let's just get on with it,' she said. She was aware that she was not handling this very well.

'Look Shannon, I am sorry, I truly am, what happened…,' Anita whispered.

'Anita this is work, let's just do what we have to and keep the personal stuff aside,' she stated, willing her voice to remain steady and not betray her true feelings at coming face to face with her arch-rival. She looked alright, she had certainly aged somewhat, too much time in the sun perhaps, in fact her skin which had once been envied by all the girls for its soft sallow tones looked a little wrinkled and old. She took consolation in that; it secretly pleased her.

'Okay, if that's what you want, if you're sure, it's just….,' she hesitated.

'I'm sure,' Shannon interrupted.

She wasn't in the form for any more excuses, she had heard enough over the last 24 hours and whatever was going on in her personal life or his for that matter really was none of her business. She was intent on changing her ways and nothing or nobody was going to interfere with that. The past was the past and it could stay there, as far as she was concerned. She didn't want to hear anymore and with that in mind she forced a smile and proposed that they just concentrate on the job in hand.

The meeting continued quite formally, with Shannon handing over the terms of business, outlining fees and letting her 'client' know what course of action she would be taking in terms of finding a suitable candidate. They didn't shake hands afterwards but exchanged a quick smile and a hasty goodbye before Shannon stood up straight and tall and departed hastily for her premises in Linenhall Street. What a morning, she thought? It was relentless! And she still hadn't eaten. She grabbed a couple of bananas from a nearby fruit shop to keep her going, before returning to the agency. She knew that she hadn't asked Anita half enough questions but, how could she? It would be interesting to see if she heard from her again. She suspected Anita would probably use another agency to avoid any awkwardness and that would be fine. The last thing she wanted was to have anything to do with the nasty little trollop who stole the only person she had ever really loved. Thankfully her manager was on leave for a week or two so there would be no interrogation about this potential new client and by the time she returned there would hopefully be a few other new clients. The remainder of the day passed smoothly although at times she found it difficult to concentrate, as her mind kept revisiting the morning's encounter. Her third visit of the day was an easy one, just a matter of visiting an existing client and checking that everything was working out with temporary staff she had supplied to them. It was an on-going contract and didn't require any effort which Shannon appreciated, as her conscience kept interrupting her thought process. She was never as glad when it came to half past five and she could leave and on reaching home she flaked out on the sofa.

She noticed the light on the answering machine flashing and found she had three messages waiting. The first was from Pete; he wanted to call round for coffee and sounded excited. No doubt his date had gone well and he was dying to tell her all about it. She made a mental note to call him back and proceeded to the second which she quickly deleted. Another one of those annoying call centre ones! There were few things that grinded on her but phone calls from call centres were up there with the worst. By the time the third message played she was halfway through preparing her coffee.

'Hi, it's me, please phone me on the mobile, same number, please… you need to know the truth. I love you Shannon, I still do, I'm sorry.'

Shannon stopped in her tracks and promptly spilt her coffee everywhere. Just the sound of his voice was utterly depressing, if not ultra-soothing and comforting. Her eyes watered, salty tears dropping on to her cheeks, as she fell to the floor, totally overwhelmed with grief. Grief for him, for what was, grief for her mum, grief for herself and who she was before all this chaos stormed into her life. The cup escaped her grip and smashed on the tiled floor. The line went dead. He wanted her to phone him. This was becoming ridiculous; it was wrecking her head. What was going on?

The sound of the doorbell startled her. Could it be him? She had had enough surprises for one day, she thought, as she gathered herself and headed to the door. She quickly peered in the mirror before wiping away her tears with a tissue. It was pleasant all the same to see Pete standing there, beaming broadly from ear to ear, and bursting with even more enthusiasm than usual. He didn't appear to notice her upset and for a few minutes she was distracted by his upbeat humour as he walked in and headed to 'his chair' in the corner of the sitting room.

'Any coffee on the go?' he hinted.

'Yeah, yeah, just making it,' she replied. 'What's up with you then? Good night?'

'The best, I had a great time. She is sweet and cute, quite quiet and unlike the usual types I pursue but I am going to see her again and you never know what will happen down the line,' he laughed, cheekily.

'Her name is Chloe by the way. You introduced me to her, I think you bumped into her at the bar but sure you had only met her five minutes when you knocked a drink all over her!! Seems you were profusely apologetic and even offered to take her home with you and give her something to wear.'

'Oh no, this just keeps getting worse,' Shannon blubbered, feeling round salty tears sprinkle from her eyes. Seeing that she was becoming visibly upset, Pete immediately regretted his words and rushed over to give her a hug. But Shannon, who had been trying so hard to retain her composure, could not hide her distress and dissolved in floods of tears much to Pete's horror.

'Come on Shan, I am so, so sorry. I was just joking; you should know me by now. Hold on, has something happened? What's going on?' he suddenly demanded to know. He could sense her shudder and shake and he stood back to look at her properly.

'I'm just tired, that's all. I have had a rough day, just a nightmare from start to finish. I wish I could crawl under a shell and disappear. Don't tell me anymore about my drunken antics, please,' she pleaded, 'I am honestly embarrassed, I can't believe I tossed my drink over the poor girl. I promise it will not happen again, I am so done with going out,' she sobbed.

'It's okay Shannon, don't worry about it. You apologised and wasn't she fine? She hasn't mentioned it since. It really doesn't matter. Anyway, that's not the only reason you are this upset? Tell me,' he probed, sensing that there was more to this outburst than initially appeared.

Well, I didn't want to tell anyone, but I ran into Steve yesterday in the shopping centre and then Anita today...' she cried, dabbing her eyes with a tissue. It was weird telling him this, somehow it made it all too real which upset her even more.

Quickly passing her a new one, Pete stared at her in confusion, his face fixed in a deep scowl.

'What? What do you mean? Are you saying that they are back in Belfast? Are you serious? I am lost for words; I don't know what to say. What did he say to you? Where did you see him? Where did he go? Was he with her? Were they together? What did you say?' he asked, his tone as cross as it was urgent and desperate for answers.

'You don't have to say anything, Shannon cried, dismayed at the tears which were starting to flow rapidly again. There is nothing to say. I just need to get a good night's sleep and I'll be fine and by the weekend I'll be back to my normal self,' she sobbed, reluctant to go any further with the conversation at that moment.

'I cannot believe he has the audacity to show his face after what he did to you,' he said angrily, unable to disguise his utter dismay.

'Yes, well, he has just phoned and left a message. He wants me to meet him. He says he still loves me and Oh Pete, I feel so confused. Why are they back? Why could they not have just stayed in London? It would have been easier that way'.

Pete gripped her in a bear hug, patting her softly on the back.

'Don't meet him Shannon; he has some bottle to think he can just march into your life again. I'll soon give him a piece of my mind if I see him,' he snarled. 'He has a nerve mentioning the word 'love' after what he put you through.'

Shannon smiled. Pete was so protective; she honestly didn't know what she would do without him.

They sat there, the pair of them, for a while on the sofa, comfortable but both lost in their own thoughts and ideas and memories. Shannon soon wanted to hear all about Chloe and Pete told her all about his hot date, grateful that he could provide some mode of temporary distraction. She was surprised he was so taken with her. It wasn't like him, but she was glad. He hadn't shown much interest in women to date. Sometimes she felt guilty because she knew that she had consumed a lot of his time but he always assured her that he wanted to make sure that she was okay and that he knew how hard it was to lose a parent especially in such devastating circumstances.

7

The following day after work, she decided to purchase a new pair of trainers. She had read her new running magazine and thought she would like to give it a go. She picked up a pair of New Balance running shoes, some headphones, a pink water bottle and a bum bag for her mobile and keys. As soon as she arrived back at the apartment, she uploaded a CD to her MP3 player before scooting to her room and changing into her 'dri fit' jogging bottoms and a sleeveless, white Adidas top. After a few light stretches she was good to go. She walked for the first ten minutes where the traffic was thickest until she reached an old, bendy road which immediately led her into the countryside. She liked the fact that it was peaceful and that she had easy access from the main buzz of city life to a rural area.   She took a swig of water, adjusted her headphones and music and set off at a nice, slow but steady pace. The soft music filled her ears and she imagined her mum singing the words to her. It was lovely, so peaceful and calm with the light wind blowing softly on her face. She never thought she would like the smell of manure as normally it repelled her; but it was just part and parcel of being in the outdoors, and she felt at one with nature and its surroundings. She couldn't believe that she had never done this before. She had friends who loved running and raved about how exhilarating it was, but she always argued that she couldn't run, that she wouldn't be able to manage more than a hundred yards. She felt a slight sweat break, but she felt completely invigorated. After a few minutes, she stopped and regained her breath before restarting, remembering some of the advice and tips she had read. She felt filled with hope like all was not lost, like she could do anything she wanted if she tried. She thought of her mother and imagined her running alongside her which made her giggle aloud. The mere thought of her mother running was just hilarious, she would never have entertained the notion even if she were alive. Getting her out for a walk was hard enough and even at that, when they did walk it took forever, as her mother loved to talk and God forbid if her mum actually met someone she knew whilst they were walking because that would have add an extra half hour at least. She thought of Steve and considered the possibility of hearing his explanation, of Anita and why she had acted as she had, both in terms of stealing her man and now as regards her offer of a reason to justify what she did. She considered her dear friend Pete who had always been there for her through thick and thin and briefly wondered if she was naive to rule him out as a potential partner but dismissed that notion quickly knowing that he was quite into Chloe who according to him was a lovely girl. She recalled again how he had been when Steve left, always by her side, phoning and texting and taking her out. She remembered the few times they had shared a kiss, but it hadn't seemed right and they had both been embarrassed afterwards. In truth, he had instigated it and she had gone with the drunken flow. Had she been sober, it would never have happened. Another reason for refraining from drink! She thought of everything and nothing. She spent an hour running and walking intermittently. She had considered taking an antidepressant a couple of years back but surely there could be nothing better than the fresh air and exercise she was getting now. Had she known that exercise would have made her feel this good, she would have started it years before. She didn't attempt to run up any hills as she was conscious of doing too much and causing herself an injury. The hills would keep and hopefully in a few weeks she would manage them with no problem. By the time she returned to the flat she was sweating profusely but felt much better. She waited for half an hour, drinking a glass of Lucozade Sport before heading for a cold shower. Afterwards, as she dried her hair she felt more energised. It had not been easy and in fact had been tough, but she would get much better as her fitness improved. Pete loved running as well. Maybe she would join him down the line, once she could manage a decent distance. To date she had always refused. She had not seen the point of getting hot and bothered and stinking of sweat but maybe it would be a fun thing to do with him. Nonetheless she would go out again as soon as possible and would ask him to join her if he had time. He had a new hobby at the minute, she thought, smiling to herself. She wanted to meet Chloe, it was important to her that they be friends because Pete was so special to her. Maybe the three of them could go running and she could show Chloe that getting drunk and out of control wasn't what she was all about, that it was just a one-off. Not strictly the truth but there was no harm in a little white lie, was there? Pete had a few marathons under his belt, so he was a real pro. She would probably hold him back. Next year she might enlist for a marathon herself or even a 10k. That would be a good start, a goal for her to work towards, an achievement down the line for someone who was always indignant that she couldn't run the length of herself. Who knows, maybe one day she could run for a charity and raise some cash; that would make her mother proud for sure. She could even involve her father and Gemma if they were interested. She really ought to go home more regularly, she didn't visit much although she talked to her dad religiously every day, sometimes twice or three times. When she spoke to him later, she would arrange to call over for a coffee, maybe they could even have a wee drink together, just the one for she was turning over a new leaf. Her dad liked a drink, usually whiskey although he was fond of a glass or two of red wine. He did not really touch spirits unless there was nothing else available. She decided that's what she would do, call over with a bottle or two of red and some flowers and chocolates for Gemma. She needed to spend some time with her dad, but she wouldn't tell him about Steve as he had been disappointed in the young man and he would start worrying unnecessarily. He had regarded him as the son he never had, that was until the day he broke his beloved daughter's heart. He hadn't said much about the split at the time knowing that his wife was far more skilled at dealing with affairs of the heart.

Two weeks later, Steve was sat in the Yellow Tree Restaurant waiting on Anita to arrive. The Yellow Tree had been around for years; it was small and cosy with paintings from unknown artists adorning the walls and framed poems which were truly beautiful sitting at eye level, so that you could read them without getting up from your table. It was a quiet and unassuming place and as he sat there, he was in sombre, reflective form. He felt relieved to have finally found a flat and although ultimately, he wanted to buy a house, this new apartment would be the perfect stopgap. He would have preferred something a little bigger, but beggars could not be choosers and he would have to bide his time for the moment. Fortunately for him, Anita had come along for the viewing and managed to negotiate a short-term lease and a slightly lower monthly rental charge. She had proved a real tower of strength in recent times and he didn't know what he would have done without her. Now he was feeling more like his old self, he was keen to move on from the awful events which had led to him quitting the country and taking off to London. He hadn't expected Anita, of all people, to follow suit by any means. They had never seen eye to eye but down the line they had come to recognise that they had been far too quick to judge one another and that they were in fact totally different to what they had initially assumed each other to be. When he had first met her, he had found her cocky and arrogant, seemingly consumed by her own self-importance, which he would eventually learn was just a front. She had been through a lifetime of untold misery brought about by an alcoholic fool of a dad and a mother too meek to take a stand. Her dad had been a drunk for as long as she could remember; a vicious, bad tempered thug who thought nothing of lifting his fist and throttling her black and blue. It would take next to nothing to rattle his cage and Anita found that it was safer to stay in her room and lock the door. Her poor mother did not escape his beltings either but had always been petrified of leaving in case he finished her off completely, or worse, still vented his rage on his daughter. Not only that, but he had never sufficiently provided for his wife or child, he permitted the bare minimum for food and did nothing to help in any way around the house or otherwise. Furthermore, any money that came into the household was used to fund his atrocious alcohol habit. Anita had explained that she was so terrified of anyone mistreating her that she pretended to be ultra-confident when inside she was completely lacking in self-esteem. She said that this was her self-defence mechanism. When she had bumped into Steve in the park one day, she had hit breaking point herself and was amazed at how wrongly she had judged him. He had confided his troubles and when she realised the gravity of his problems, she had urged him to leave and let the dust settle for a while, and he had taken her advice and fled with a heavy heart. When, a fortnight later, she arrived unannounced at his poky bedsit in South London he was overawed with emotion. It had been by pure coincidence that they had met in the Botanic Gardens three days before he left. Anita had been walking a friend's dog and he had been just sitting there, head in his hands on a shabby, old park bench, close to the Ulster Museum. She had approached hesitantly as the little black Alsatian pup with her chocolate eyes skipped around his feet and wagged her tail. Before he knew it, she had joined him on the bench and he was pouring out all his problems. He remembered now her look of pure bewilderment. She thought it was all very disturbing. She had considered him a loudmouth up until that point, someone who liked to take centre stage, but the truth was the exact opposite. He was pleasant and civil and extremely distressed. He recalled how quiet she had become as he recounted the whole sequence of events that had occurred. She was sympathetic and compassionate, and had listened carefully, at times asking him to slow down because the enormity of the situation was so hard to absorb. They had sat there for a couple of hours and Anita had agreed that the situation was very serious and quite possibly very dangerous. She wasn't normally one to dish out advice, but she thought he should consider disappearing for a while, until things calmed down. He believed himself that indeed it was the only solution and it tore him in two to carry it through. When she arrived there on his doorstep, he was at his lowest ebb unable to make sense of any of it. He knew he looked awful, with his stubbly beard and his eyes were empty and haunted. He had lost weight, at least half a stone, maybe more and his frame seemed out of proportion. It was clear that he was not eating properly and that he was distraught and depressed. When she turned up out of the blue, he couldn't have been more appreciative, and she really was his saviour, for left to his own devices, he wasn't sure where he would be. Anita had been great and now as he waited for her to arrive at the restaurant; he wondered what she would make of the latest development in this twisted saga.

The waiter approached, and he ordered a large cappuccino, keeping a watchful eye on the pedestrians, going about their everyday business outside. It was a cold day, but he was in his standard jeans and t-shirt which hugged his thick biceps and shapely shoulders, courtesy of hours upon hours of hard graft in the gym. He was sinewy, stronger not only physically but mentally too. He had attended extensive counselling and was now no longer taking antidepressants. He did not feel as nervous or fretful and was prepared to do whatever it took to win back his girl. Furthermore, he knew that Anita would be behind him every step of the way.

He looked up suddenly and she was there, smiling as usual.

'Hi Anita, how are you?' he asked, rising quickly to greet her with a peck on the cheek.

She was such a petite wee thing, barely five foot and he towered above at six foot three.

'Hi Steve, it's so good to see you, you look fantastic,' she cried happily, genuinely pleased to see him. She took a seat opposite and looked at him curiously,

'Dare I ask if you have had any news?'

'Not a dickybird since Anita, obviously you already know that I ran into her in town, but she scuttled off as quickly as possible. I asked her if we could talk, if I could explain myself and why I behaved as I did. She didn't want to know; said I was two years too late. She seemed different somehow, she was very cool but then what else can I expect?' he grumbled, sadly.

'It will all work out Steve, she was probably shocked. I'm sure you were the last person she expected to see after all this time. She's bound to be cool, she doesn't know your side of the story. I saw her too by sheer coincidence when she came into our premises for an appointment with me. I dare say if she had realised in advance that it was me she was meeting, there is no way she would have shown up or else she would have just designated a colleague to take her place. I could tell by her initial reaction that she was shocked, but she put on a good front of behaving unbothered. The meeting was purely business, she didn't want to talk about personal stuff. I tried to explain but she was adamant that the subject was off limits. She was by no means rude, but she had her head together and although pleasant, she made it crystal clear that only business was on the agenda. Besides, Steve it's much better to come from you than me,' she mumbled, clearly perturbed.

'Don't worry Anita, you did your best. It is just one big, ugly mess, I phoned her and left a message, but I don't know if she even got it and if she did, then she's obviously made up her mind,' he replied, gloomily.

'Steve don't give up, these things take time, it might take months, years to sort out but I have faith that it will all come good in time,' she consoled.

After a light lunch, they sauntered through the park towards Anita's new apartment which turned out to be the trendiest, coolest place he had seen in a long time. She had done well for herself returning home and obtaining a decent job and a nice place so quickly. Later when Steve returned to his own place, he felt inspired to give it a thorough clean. He changed the sheets, dusted and vacuumed. He sorted through his clothes and dumped the ones he had not worn in a while and when he had finished, he poured himself a glass of wine and retrieved his old photos.

He examined all the pictures of himself and Shannon, one taken at the Eiffel Tower when they had only started going out, others from their weekend in Amsterdam not to mention countless holiday snaps from exotic locations within Crete and Spain. He had fallen in love with her immediately. He hadn't expected that to happen, but he couldn't help himself. She was funny and kind, and sweet and beautiful, so beautiful inside and out. He loved her raven black hair which seemed slightly shorter now and her gorgeous, sparkling eyes set in a face that looked like a porcelain doll. He loved how she was so organised one minute with everything having its place and then the next she was totally absent minded. He loved the stories she told about everyday things that happened, she always seemed to get herself into these weirdly, bizarre situations.

He loved her personality, and the fact that she could hold an intelligent conversation with anyone no matter what the topic.

She was warm and friendly, and she had wit and charm that far excelled that of anyone he had ever met in his life. She was everything to him, nothing had changed, and he would fight for her. He would do whatever was necessary to persuade her to see him and after he managed that he would explain everything that had gone down a couple of years before, and they would get back together come what may. He would give her a few days grace and then he would call again. He was absolutely determined that she knew the truth. She had been the love of his life and nothing had changed in that respect. He had moved in with her quickly after they met, and she had made him the happiest man in the universe. They had made all sorts of plans together from backpacking around Australia to trekking across the Inca Trail in Peru. They had talked engagement and babies and discussed moving out into the country at some stage in the future. It had been perfect. Of course, there had been a few heated rows along the way but never anything serious. There would be one hell of a row now though. He had to tread carefully. He knew without a shadow of a doubt that he wanted to marry her, he had always known that, and nobody would ever come between them again, and especially not Pete Mc Glynn. Indeed, he would win back her affections and then he would marry her and they would spend their lives together. That was his goal, his dream! He knew that it was going to be difficult and could potentially be dangerous but that was a risk he was prepared to take. Unfortunately, he had no idea how close Pete was to Shannon, he would discover that soon enough.

8

Pete was not happy about Steve's return. In fact, ever since he had heard that he was back, he had been stomping around like a bear with a sore head. He was worried and he had every reason to feel as such. Later in the week he decided to head over to the girls' flat to catch up. Normally he would phone first, but he didn't bother this time. Chances were one of them would be on the phone and he would get the usual message informing him to try again later. He called regularly with the pair but now with Steve showing up, he was anxious to hear if there had been any further developments. When he arrived, there was no sign of life, so he let himself in. It was handy to have his own key, he thought. He liked slouching around Shannon's pad – it was a palace compared to his poky, wee bedsit.

'Shannon, Mel, anyone home?' he yelled.

There was no reply. They were obviously both out but undoubtedly, they would not be far away, so he decided to wait. He would have a hunt for his bank card in the meantime. He had already searched his place high and low for it, but to no avail. He knew that he had it the Saturday they had been out drinking as he had used it for a withdrawal, but he hadn't seen it since. He had another one and he had been withdrawing cash from that account, but he needed to find the one he had lost or else inform the bank so that he could be sent a replacement. He made himself comfortable, removing his trainers and socks before sauntering into the kitchen and switching on the kettle for a cuppa. He noted that the breakfast dishes were stacked up on the worktop and quickly retrieved a large, clean mug from the cupboard. Where were they anyway? And why did they always insist on instant coffee when they had a proper coffee maker, he sighed. He had bought them the coffee maker as a Christmas present but for whatever reason they never seemed to use it. He doubted they even knew how to use it. They were obviously still drinking the instant stuff. There was no comparison between the two, as far as he was concerned. He liked real coffee! The phone started to ring and he debated on whether or not to answer it but decided he wouldn't bother. He figured if it were important enough, they would ring back. He stretched out on the sofa and switched on the television but promptly switched it off again when he heard the voice on the machine, Steve's voice. He sat up straight and listened, every muscle in his body tensing with deep fury. What the hell was he doing ringing here? Could he not just leave Shannon alone and stop chasing her like some crazy stalker? This was not good enough. Shannon would freak out completely. Poor girl! He replayed the message and listened intently, but he was boiling with anger, a cloud of red-hot rage enveloping his usually handsome face. Suddenly, he heard footsteps and the sounds of the girls laughing outside as they made their way up the path towards the front door. He quickly pressed the delete button on the answer machine and flicked on the TV channel to Sky Sport before assuming his previous position on the settee. The two girls burst into the room giggling, their faces devoid of makeup, wearing gym gear. Neither of them noticed him at first but they glanced at each other knowingly. There was only one person who watched Sky Sport and had a key.

'Hi ya Pete,' they chanted simultaneously, still laughing.

'Well hello there you two, you could knock you know!' he laughed.

'The cheek of you, it's my house,' stated Shannon, playfully punching him on the arm.

'What are you doing here anyway?' she asked, popping out to the kitchen and returning with his missing bank card which she was waving in the air.

'Was this what you were after? I sent you a text when I found it, after I cleared your account that is,' she sniggered.

'It must have fallen out of your trouser pocket when you were sleeping. I found it when I was vacuuming.'

'Thank goodness for that,' he said, 'I've searched everywhere for it and no, I didn't get your text because my mobile needs charged and I can't find my charger anywhere,' he groaned. 'Anyway, I will have to love you and leave you, I am meeting Chloe for a quick drink,' he said, hastily pulling on his socks and shoes and bolting for the door.

'Oh hang about, where are you off to? Do you have to go so soon? Did anyone ring when we were gone?' she asked.

'No, no calls,' he lied, giving Shannon a quick hug before quickly shutting the door firmly behind him.

'He's in a hurry, isn't he? He doesn't hang around,' Mel yelled from the spare bedroom.

'He does seem rather preoccupied. It's not like him to rush off like that. Not like him either to go off on a second date so soon. Maybe this is the one,' she commented.

'The one is you, but you don't need me to tell you that. Can't you tell the way he looks at you? It is so obvious!' Mel groaned.

'Oh Mel, come on, give over. Seriously you are like a broken record, there is nothing between us. We just enjoy each other's company, end of,' Shannon retorted, sternly.

'I know, I'm just envious that you have your own personal bodyguard Shan,' her friend whispered, irked with herself for opening her big mouth.

'Tea?' Shannon suggested.

'Sounds good,' Mel replied.

'Mine is black with one sugar,' Shannon laughed, before curling up on the sofa and flicking on Coronation Street, whilst Mel went off to the kitchen to make a brew relieved that Shannon wasn't upset with her.

Meanwhile, Pete was on a mission. He rushed home to his bedsit and peeled off his clothes before quickly jumping into the shower after which he hurriedly rummaged through his wardrobe and picked out a clean pair of jeans and a shirt. He pulled the shirt on so quickly that he didn't notice the red wine stain down the front and he promptly tore it off. Swearing to himself, he scanned the room for something else to wear but it was such a mess he couldn't see anything suitable. Clothes were piled in various corners of the room, some were clean, but most were dirty and he needed to go to the laundrette. There were empty beer cans lying around and the remainders of the Kentucky he had consumed the night before. He finally located a pale blue t-shirt and pulled it on quickly. He lifted a bottle of Paco Rabanne aftershave and managed to squeeze out a drop or two before casually tossing it on the floor along with all the other garbage. He kicked a few old papers and magazines under his bed and managed to break a clock in his rush around the room. It was a depressing sight but the least of his worries. He would get around to cleaning it when he was good and ready and it wasn't as if he would be bringing anyone back. He had never brought anyone here! Not even Chloe, he said aloud. All this nonsense about Chloe and they had believed every word of it. There was no Chloe, there would never be a Chloe for there was only one woman in the world for him and he would stop at nothing to win her over. Steve could go to hell. If he wanted a battle, he would get one. He should have stayed where he was, he should never ever have come back.

He has made one hell of a mistake, he growled to himself, grabbing his bank card and slamming the door behind him. After a few minutes he managed to flag down a taxi and ordered the driver to bring him to The Red Tiger, a trendy, upmarket bar in May Street, right in the city centre. Steve was going to get one hell of a surprise when he sauntered in. He had a gall to phone Shannon and leave a message like that, begging her to meet him in town. Thank goodness he was in the flat when the message came through and was able to delete it in the nick of time. The traffic was busy, and the taxi driver stopped unexpectedly for another fare. A pretty girl jumped in and Pete noted her scanty clothes and made up face. No doubt she was going on the manhunt, silly girl. She started to converse with him, but he simply nodded and wished for the journey to hurry up and end. He was in no mood for small talk. He looked at his watch impatiently and realised he was late but that wouldn't matter because Steve would probably wait all night if he thought she would eventually turn up.

Finally, the taxi pulled up outside the Red Tiger and Pete stepped out, handing over his share of the fare. The girl smirked, she probably expected him to pay all of it but why the hell would he. He didn't know her!

He smirked back and wandered up to the entrance of the bar, acknowledging the bouncers standing outside.

'Sorry Sir, no jeans I'm afraid,' one of the doormen stated, blocking his entrance with his bulky form.

'But I've arranged to meet someone; I don't mean to hang around.'

'Rules are rules, no jeans here, if you are meeting someone send a text or phone whoever it is because you are not coming in here tonight and that's final.'

Pete was livid, he didn't have his mobile phone as he still hadn't found the charger and he didn't have Steve's number anyway, it would have to wait. He glared angrily at the two burly bouncers and stomped off in search of another taxi. What a waste of money and time! There was no point in him trying to argue his case. Those boys would stick to their guns, forcibly if required. He contemplated returning to Shannon's pad but given that he had lied that he was out with Chloe he had no choice but to return to his own pad. That was probably the best option anyhow as he wasn't sure that he'd be able to disguise just how annoyed he was feeling.

He started towards the taxi rank but on passing a busy bar decided to have a quick pint. In fact, he might have two. He elbowed his way through the crowds of young revellers to the bar and ordered a Carlsberg, before heading over to a corner booth, the only unoccupied one in the bar. He hadn't taken more than two sips of his beer when the scanty girl from the taxi rushed over, her mini dress barely covering her ample charms. It wouldn't have been so bad he thought if it fit, but there were more bulges than he cared to count.

All the same, fair play to her, he thought, as there was too much emphasis on size zeros these days. He would rather someone with a few curves than a beanpole with none. She was a curvy girl, but she needed someone to teach her how to dress.

'Did you get stood up then?' she demanded to know.

'No, someone else did,' he grimaced.

'Ah, too bad, their loss and dare I say my gain?' she chuckled, flirtatiously.

'You never know your luck,' he answered, wondering how on earth he had had the misfortune to run into her again.

'Did you get stood up?' he fired right back at her. He didn't care if she had been or not but couldn't think of anything else to say.

'Not on your life, I was meeting my sister tonight, but I had to persuade her to leave her husband behind and come out on her own. Got herself a bit of a sugar daddy, if you don't mind. To be honest, I can't believe I quite coaxed her to hit the town, but it seems he was more than content for her to come along,' she said. 'Told her it would do her good, getting out for a night with her little sis.'

'Is that right?' he answered, forcing a smile.

'Of course, he is a lovely man, her husband, and she is lucky to have found him, so now she is well settled whereas I am still out on the party scene, doing the same old thing, strutting my stuff. If you've got it flaunt it, that's my motto.

Anyhow, they have just informed me that I am to be an aunty so of course I am thrilled to pieces,' she droned on. Just then a tall, very pretty blond approached the table.

'Gemma, Gemma, come and meet someone... oh I am sorry, what is your name?' she demanded to know.

'My name is Pete,' he replied, wondering how on earth these two girls could possibly be related. They were so different. The sister could flaunt it, he thought, with a figure like that, and her pregnant too!

'I believe congratulations are in order, can I get you a drink?' he asked politely.

'Cara, how could you? You know we are keeping it quiet. Gerry hasn't even told his daughter yet and there you are spouting off to strangers, no offence Pete. My little sister has a mouth on her the size of a truck,' she protested, glaring at her sibling.

'Ah sure it's great news, especially at his age, I am just so elated for you, I cannot wait to have my own little niece to dress up,' Cara argued.

'Less of the age business if you don't mind. We haven't got our bus passes yet and we don't know for sure that we're having a girl either. I wish you could put a zip on it sometimes. That mouth of yours is going to get you in big trouble one of these days,' Gemma protested, in annoyance.

'Ah sure come and sit down, your secret is safe with me,' Pete insisted, sliding over in the booth to make room for her. For the next two hours the three of them sat chatting and ordered another few rounds of drinks. Gemma sipped orange juice and whilst they tried to tempt her with a half pint of Guinness emphasizing the benefits of its iron content, she wasn't interested. Meanwhile Cara knocked them back and the more she had the flirtier and louder she became. It was clear she fancied the pants of Pete, but Gemma observed a distinct lack of interest on his part. It was obvious he had a lot on his mind and whilst relatively civil, he was quite monosyllabic in his answers. She couldn't blame him either because Cara was giving him the third degree, questioning him about his work and what he did for a living but more importantly trying to gauge if he had a girlfriend. Eventually, after an interrogation from Cara he confided that there was someone special, but it was not straightforward, in fact it was complicated. He outlined how he felt he had made some headway but that unfortunately her ex had reappeared on the scene and was starting to make a nuisance of himself. He even described how he had invented a girlfriend called 'Chloe' to try and push things along, make the girl he loved jealous. He explained how he had pretended he was on a date with her tonight when in fact she didn't even exist. He appeared angry at times and after a whiskey or two became quite vocal and aggressive. Gemma wondered whether he had a split personality. There was something about him that bothered her, but she couldn't quite put her finger on what it was. Of course, Cara didn't notice and continued fluttering her eyelashes like butter wouldn't melt in her mouth.

'Pete, why bother with someone who blatantly isn't interested in you, perhaps she still loves her ex and...'

'Stop right there. 'You know nothing about it, what we have is special and she feels the same, she just hasn't realised it yet,' he boomed. Cara giggled nervously but his expression seemed to soften quickly, and he apologised for his outburst claiming he was just a bit stressed out. Gemma was not impressed by his tone and smiling at both, excused herself on the pretence of needing the ladies. She sent her husband a quick text and told him she couldn't wait to get back but that she wanted to ensure she got her sister home safe first. She lied that she was having a good time, but the truth was she had had enough. She hadn't wanted to go out in the first place, but her younger sister had pleaded with her until she eventually relented. Gerry was more than glad for her to go, told her it would do her good and that he would wait up for her, enjoy a glass of wine or two and watch a movie in the meantime. She heard her mobile bleep, read his reply and smiled. She was so lucky to have met him for he was everything to her. Friends were initially shocked that she was seeing a man so much older than herself but when they met him, they immediately saw the attraction.

He was a fine figure of a man, startlingly handsome with his blue, blue eyes and tanned skin. He was her very own silver fox, a cross between Philip Schofield and Richard Gere, only taller and broader, she thought. Not only that but he was as nice as he looked with a witty sense of humour and so much charisma that she quite simply fell in love at first sight. She later learned that he was widowed and was dismayed to hear that his wife had been killed tragically. She was also extremely cautious when he first asked her out but within a matter of days all caution flew to the wind as she found herself head over heels in a whirlwind of romance. Now instead of curling up beside him on the sofa, she was in a rowdy bar watching her sister make a fool out of herself, fawning over some strange weirdo who quite obviously had no more interest in her than the man in the moon. She strolled slowly back to the booth and was even more taken aback to find her sister sprawled across this Pete guy, making out like there was no tomorrow. She coughed a couple of times before they came up for air and looked at her slightly embarrassed.

'I'm going to head now Cara, I am pregnant after all and this just isn't my scene.'

'Oh, come on, I am just getting started sis,' she squealed.

'I can see that Cara, but I want to get back. It is nice to meet you Pete, but I am taking my sister home. I could give you a lift if you like,' she offered hesitantly, hoping that he would decline.

'Yes, that would be great Gemma, thanks,' he slurred, standing up somewhat unsteadily whilst Cara tittered hysterically beside him. Honestly, her sister had no shame.

They made their way outside to Gemma's black Mercedes Benz and the pair of them climbed in the back. Pete gave her directions and they stopped outside his pad twenty minutes later, the longest twenty minutes Gemma ever had to endure with all the smooching and petting back there. Honestly, they should just get a room, she fumed silently, or else at least show her a bit of respect and refrain until they were alone. She switched the music up louder and wished to God that she could turn the mirror around, so she didn't have to see them cavorting. She busied herself for a couple of minutes checking her Facebook notifications as Cara stepped out of the car to say goodbye. She noted the pair share a last, lingering kiss and felt mildly nauseous as she waited patiently for them to separate.

'Thanks Gemma,' he said, 'nice to meet you Cara,' he added, grinning stupidly.

'Oh, are you not going to invite us in for a nightcap?' At least let me have your number and maybe we could have a repeat performance,' she persisted.

'Nothing like being assertive young lady, here you are, my mobile number,' he agreed, handing her his details which he had quickly scrawled on the back of an empty cigarette box. He leant over and pecked her on the cheek before thanking her sister and taking off up the path like a drag queen in the highest stilettos you could imagine.

'You have no self-respect Cara, have you ever heard of playing it hard to get?' Gemma remarked, gazing at her, with a mixture of sympathy and annoyance.

'It's alright for you, married with a baby on the way. What am I meant to do?' I liked him, I met him in the taxi on the way into town and he's the first person in ages to take my fancy.'

'You don't even know him for God's sake. He could be anyone, a serial killer for all you know. No offence little sis, but I wouldn't trust him as far as I'd throw him and you do realise that he is totally besotted with someone else or were you missing for that part of the conversation,' she said sternly.

'Oh, give over Gemma. He's gorgeous and I am a single girl. Wind your neck in and leave me alone, I appreciate your concern and I am sorry that I disappoint you but see it from my point of view please. I am fast heading for the shelf, I only have a couple of good years left in me and then everything will go downhill, I will be past my sell by date in no time,' she whimpered, feeling hurt and annoyed.

Gemma apologised, she did understand because she had felt that way herself before Gerry had turned up and changed everything. True, she had been with Alan for a couple of years, but he had been unreliable and unpredictable and he had no get up and go whatsoever. His idea of a perfect night was watching a football match in the house with a few beers whilst she waited on him and his friends playing the dutiful girlfriend. She always hoped that he might change but a chance meeting at a petrol station altered everything. It had been raining that day and she had just put thirty pounds of petrol in the tank. However, as she was hurrying into the filling station to pay, she slipped and fell over in her high heels, hurting her ankle and her pride. She reckoned that despite the pain in her ankle the embarrassment was far more painful. Grimacing with pain and humiliation and aware that the contents of her handbag were spewed all over the forecourt for everyone to view, she attempted to get to her feet and rescue her belongings. That was how she met Gerry Dobberty. He was on his way out of the garage and came upon her sprawled on the ground by the double glass doors of the main entrance. He looked at her for a second, as if mildly puzzled before immediately crouching down beside her to see if she was okay. Before she had even replied and as if sensing her discomfort, he had swiftly scooped all her scattered personal items back into her handbag which embarrassingly enough contained her tampax and panty liners. That done he offered her his arm and helped her to her feet. Even now, she would redden thinking about it. Aware that she seemed quite shaken, he had proposed a coffee in the little restaurant next door so that she could get herself together. She had gladly accepted, not wanting to get back behind the wheel until she had composed herself. Besides, he seemed such a gentleman, coming to her rescue like that. She was glad to have a coffee with him and they had sat for a long time talking. Gemma found him extremely attractive and was drawn to his magnetic personality. He had worked for years as a Principal of a reputable grammar school and he was also well travelled and well read. She had noted the absence of a wedding band on his finger and wondered if he was married or divorced. That became clear a few weeks later when he explained everything. The coffee that day marked an end to her stale relationship and low and behold, Alan was history and Gerry quickly became her future. She did appreciate how hard it was to meet people these days, but Cara did herself no favours. She was going about it the wrong way, wearing revealing clothes and getting blocked – she was a sweet girl with so much going for her, but she was attracting the wrong sorts. Some things just never changed, she thought sadly. She wanted her sister to meet someone nice who would look after her and treat her well, but she really didn't think that meeting a nice guy in a pub after a feed of drink went hand in hand. Cara was just coming across too easy as far as she could see.

As they pulled up outside Cara's quaint little cottage, Gemma thanked her for a great night and watched as she trundled to the front door and fumbled for her keys. Satisfied that she was finally safe behind closed doors, she drove off waving at her younger sibling who was peeking out at her from behind the curtains. She would phone her in the morning and check that she was okay. She knew that she had upset her, but she just wanted her to know her own worth, stop settling for bad boys and find a good, decent man. She really thought it more likely to happen in a gym, or at an evening course or bloody hell, a filling station. Cara was getting too desperate and there were certain men that could smell that desperation and would take advantage. Pete, she was sure, was one of those. He would take what he could get and be gone just like the guy before him, and the one before that. The only decent one had been Matthew and he had been crazy about her but Cara grew bored with Mr Nice Guy and by the time she changed her mind and saw the light as it were, he had got hitched to someone else and moved abroad whilst Cara involved herself in a series of ill-fated, casual flings, all the while regretting what could have been, had she played her cards right in the first place. She thought that the grass was greener on the other side but soon learnt that was not the case at all.

Now, she was lusting after this Pete guy, whom she was sure, had only one thing on his mind and knowing her sister; she would throw herself in deeply as she always did and end up nursing yet another broken heart.

9

Meantime, Pete was throwing off his clothes, scowling at the litter bin that had become his home. It had been a good enough night, not entirely satisfactory though considering he had been declined admittance to the Red Tiger. Too swanky for jeans? Indeed. Steve was obviously going all out to make an impression, but he was fighting a losing battle. Soon enough, he would be on his way again if he had anything to do with it. He was only a coward anyway, tall and thin with his long neck and big head, just like a baby giraffe, he smirked. However, the night hadn't been all bad! The girls had been fun, more than he had expected. Gemma was particularly striking. If it wasn't for Shannon and if it wasn't for her being pregnant with some old bloke, he might have been interested. She was a bit stuffy though although a few drinks might have loosened her up a bit. She was a true chaperone to her sister as well and God knows the sister needed it. She was so easy looking in that cheap dress and heavy make-up, but she might have her uses he surmised. She was full on, but she was good fun and apart from her constant stream of questions he found he had enjoyed her company. Suddenly it occurred to him that perhaps Steve had phoned Shannon again and managed to entice her to meet him.

He poured himself another drink and lifted the phone. When she answered, he hung up. At least she was home; he smiled to himself, quickly downing a double vodka before diving into bed. He would get a good night's sleep, tidy up the place in the morning and head to the cottage in the country for a couple of days. He loved that old cottage which his parents had left to him in their will. It was as ancient as the hills and required a massive refurbishment but for now, it suited his needs perfectly. Located next to a river and surrounded by lots of green trees and endless fields it was the ideal location for him to retreat, think things over and devise a plan of action. Yes, that's what he would do; take himself off for a little break and some quiet, peaceful meditation. On those thoughts, he fell into a deep sleep and when he awoke the next day with a throbbing headache, he poured himself a large glass of water and swallowed it down with two paracetamols. He then quickly set about the mammoth task of cleaning the bedsit. He emptied bins, gathered up all his clothes and put them in a giant, black bin bag which he would deliver to the laundrette on his way to Killywillin. He washed the dishes and dried them before tackling the shower which now in the light of day seemed so much grubbier than he had imagined.

He even managed to find his charger underneath the avalanche of paperwork and magazines he had thrown beneath his bed. He would charge up his phone when he arrived at the cottage and check his messages. He switched on the coffee machine and hunted out his sports bag before loading it up with everything he needed for a couple of days in the country. He thought about ringing Shannon but figured he would get on the road as soon as possible and perhaps call her later. Shoving his phone and charger in his pocket, he gulped down a milky coffee and after tossing the cup in the sink, switched everything off and locked the door behind him. Two hours later, having completely forgotten to stop by the laundrette with his dirty washing, he reached the cottage and the first thing he did was charge his phone, before lighting a roaring fire and switching on some light, classical music. How he loved this place! His parents had wanted to sell it years before they passed away, but he had told them that was unreasonable, that after they had gone, it would be all he had to remind him of them. He had reassured them that one day he would like to settle here and that he would bring life back into the place; that they would live on through him and his children. They, in their old age had agreed and said that nothing would make them happier. Of course, he was no further ahead a decade later of producing any offspring, but he was determined that that would change soon. The next couple of days he would spend working at the house, he would tidy up, paint a few rooms and do some light gardening. He could not wait to prepare the house for her arrival. She would be so pleased especially when she saw the lengths he had gone to, to win her approval. He would get started on the master bedroom he decided and take it from there. The master bedroom after all was the most important. He was interrupted by the sound of his mobile ringing but happy when he saw Shannon's name flashing up on the screen.

'Hi Pete, it's me. I was just wondering if you fancy doing something?' she asked.

'Sorry Shan, I am absolutely up to my eyes here. How are you though?' he asked gently.

'Fine Pete, fine, what are you doing? How did it go with Chloe? Where did you go last night?' she asked him.

'I am fine, everything is fine. I have come down to Killywillin to the cottage. I have some clearing up to do so I thought I'd best get on with it,' he answered.

'And how are things with Chloe? Is she in Killywillin with you?' she asked.

'Chloe is fine, she is with me, in fact,' he lied.

'Must be love, love,' Shannon sang down the phone.

'Yeah must be, look I'll give you a call back,' he laughed, ending the conversation more abruptly than he had intended. Never mind, he thought. He would call her later, he had far too much to get through. Why had he told her that Chloe was with him? It couldn't do any harm, he reckoned. She had never seen him with anyone or heard him talk of a girl, perhaps it would ultimately give her food for thought. Make her a bit jealous, make her realise that he was the one; she would know that soon enough when she saw the huge effort he had gone to for her. He had wasted enough time already and he sure as hell wouldn't waste anymore. All these years he had loved her and been too cowardly to admit it for fear of rejection but now he was going to take the bull by the horns and she would be left in no doubt, no doubt at all. He had been patient with her and God knows it was hard sometimes. When her mother had died it had been the perfect opportunity to get closer to her especially since Steve was off the scene. Not that he would have wished for it to happen that way, her mother had apparently been a lovely lady and no-one deserved a fate like that but as it happened her mother's death had pushed them together more than ever. He had not known either of her parents; he had seen them when they had picked her up once or twice from the youth club in their younger days, but they had never been introduced. Besides he was a lot more awkward then and even his own parents had no idea that he visited the club at all. He would just pretend he was going out on his bike for a while and disappear for a couple of hours. Of course, he had to cycle about three miles to reach the little village where the youth club took place. He had gone along to the wake to pay his condolences when Shannon's mother had died but her father had been resting at the time, worn out physically and mentally. Shannon's mother had been laid out in the downstairs living room and she just looked like she was sleeping. He didn't recognise her face as obviously a long time had passed since he had seen her, but he could easily identify the striking resemblance between mother and daughter which was also evident by the numerous photographs hanging high on the walls. He heard his phone bleep and smiled to himself. She was missing him already but when he read the text he swore impatiently as it was from none other than Cara. She sure was persistent, he mused, and he set the phone on the chair, not bothering to reply, at least not for a while. He wouldn't rule her out completely though, not yet. She might just come in handy!

10

A couple of days later, Mel was on her lunch break and decided to make good use of the time by going to the leisure centre. It had been busy in the salon and she quite simply couldn't wait to get out. Whilst she loved her job, sometimes it could be difficult. It was tiring standing on her feet all day and whilst generally speaking she enjoyed chatting with her clients, there were days when she wished she could just do her job without uttering a single word. As it was, she was always up to date on all the gossip. She could rhyme off all the names of local people having affairs or coping with divorce or drink problems. All she ever did was nod but she deliberately never made comment. She knew too well that loose comments could be repeated and misconstrued and she was not going to be a victim of her own lack of discretion. Anyway, exercise always gave her a boost and she felt sure that a twenty-minute workout on the treadmill with a few lengths of the pool to finish would set her up for the rest of the day. She felt inspired by Shannon's new fitness drive and decided to follow suit, not so much with the running as she had injured her foot some years before but maybe a brisk walk on the treadmill would get her started on the right path.

She hurried along to the centre and quickly changed into her sports gear. She enjoyed the treadmill, but the pool was the highlight and after 10 lengths she felt bursting with energy and raring to go. She loved swimming and had won a few competitions years before but unfortunately, she had let it go as her social life took over. She hoped that if she started off gradually again that she could build it up to a good standard once again. After a quick shower at the leisure complex she quickly pulled on her clothes and with her hair still soaking wet she made her way to Tesco's Express. She quickly opted for a meal deal, tuna and cucumber sandwich, packet of crisps and a diet coke, before rushing off to the salon for the afternoon rush. She wouldn't eat the crisps, she decided. There was no point burning off all those calories to immediately cancel it out with fattening junk food. With ten minutes of her lunch break remaining before her first appointment of the afternoon, she munched quickly whilst doing the Mail crossword. She had a passion for crosswords and she reckoned that it had improved her vocabulary somewhat. If she couldn't work out an answer, she could Google clues on her mobile so next time she would remember.

'Your client is here Mel,' yelled Claire, a young trainee who had only recently started working in the salon.

'Be right there,' she yelled back, before quickly rinsing out her cup and checking the diary. Wash, colour and highlights, she noted, quickly fixing her own hair which had gone mad curly after the swim. It was always the same when she didn't blow dry and straighten it immediately afterwards. Some example I am setting, she thought to herself. She made her way out to reception and came face to face with Anita who of course had no idea she worked there, having been away for so long.

The two girls stared at each other in confused silence before Mel spoke first,

'Hi Anita, are you my appointment? I have a wash, colour and blow dry,' she stated, looking around to see if there had been a mistake or if someone else was waiting nearby.

'I guess so. Is that okay? I mean if you feel uncomfortable, I could go somewhere else,' she mumbled. 'I'm not here to cause trouble, I just….my hair is in an awful mess,' she babbled, anxiously.

Mel was flabbergasted. What could she say? She was the last person she wanted to see but she couldn't exactly kick her out, that wasn't her call or maybe she would have considered it.

'No, it's fine, I'm just a little surprised to see you after all this time, that's all,' she said, 'can you just put the black cloak around you to protect your clothes and I'll gather up what I need.'

Anita did as she was asked whilst Mel fled out the back and took a few deep breaths. She felt flustered. She didn't want to encourage conversation, but she had to remain polite. She had her job to do and she took great pride in her work. Maybe she would mix the colours a little, overdo the tones or add a little green or pink. She just couldn't believe the coincidence, of all the salons in the town Anita could have chosen and she had ended up here. She sighed heavily before making her way back towards Anita and the job in hand. Together they studied colours and styles and decided on a short casual bob. Mel began carefully trimming off the split ends. Then she added the colour and told her that she needed to wait 20 minutes for it to take. She offered her a coffee and a biscuit which was gratefully accepted and handed her a copy of the local community magazine. Ten minutes later, Mel checked how the colour was progressing and they talked again briefly. Anita asked after Shannon and said she had seen her in her office but that they did not really get a chance to chat. Mel already knew of their meeting and informed her that Shannon was in great form and had taken up running. She said how she was planning on her very first 10k soon with the intention of doing the Dublin marathon later in the year, perhaps with Pete. Anita asked about him as well and what he was up to these days and Mel said that he was fine, he was a regular visitor to the flat and that as far as she was concerned they were meant to be together and that it was only a matter of time. Anita showed no emotion although deep down, she was very concerned.

'Steve has tried to get in touch with Shannon, you know,' she said.

Not wanting to be drawn into this line of discussion, Mel studiously checked her hair,

'Right, that's you, let's wash this out and see how you look. Come on, follow me.' After a relaxing shampoo and deep conditioning treatment Anita was sat in the chair again whilst Mel set about shaping her hair before blow drying it and using the straightening irons. She was glad that she was almost done and the whirring of the hairdryer made conversation virtually impossible. She massaged serum throughout and a quick spray completed the look. She had done a good job and probably had knocked a few years of the girl's age. Shannon had said she looked awful the day she saw her, but Mel considered her looking quite well despite the false tan which when applied densely did no-one any favours.

'What do you think then? Are you happy with it? Is the back okay?' Mel enquired, holding the mirror up and turning it around so Anita could get a good view.

'More than happy Mel thanks,' she smiled. 'It's great. Please tell Shannon I was asking after her and I hope her and her family are well, it would be nice if she would grant Steve a chance to explain himself,' she added.

'For your information Anita, Shannon's mum died three months after you two took off together, so I don't expect she'll be interested in hearing any explanations. It was not a good time. Thank you for coming in, I do hope you like your hair and I'll see you in here again, perhaps,' Mel retorted more sharply than she intended, before moving on to one of her regulars who was awaiting a perm. She could tell that Anita had lost the power of speech and was shocked to see the girl's eyes well up as she quickly handed her some cash and told her to keep the change. She practically raced out the door and took off like a hare down the street, almost flooring a little, old lady in her rush. Mel felt a stab of regret, perhaps she had been too harsh, but she had to state the facts. She didn't want to have the discussion in the first place and now she had upset a client and whilst that client was an ex friend she knew now that she would fret and worry because there was nothing she hated more than causing any degree of misery to others. It was evident that Anita knew absolutely nothing about the tragic events surrounding Maeve Dobberty's death and that probably hit home because Maeve was very popular amongst all Shannon's friends. She had assumed that Anita would have known or heard from someone but that did not appear to be the case which probably meant that Steve was also unaware of the dreadful accident hence his failure to attend the funeral or even send a card. Over the next few hours Mel tried to focus on her work but far too often her mind would roam and she would find herself thinking about Anita. There was something weird about the whole thing and she wondered if there had ever actually been anything between Anita and Steve. In fact, Anita had seemed eager that Shannon see him. It was really puzzling. It wasn't what she would have expected. Now she had to figure out whether to tell Shannon and risk upsetting her or say nothing at all.

When the last client of the day had gone, she quickly set about brushing the floor, washing the sinks and rinsing the hair appliances, after which she lifted her sports bag, said goodbye to the remaining staff and headed off down the road towards home.

11

Shannon was already in the kitchen when she arrived back, her head buried in a mountain of bills and paperwork from the office. The place was totally spotless and had been given a thorough spring clean. Mel offered her a coffee, but Shannon favoured a green tea for a change. After all, if it could boost the metabolism it was a healthier choice. Mel hated green tea with a passion and so settled for her usual Nescafe before joining her friend at the table.

'How was your day?' she probed, still wondering if she should tell her.

'Same as ever, went to work, prepared CVS, interviewed candidates, worked on the computer, interviewed more candidates, made some business development calls and that was it. I had to send Anita Dolan the CVS I promised, which was fine because better that than to have to hand them over personally. Of course, I will still have to phone her to see if she would like to interview any of them, but I can handle a phone call I think.'

'I saw her today....' Mel stuttered, realising that there was absolutely no point in retaining the truth. It might hurt now, she figured, but it would hurt more later if Shannon discovered that Mel had been dishonest. Mel studied the look of confusion on her friend's face and was dismayed to see her eyes fill up.

'But how, why...did she get in touch with you?' Shannon cried in disbelief.

Mel interrupted quickly, 'She came into the salon, she had made an appointment, she didn't know I worked there and I didn't know what to do. I couldn't refuse to do her hair. I would have got myself fired. She asked about you, she wanted to know how you were and how was Pete, she asked about your family too. She didn't know Shan. She didn't know about your mum. She was very sorry. There were tears in her eyes and she looked very remorseful. I've been feeling really bad all day since she left, I was really sharp with her.'

Shannon looked stunned. 'I can't believe that she didn't know about my mum. Surely someone would have told her. Do you think that means he didn't know either?'

'If she knew then all I can say is that she is a fine actress. She was really distressed,' Mel answered.

Did she mention him?'

'Yes Shannon, it seems he is really wanting to talk to you and she seemed all for it. Don't ask me what is going on, I just can't work it out.'

The phone interrupted their conversation and Mel ran over to answer it glad of a quick pause in the discussion which was intense to say the least. She lifted it, said hello and then hung up.

'Weird, no-one there,' she mumbled.

'Not again, that's about the fourth or fifth time that's happened. You don't suppose it's him, do you?' he asked. 'It happened last night as well, as soon as I picked up the line went dead.'

'If it is him, then he is more of a coward than I thought. Why would he bother ringing just to hang up? Sounds like a waste of time to me.'

'Yes, it doesn't seem his style,' Shannon agreed.

'Any word from Pete, Shan? What about him and Chloe? Is she still on the scene?' Mel asked next.

'He's down at the cottage with her. I reckon it must be serious because in my knowledge he has never brought anyone there before. I called him the other day and he was meant to call me back, but I haven't heard from him since. However, 'no news is good news' and he is probably having a whale of a time. Besides, I don't want to be ringing him when he is away with his new girlfriend. It is not fair on her,' she added.

'And you're happy with that Shan, are you?' Mel enquired.

'Please get it into your head Mel, that nothing is ever going to happen between myself and Pete, I am not interested in him that way, I haven't been since I was about 11 years old and believe me that is a long time ago. I know we have kissed a couple of times and that was wrong. Neither of us would want to jeopardise the friendship we have by making it into something that it is not nor never will be.'

'Okay I believe you Shan, I really do this time. Maybe…. I just thought, because you had become so close that it would be a shame to rule it out, but if you're not interested then you're not interested. Anyway, what do you say we forget about all this for a while and go out and grab a bite somewhere? I fancy something nice for tea,' she suggested.

'Great idea,' Shannon agreed and with that they both took off to their rooms to freshen up. A half hour later and they were both ready, dressed casually and Mel had managed to wash her hair and tidy it up somewhat. They decided to check out a little pub called The Wasp's Nest as they always served decent food there at reasonable prices. Shannon ordered her favourite scampi dish with mushy peas and chips and of course a portion of tartare sauce whilst Mel opted for lasagne with side salad and garlic potatoes. They had a couple of glasses of wine with their meal and reminisced about their student days and places where they had gone together and as usual, they both had the tissues out to wipe away their tears of laughter. They kept the conversation light-hearted and steered away from any talk of Steve and Anita. Afterwards, they strolled home, arm-in-arm, still chuckling together. When they returned to the house the answering machine light was flashing to indicate two messages. The first was from her Dad asking her if she could call by the following day for a chat. He had something that he wanted to tell her and Shannon detected a happy, relaxed tone in his voice. She wondered if he had bought himself yet another gadget. The second message was blank and when she dialled 1471 the number was withheld. She glanced at her friend and merely shrugged her shoulders and smiled. It seemed odd but she was shattered now and without further ado said goodnight to her pal and headed off to bed.

12

Meantime at her dad's house, Gemma was feeling awful. She thought the morning sickness would have passed by now. She was nearing the middle of her second trimester and it still hadn't eased. She constantly felt nauseous and hopelessly tired. Gerry was being great, giving her lots of attention and constantly keeping an eye on her, ensuring that she rested and eased off on housework. She didn't know what she would do without him.

When she realised that she might be pregnant, she had locked herself in the bathroom to do a test and whilst waiting impatiently for the result yelled at him to come upstairs. Gerry had rushed in moments later to find her perched on the edge of the bath, tears of joy rolling down her face, clutching that little stick like it was the last penny in her pocket. They were absolutely delighted to see the two strong blue lines revealing a positive result. She kept the test for a few days so she could repeatedly check that she really was expecting a baby. Of course, they had discussed the possibility of having children of their own but knew that they were no spring chickens and that they might have been past their sell by dates in that capacity. They had also recognised that as older parents there was an element of risk, the baby might have Downs Syndrome or God knows what else, but it was a chance they were willing to take and as far as they were concerned, they would love their baby, no matter what difficulties might arise. They figured that if it was for them it would not go by them and either way so long as they had the love of each other then life would be great whatever way it turned out. She hadn't bargained for the awful prolonged sickness though, not for this length of time anyway. She thought that once she had reached the three-month milestone; that she would be full of energy and raring to go. The only place she was raring to go now was her bed but that was not an option. Today,

Gerry's daughter was visiting and she had a mountain of things to do. She decided the first thing would be to tidy herself up a little, look more presentable. She looked like she had put on a few pounds as opposed to looking pregnant. Friends of hers had said it was a tricky stage because you never looked pregnant, just fat! She was looking forward to having a proper bump. Nevertheless, she knew that she was extremely fortunate to be expecting a baby and she did not plan to be negative, especially as regards to a bit of weight. A few hours later, she had showered and dressed and washed her long blonde hair which was shining in all its magnificent glory. She had been to the shops and picked up some fancy queen buns and various nibbles, including cheese and pitted olives, as well as a bottle of Westland wine, in case father and daughter fancied a drink. She had even managed to give the house a quick clean, she was very house proud but had let things slip recently due to her condition. At 8pm on the dot Shannon rang the bell and she rushed out to meet her. She had told her several times that she had no need to ring the bell, that it was still her house and she should come on ahead in, but Shannon simply told her that she preferred it that way.

Gemma opened the door and greeted her stepdaughter with a hug. She was very fond of her and hoped that their friendship would develop; she also hoped that she would be happy with the news that they were about to impart. She was worried that Shannon would be offended that they had not told her of the pregnancy sooner, but they hadn't seen her in a few weeks and it was not news to deliver over the telephone. She didn't want her to be a stranger; indeed, she understood why she had stayed away so much and for so long but deep down she longed to be friends and get to know her better. She really didn't know her well at all and she had never met any of her chums and whilst Gerry spoke so lovingly of her, as any father would, he didn't share much, despite her occasional interrogations.

That was his type, he didn't believe in gossip for the sake of gossip, and whilst he had confided in her about his daughter's failed romance, it hurt him too much to go into the detail.

'Come on in Shannon, it's great to see you, your dad is just pottering about the garden and I thought we would have a cuppa out there on the patio, as the day is so nice.'

'Sounds great,' Shannon answered, her eyes taking in the new, cream coloured wallpaper in the hall. It was so tasteful and really seemed to brighten up the place. It had been quite dark and dreary before. Seemed odd that a lighter wallpaper could have such a dramatic impact, she thought.

'I'll just pop out the back and say hello to dad,' she said, removing her navy-blue denim jacket and carefully placing it over the back of a chair.

'You do that, I'll bring out some coffee in a minute,' Gemma replied, hurrying towards the kitchen. She really hoped that this would go well and was already feeling a little nervous and queasy but wasn't sure if this was as a result of her pregnancy or the thought of revealing it to Shannon. It was major news for her and Gerry at any rate and she hardly dared hope that Shannon would be just as pleased.

'Hi dad,' Shannon yelled. 'Still pretending you're the next Alan Titchmarsh, I see?'

'Ha ha, what do you mean, pretending?' he laughed, scooping her up in a big bear hug. 'I am so glad to see you, come and see my new toy.'

He led her excitedly by the hand over to the garage to reveal a massive ride on lawn mower and lovingly patted it as you do a new dog.

'Bought this the other day, it's fantastic, it takes me no time now to get the lawns done, plus it's so much easier on the back; a real blessing.'

Shannon knew that from time to time his back played up on him and she could tell he was over the moon with his new purchase.

'Showing off his new toy?' Gemma laughed, appearing beside them with a tray laden with coffees, sandwiches and buns.

Gerry smiled, swiftly moving two chairs back so they could sit down. Once they were comfortable, Shannon scanned her dad's garden appraisingly. There were lots of pretty shrubs and flowers, and he had his own prized vegetable patch where he grew potatoes, scallions, strawberries and even rhubarb which if the truth be told, she didn't really like. She recalled the rhubarb tarts and crumbles that religiously followed the Sunday roasts she had when her mum was alive. For some reason, she had never really been a rhubarb fan, a fact that had not gone unnoticed by her folks. When the sun was shining brightly, this was her favourite place in the whole world. After several minutes of light-hearted conversation, Gerry suddenly grew serious and taking both Shannon and Gemma's hands in his, he looked at his daughter earnestly.

'We have some news for you love,' her dad said quietly. 'I, we are hoping that you will be as happy about it as we are,' he added.

'Dad?' Shannon said, looking anxious.

'We are having a baby.'

Shannon glanced up quickly, wondering if she had heard him correctly.

'Gemma is expecting; she is in her second trimester.'

As the words sank in, Shannon leapt to her feet and threw herself into the open arms of her dad before literally pouncing into the arms of her stepmother and squeezing her tightly.

'I am so happy, oh my goodness, when?' 'I'm going to have a sister or a brother?' she yelled, starting to dance around the patio area.

The reaction was better than Gemma could ever have hoped. Shannon was ecstatic! She asked question after question and was bubbling with happiness and enthusiasm. They opened the bottle of Westland and had a drink to celebrate. They talked about the baby; that they felt sure it was a girl but that they were going to decorate a nursery in neutral colours and wanted her to be involved as much as possible. Shannon bombarded them about names and scans and eventually when they were talked out about 'babies' she told them all about what had been going on in her life. She decided to tell them about meeting Steve and her encounter with Anita, she talked about Mel and how she was being as supportive as ever and she mentioned Pete and his new girlfriend Chloe. She described with great passion how she had taken up running and that it was doing her the power of good. An hour or so later, they were joined by Cara, Gemma's sister, who had decided to pop over and they had another drink or two with her. By this stage, it was clear that no-one was going home as they had consumed too much alcohol to drive. Shannon had only met Cara a handful of times in the past but the two of them hit it off like a house on fire. Gemma asked Cara about her new love interest and Cara explained that she had heard nothing from him since to which her sister advised her that she was fighting a lost cause and to let it be.

'He may be a handsome looking guy but looks aren't the be all and the end all. It was crystal clear that he is obsessed with his friend. For God's sake, he has even invented a 'fake' girlfriend to try and make her jealous. Besides there was something about him which freaked me out a bit. One minute he was nice and the next quite aggressive. I am sorry Cara, I just worry that you are setting yourself up for a fall, I really do. I am only telling you this because I love you and don't want you getting hurt.'

Cara felt a flush of embarrassment. She felt like she was being given a dressing down but joked it off knowing that her sister was only doing it out of concern. 'You have to kiss a lot of frogs before you meet your prince and there are plenty of frogs out there,' she cracked. She talked about meeting Pete and admitted that she had been quite forward but 'nothing ventured nothing gained' was her motto. The others were amused by her banter and listened and laughed as they consumed a good few drinks. When the night cooled, they moved indoors and talked some more. Gemma eventually succumbed to her tiredness and went to bed. The others followed suit in the wee small hours, having enjoyed a great night's crack telling stories. Gemma was thrilled that the news had gone down so well, Gerry felt relieved, and Shannon felt chuffed to pieces. She would be the best sister in the world, she thought as she snuggled under her duvet and fell into a deep, peaceful sleep.

Gemma was first up the following morning and softly crept downstairs, her stomach as usual, churning around like a washing machine. Despite the horrible nausea, she was in good spirits and as she cleaned up, she sang softly to herself. She was surprised when less than an hour later; the others joined her in the kitchen. She did not expect to see any of them before mid-day, but they were all up and raring to go.

Shannon asked some more about the baby and reiterated how happy she was. After some lightly buttered toast and a strong cup of coffee, she said she had best get home as she had a to do list the length of her arm. Gerry walked her to the car and after seeing her off, joined Gemma and Cara in the sitting room. He smiled lovingly at his wife and said,

'You see, I told you so, you worry too much....... Shan is overjoyed at our news.'

'I know Gerry, you were right, it could not have gone better. I am so happy; I just wasn't sure how she would take it. I was worried that she would be annoyed that we are only telling her now, but she just seemed to take it all in her stride.'

'That's Shannon for you Gemma. She is quite laid back. She is beyond thrilled and her reaction has exceeded my expectations so you can stop worrying now,' he reassured her, clutching her hand in his.

'Do you think she seemed okay Gemma? This business with Steve seems to have hit her hard. It is obvious that she is very mixed up what with him suddenly turning up again. I just hope she doesn't cut her nose off to spite her face,' he said, anxiously. 'I was fond of him too, but it was all very bizarre, they were happy together, really content, I would have been glad to have had him in my family, I just think that she should hear him out. I, for one, would be interested to hear his reasons for behaving as he did. I still just don't understand it.'

'She is a grown woman Gerry, she'll do what she thinks is right but I honestly think that if she loves him, and I believe she does, that she should hear him out, as you say, see what he has to say for himself,' Gemma agreed.

'It's just that she seemed to be on the right path, getting back to her old self again, she took the whole thing very hard and then she had to deal with her mother dying. Sometimes I wonder if I could have done more,' he stated.

'Oh, listen to you two, Shannon has her head firmly on her shoulders, she isn't as soft as she looks, she is just like me. There are plenty more fish in the sea to fry,' interrupted Cara.

Gerry and Gemma looked at her, then at each other before bursting into fits of laughter, for they knew that the pair of them were like chalk and cheese.

13

When Shannon arrived back at the flat, having stopped to run a few errands on the way, she had four messages waiting. One was from Mel who had decided to stay over at her Mum's for the night. Apparently, her mother was feeling poorly and Mel decided to stay home and look after her. Typical of Mel, so kind and considerate! It was such a shame that Mrs Black was ill but Shannon knew that Mel would wait on her hand and foot until she was well on the road to recovery. It was a pity that she would have to postpone telling her the amazing news as she would be just as elated as her. That could keep though. The main thing was that Mel's mum got over her illness and got back to her old bubbly self soon. The second message was from Pete advising her that he was still in Killywillin and that he was doing lots of work to the cottage. He sounded cheerful and said that he would call over as soon as he came back to the city. The third was from her dad checking that she had made it back safely and to phone him as soon as she came in to confirm her arrival. She smiled when she heard his voice as she knew what he was going to say as soon as she heard him speak. He always phoned her to make sure she was safe. The fourth, which caused her to immediately sit down, was from Steve pleading with her to call him and mentioning something about the Red Tiger and her not showing up. This, she didn't understand! What did he mean? She replayed her saved messages wondering if there was a possibility he had phoned and Mel had forgotten to let her know. That didn't seem right though! She would ask Mel later when she came home. She replayed the message, saved it and sauntered into her bedroom. She needed to get out of the house and get some fresh air. After quickly ringing her dad back and confirming that she was indeed home and safe, she popped on her trainers, shorts and a t-shirt and headed for the forest. She managed to run at a good pace for twenty minutes this time without stopping and felt very proud of herself. She would not dwell on any negativity. There had been good news. She would have a new baby sibling shortly. She was reading Self-Help books and felt that she really could change her ways. She was particularly taken by a book called 'When I loved myself enough' by Kim McMillen. She was determined to look after herself better but how could she do that by seeing Steve – it would be like one step forward and ten steps back. Her mind was in turmoil, so many conflicting emotions spinning around in her brain like a tornado, powerful and totally destructive. She plugged in her earphones as a distraction from the storm of thoughts invading her brain and tugging at her heart and started the return run as Lady Gaga took over with Poker Face. Listening to the music, she let all other thoughts drift away and began her journey back enjoying the familiar feel of the light, evening air caress her face. When she finally unlocked her front door, she was surprised that she had been gone for a couple of hours. It hadn't felt that long! She glanced at the answering machine and felt relieved that no light was flashing. She hurried through to her bedroom and stepped into a cold shower. She would have to contact Anita this week to see what she made of the C.V.s she had forwarded. She made a mental note to do that and after pulling on a nightshirt sat in front of the television, with a mug of steaming hot chocolate in her hand. She was exhausted though and found it hard to keep her eyes open, so she locked up and got ready for bed, sprinkling a little lavender on her pillow before flaking out on top of the duvet and falling fast asleep.

It was the middle of the week before she managed to get hold of Anita who had requested to see two of her applicants for interview as soon as possible. She declined her offer of lunch and again reiterated that she did not want to discuss anything of a personal nature. Anita told her that she really should see Steve and Shannon, without raising her voice, left her in no doubt as to what she now felt about him. They continued their discussion with Shannon checking Anita's schedule to organise interviews. After obtaining an email address in order that she send a confirmation of suitable times and dates for interviews, Shannon politely said goodbye and hung up.

As it turned out, Mel's mother had developed pneumonia and Shannon did not see her for a couple of weeks. Mel eventually returned looking totally drained. The girls talked but Shannon refrained from spilling her worries to her pal. She had been through enough and was tired out. She did however tell her about Gemma's surprise pregnancy and Mel was just as delighted as Shannon thought that she would be. She just hoped that everything would go well and that there would be no difficulties. Joe popped around for a couple of hours and the couple headed out for a bite to eat. They invited Shannon to join them, but she declined, aware that they needed some time together. Joe was a lovely guy, very together and level-headed and Shannon hoped that indeed one day they would walk up the aisle. She could not think of anyone more suited to her friend and it was a bonus that she got on so well with him. Pete was now back and strangely hadn't called round but maybe he was too caught up in his new girlfriend. He had rung her a few times and seemed somewhat distracted but assured her that everything was fine and that he would see her soon. He asked about Steve and whether he had been in touch again, but Shannon told him that all was quiet on that front. Pete seemed satisfied and after hanging up began getting ready for his date with Cara whom he had agreed to hook up with for seconds.

Cara had been pleasantly surprised by his proposal of a second date and had suggested the Bluebell Tavern, a short taxi journey from her cottage. He had not offered to collect her and she wondered if he was trying to play it cool. She knew that he would hail a taxi rather than drive himself so realistically he could have picked her up on the way, but she wouldn't dwell on something so trivial at the minute. If he was playing it cool, she would too. Two could play that game, she decided, slipping on a little, black number and a pair of pointy, patent stilettos. She looked at the mirror and frowned. She had put on weight and she wasn't sure if the dress did her any favours. She didn't want to give him any ideas either. She sighed as she quickly pulled the dress up over her head and slipped into a pair of white linen trousers and a casual top instead. Satisfied, that she looked more sophisticated, she slipped on her leather jacket and a coloured scarf before contacting her regular taxi firm. Fifteen minutes later she was sipping a vodka and diet coke in the tavern waiting on him to turn up. When he eventually arrived a half hour late, he mumbled an apology for his delay before sitting opposite her in the booth.

'You look well, I must say, though you're a persistent young lady,' he said, smiling. She noticed that he had had his hair cut quite short and it suited him immensely.

'Persistent or pushy?' she enquired, laughing.

'I wouldn't want to say, he replied. So, how are things with you?'

'Good,' she replied, trying to cover her annoyance that she had been sitting on her own for the past 30 minutes twiddling her thumbs. She didn't like anyone keeping her waiting especially a bloke. However, a drink or two later and there was no stopping the conversation, at least on her part. She told him about her work in Sales and how she was seeking a career change. She said she would prefer to be more office based because as a Medical Rep her job was taking her all over the country and she was fed up with the driving and ridiculous hours. She also outlined how competitive a market it was and how her performance was target driven with immense pressure which seen her working many a weekend. It was dog eat dog and she was keen to resign, the deadlines and targets becoming increasingly difficult to achieve. She described how she had been to University and completed a Business Studies degree with French. She had graduated with a first-class honours and had intended to go off to Paris but circumstances had intervened and she had stayed in Ireland. She was not totally unhappy with her work, but she just wanted a break from the normal, to try other things whilst she was still young enough. She absolutely loved French but knew that to pursue it properly, she would have to go to a French-speaking country. She asked him about his work, but he was not forthcoming and preferred to hear about her than talk about himself.

'How is your sister doing these days?' he asked, summoning the bar tender.

'She is getting along fine, she is suffering the most terrible nausea and feeling quite uncomfortable, but she really only has a few more months to go and it will be all over. Then, the fun and games will really commence,' she declared.

'Would you like kids one day?' he enquired.

'One day,' she answered quickly. She didn't really care either way but thought that she should handle his question with caution.

'I definitely do but I've got to meet the right woman first,' he admitted.

'And dare I ask, how is that going?' she sniggered, feeling herself blush.

'That is not going too well right now,' he laughed. Then looking at her with a more serious expression he said,

'Look Cara, I like you, you are a nice girl, but you are wasting your time with me! I really am in love with someone else. My heart belongs to her.'

'Okay, okay, let's not talk about that, let's just have some fun. I'm not after anything serious,' she protested. Inside however, she felt slightly devastated. It was not the response that she expected. She would almost have preferred if he had lied than be so blunt.

'I just want to be honest with you, that's all, but if you are happy with that, then who am I to complain?' he answered.

After the pub closed, he offered to walk her home and she accepted. Slightly giddy from her few drinks she offered him a nightcap and was pleased that he accepted.

She had a bottle of brandy in the cupboard and they knocked a few back before he admitted that it was away past his bedtime and he should go. Cara was having none of it though, and brashly made a move. She knew deep down that he wasn't really interested but she couldn't help herself and as she led him to the bedroom all thoughts of sanity totally deserted her. He had been polite the whole evening, and she thought he was gorgeous. He had also been entirely honest with her and part of her still hoped, that maybe given time, he might want to become more involved. At any rate, she would enjoy the moment, as it were, because they were few and far between. She hurried into the bathroom and emerged a couple of moments later in her silk negligee. She didn't remove her makeup as she didn't want to scare him off completely when he already scared so easily. He was already half undressed in her bed and she hopped in beside him flicking off the lights as she did so. The darkness made her braver and as she moved towards him, all thoughts of playing it cool died. She knew what she wanted and even though her subconscious was screaming at her to refrain from sleeping with him she had no intention of listening. She was madly attracted to him and nothing, not even her very own Catholic guilt was going to stop her doing what she wanted. He was hers for now and that was better than nothing. She had every intention of making the absolute most of it for however long it lasted. Unfortunately, that wasn't very long at all, she thought afterwards. In fact, it was quite disappointing.

As they lay there for a while each in their own thoughts, she wondered whether maybe he was just a bit nervous or perhaps it had been a while since he had been with a woman. Either way, she had expected more experience. 'Perhaps he just needs more practice, hopefully I can teach him,' she laughed to herself. 'Or maybe it is because he is madly in love with someone else,' her inner voice scorned. He was already asleep and she curled up behind him, enjoying the warmth and comfort of having someone she really liked in her own bed. There was no way she would be sharing this news with Gemma. She couldn't take any more lectures from Miss Prim and Proper. It seemed no time before the sound of the alarm startled her, she switched it off and rolled over to the other side of the bed, but it was empty. He had gone! She wiped the sleep from her eyes, smudging the rest of her eye makeup all over her face, before jumping up and running around the house, shouting his name, like a woman possessed. She couldn't believe that he had gone and she hadn't even heard him go. You had to really slam the front door shut because it was so stiff, yet he had managed to do a runner without sight or sound. It was then she spotted a tissue lying in the middle of the coffee table and written in a scrawl in black marker was one word - Thanks!

'Oh no, what have I done,' she uttered aloud.

'Thanks', 'Thanks', he says.

'Told you so,' she heard back.

She was devastated. She slowly made her way back into the bedroom and flopped on the bed, tears trickling rapidly down her face. She sobbed and sobbed like there was no tomorrow. How could she have been so stupid? So much for playing it cool and trying not to seem desperate! She was so upset with herself but the upset soon boiled into anger. How dare he treat me like that? Who does he think he is? Brad bloomin Pitt? Not likely! Does he think he can discard me like a sack of dirty rubbish? They had a nice night, good conversation although ultimately, she did most of the talking; he had walked her home and accepted her offer to come in for a drink. Why did I throw myself at him? she screamed. She rang in to work and booked the day off because she couldn't face it. If the truth be told, she couldn't face anyone, not even herself. She felt desperately lonely and rejected and she didn't know what she had done wrong. Her head felt sore and she chided herself for not drinking water before she hit the sack but then again water had not been the first thought in her head last night. She popped an aspirin and slipped back under the duvet. Thank God, they had taken precautions because the last thing she needed was the worry of an unwanted and unplanned pregnancy. A few hours later, she was still suffering from a dreadful hangover not to mention the sheer guilt and despair at what she had done. She had also been violently ill which was hardly surprising given the brandy and wine she had foolishly taken. Maybe this will be a lesson, she thought trying to find something positive from the experience. She really wished she could talk to Gemma about it, but she could not bear to hear the disappointment in her sister's voice – again! She heard her mobile bleep and reached across to her bedside cabinet to check the message.

'Sorry, had to rush out like that, I had an appointment first thing and totally forgot about it. See you soon x,' it read.

Her mood changed instantly. She was ecstatic. She leapt up from the bed, raced into the shower, washed her hair, and applied her full make up whilst listening to Pink at full volume. She wouldn't reply just yet. No, this morning's emotions had been the wakeup call she needed. She had been silly and irresponsible and maybe it was time to take a leaf out of Shannon's book and behave a little better. Maybe, she would even take up running! She knew that Shannon had discovered a passion for pounding the pavements and thought that it was wonderful, a great stress booster not to mention toning up the physique. She had learned a very hard lesson this morning and whilst much happier now that at least he had made contact, she would not forget how low she had felt in the last couple of hours. Gemma was right. She needed to up her game!

14

Pete didn't have an appointment at all. He had woken up early and decided to get back to the bedsit and give it a good clean. She had been fast asleep when he decided to slip out. Had he woken her up she would have started to talk and he would never get away. He hadn't planned on a nightcap or what followed but he simply couldn't help himself. It had been a long time since he'd been in bed with a woman, too long he thought to himself, grimacing as he recalled their 'quick' encounter. She was quite nice, bubbly and enthusiastic. He could do a lot worse than have her as his girlfriend but being with her had not diminished the fact that it was Shannon he loved more than anyone. When he returned to the bedsit he cleaned up and it was beginning to look a lot tidier – he could see the carpet again. Everything was starting to fall into place and he was feeling upbeat. There was still a lot of work to be done to the cottage but there was no immediate rush. They had their whole lives to finish decorating it and he didn't want to alter too much in case she wanted to make her own changes when she arrived. He had kept the colours light and bright throughout and he had even gone to Ikea and bought new wardrobes, sets of drawers, a coffee table and all sorts of other items which he thought were cool and modern and which he was positive she would like too. Shannon was a big fan of Ikea and had dragged him round it several times, so he had a good idea of her taste which had to be both modern and practical.   Pete didn't particularly like big stores, particularly furniture ones as a rule, but he would do anything to spend time with her, so if she fancied a trip to Ikea then that was good enough for him. He knew that he would have to come clean soon, confess his true feelings; he couldn't keep putting it off. Steve was an obstacle for sure but not one that would be too problematic. He had scarpered the last time and he would do the same again, of that he had no doubt. It had worked out perfectly that Anita had followed suit, it had been so easy to put two and two together and make five. If he had planned that one out, he could never have planned it so well. Naturally, it was very hard to see the love of his life going through such pain and grief, but that was how it had to be. Life was tough sometimes. There was absolutely no way that he was going to sit back and watch their relationship blossom all the way to the altar. He could not for one moment contemplate that possibility. Now, he would just bide his time and in the meantime, perhaps see Cara again. He liked her, she was quite pretty with a fun personality and if it weren't for his love of Shannon, maybe he would pursue her. Why would he have a burger though, if he could have steak? He hadn't meant it to go anywhere and especially not to the bedroom, but it was obvious what she was after and who was he to refuse an offer like that? Yes, it had been fun and perhaps he would repeat the experience, but there was no way it would progress in any other capacity. Part of him felt sorry for her, she had an air of desperado. It occurred to him that women were all the same, they all got a bit desperate when they hit thirty. All that body clock ticking stuff really started to hit home once they came of a certain age whereas men weren't that bothered. It's a man's world, he thought, arrogantly. He would send her the odd text, keep her sweet and treat it as it was; nothing really! It wasn't as if he hadn't been honest either, he had told her in no uncertain terms that he was in love with someone else. It was up to her whether she could accept that and if she could then great, if she could not that would be fine too.

15

That evening he was going to the pub with Shannon, Mel and Joe. He was fond of wee Mel. She spoke a lot of sense and was always very welcoming to him. Joe was a decent bloke too and was always up for a laugh. He was glad that the four of them were heading out as they hadn't seen much of each other in recent weeks what with all his treks to Killywillin and his supposed romance with the mysterious Chloe. He arrived first and was glad that pub grub was still being served as he was starving. He ordered a large cheeseburger with chips and a pint of lager and scoffed it down in no time. As he finished his pint, the others charged through the door and settled down beside him. Drinks were ordered and everyone sat around chatting. Pete had to try hard to keep his eyes off Shannon. She looked stunning as usual in a simple teal coloured maxi dress and flat sandals. She always looked perfect. Of course, they were all very interested to hear about Chloe, but he played it down and admitted that whilst he was still seeing her, he wasn't ready to settle down just yet. He did tell them about his work on the cottage and told them that when it was completed, he would hold a great, big party to celebrate.

'Seriously guys, you would love it down there. It is so peaceful and tranquil; there is not a house nearby, just lots of trees and fields all around. At night-time you can hear the river gushing along and in the morning time, you are awakened by the birds chirping outside,' he described.

'Sounds a bit spooky Pete,' cried Mel.

'On the contrary Mel, it is quiet and calm, sometimes in the mornings I bring my coffee down to the water edge and sit there, occasionally someone will walk or run alongside the banks of the river but apart from that, I guess you don't see too many people. I don't mind though, it's beautiful, the ideal home.'

'Would you live there full time?' Shannon enquired.

'For sure Shan, who wouldn't?' he replied.

'It sounds delightful, how far does the path go?' she asked.

'It runs for several miles Shan, it's not very smooth in places though, it gets a bit bumpy here and there, but it is a great route for running or walking.'

'Sounds perfect', she sighed.

Pete was very pleased with the interest that was being shown, particularly from Shannon. She was going to be so overwhelmed with joy when he admitted that she formed a major part of his plan. He couldn't wait to tell her. He was so engrossed in his own thoughts that he hadn't realised that suddenly things had become ever so quiet. He looked up and realised that his three companions were staring at something or someone very intently. He immediately followed their gazes to the couple who had just walked in and sat themselves down in a booth in the corner. His gaze quickly turned to a fierce scowl as he realised just who had become the focus of their attention. Knowing that his group had not yet been spotted, he turned to the others,

'Okay, right, let's just go quickly, they don't know we are here. We can get our coats and go somewhere else,' he suggested.

'Are you out of your mind Pete? This is my local and I am not budging,' Shannon cried, indignantly.

This could be tricky, Pete thought staring at his rival. He looked different, and he was trying to work out why. He had always been rather weedy in appearance, but he had quite evidently been spending time at the gym because he was built like a tank. He shuffled uneasily in his seat. This was not good. He didn't look so wimpy now; he looked fit and athletic. Just then, Steve caught his eye and retaining intense eye contact, sprung to his feet and made his way towards him. He looked irate, Pete thought, feeling a tightness grip his chest, as he squeezed his sweaty palms under the table.

Acknowledging the others with a warm smile and a nod Steve turned to Pete and spoke purposefully and without fear,

'Well, well, well, if it isn't Mr Mc Glynn, I was wondering when I would have the fortune of making your acquaintance again.'

'Now is not a good time, in fact it is never a good time so why don't you just do one and leave us in peace,' Pete responded scornfully, leaping up to face him straight on.

Shannon glanced from one to the other. She had never seen Pete behave so aggressively in her life and she would never even have thought that he was capable of it. As for Steve, it was difficult not to detect the sarcasm in his tone, the tension between the pair was immense, but she could not for the life of her understand why.

'Steve, just go, Pete has nothing to do with this. You made your bed and now you have to lie on it,' she pleaded.

'Shannon, as always it is lovely to see you and I am disappointed that you won't give me the chance to explain. Perhaps Pete will explain? Will you explain Pete?' he demanded, his eyebrows arched high as he waited for a reply.

'Pete will explain what? What are you talking about? Seriously Steve, just go now, please just go, I don't know why you are involving Pete,' Shannon said, confusion written all over her pretty face.

'Pete is very much involved, aren't you Pete?' Steve growled, sarcastically.

'Get lost Steve, she is not interested. Look, here comes your girlfriend, Anita,' Pete barked, as Anita slowly approached the group.

He had to keep his cool, on no account display any indication of exactly how enraged he was feeling. He felt ready to explode and the sooner he got out of here the better for everyone.

'Come on Steve, there is a time and a place and this is not it, let's just go,' Anita muttered nervously.

'Okay Anita, he answered softly, before turning towards Shannon and saying, 'you have got this all wrong, I will never give you up, not ever Shan,' he finished. He stepped towards Pete, the tension between the pair of them dark and oppressive, 'you tell her the truth Mc Glynn and you tell her very, very soon.'

With that the pair of them turned on their heels and walked quickly out of the pub and the four that were left sat in stunned silence.

'Pete?' Shannon finally whispered, slowly bringing her eyes up to meet his and ending the deathly silence lingering in the air.

'Shannon, I don't know what he was talking about, he has obviously been on a pub crawl and has had one too many. I have never heard such bullshit in my whole life. He wants you back and somehow or other, he reckons that I'm to blame for everything,' he said angrily.

'But Pete, what did he mean? I just don't understand, I have never seen him like that. And Anita? What is going on? I have doubts as to whether they were a couple in the first place – he is being very open in front of her. If they were ever an item, it would seem very insensitive to be saying such things so publicly. She was totally unfazed by everything freefalling from that loose tongue of his.'

'Look, Pete's right, when the drink is in, the wit is out. Sure, isn't that what folk say?' Mel interrupted, glancing at Joe for some support.

'I don't know what's going on here, I am completely at a loss to understand it,' Joe replied, glad that the confrontation was over without anyone getting hurt.

'Yeah, I guess so. Nevertheless, I am ready for home. I've had quite enough excitement for one night,' Shannon muttered. 'What about you Pete? Do you want to come back to ours?'

'No, I think I'll hit the road and get an early night,' he answered apologetically, briefly draping his arm around her shoulder. 'I feel really bad, he must be jealous, to spurt all that rubbish. I just don't get it at all. He obviously wants to make amends and is dropping all responsibility at my door. The man is mad; he has obviously totally lost all sense of reality.'

'I don't get it either Pete. He knows how close we are. You and Mel mean everything to me. You have been there for me through thick and thin. Don't give it another thought. Quite frankly, I have neither the time, nor energy for all this drama.'

Pete gave her a kiss and set off into the night, shaking his head as he walked away. He was ripping mad. How he had managed to disguise just how irate he was, he didn't know.

'Poor Pete, he is so upset and he is not the only one,' Shannon yelped, linking arms with Mel and Joe as they slowly trundled home.

'Pete will be okay, he can handle it, it looked like they were about to come to blows in there though,' Mel replied.

'You know, folks, I think I'm going to get away for a week, somewhere in the sun, maybe one of the Greek Islands or Spain. It is going to be busy in a while what with the new baby and now is probably the best time to head off and get my head cleared.'

'That sounds like a fabulous idea, I would love that,' Mel said quickly, before glancing at Joe for a reaction.

'Why don't the two of you head into town tomorrow and get a last-minute deal, you've both had a lot of stress lately and whilst I'd love to go too, I would not be able to get time off. That doesn't stop you two, though,' Joe insisted.

'You wouldn't mind Joe? I could do with it,' Mel squealed, happily.

'I would be happy for you to go, so long as you bring yourself back in one piece,' he assured.

Shannon was delighted. A week with her friend abroad was just the tonic she needed.

'What about Pete? Do you think we should ask him?' Mel enquired.

'No, he is loved up with Chloe and I would not want to rock the boat, sure, it would be lovely if he could come but it would be unfair. I don't want him to feel under pressure.'

'Probably, a good idea,' Joe agreed.

The following morning the two girls headed into town to the travel agents. After pricing various deals in the Canary and Greek Islands they eventually booked a break to La Manga Strip in Spain. They would fly into Mercia and be collected at the airport and taken by taxi to their five-star hotel where they had chosen an All-Inclusive deal. Shannon phoned Pete to tell him their plans and ask him to keep an eye on the place in their absence. He was very quiet.

'I wish I was going', he whispered.

'I was going to ask you to come but I didn't think it fair on you or Chloe. I don't anticipate she would be happy for you to holiday abroad with two girls.'

'I understand,' he replied, but he was absolutely fuming when she finally ended their call. Things were not going how he had planned. How perfect it would have been to spend a whole week with Shannon in the sun and he had messed it up all by himself. All those silly lies he had invented and now they had backfired badly. He could have done with a break to gather his thoughts. He was extremely troubled by the incident involving Steve and Anita and felt that time was closing in on him. If he didn't start to act quickly, everything was going to start crumbling around him. When he had returned after that night at the bar, he had gone berserk, he had wrecked his bedsit, drank copious amounts of whiskey whilst trying to concoct some sort of sensible plan to resolve all the matters troubling him.

16

The next day he phoned the girls early and offered them transport to the airport for an early afternoon flight. It was pouring down at home and he felt extremely envious that they were escaping the awful weather which was forecast to last at least ten days. As he loaded their suitcases into the boot of his car, he couldn't help smiling at the excitement the two were displaying. It was as if they had never been abroad in their lives. Upon instructing Mel to look after Shannon and not let her drink too much or do her idiotic party piece he waved them off and watched as they skipped through the main airport entrance with their brightly coloured luggage. It was only a two-hour flight to La Manga and before long the pair had checked in to what would be their new home for the next week. The air was warm, the skies blue and clear and from their outside balcony they had a perfect view of the Mediterranean waters on one side and the Mar Menor on the other. The Mar Menor was a beautiful lagoon, described as the biggest swimming pool in the world. They spent their days swimming in its warm, shallow waters and only ventured to the Mediterranean side once. The waters of the Med were colder and rougher and they didn't hang around that part too long. Instead they bought a couple of lilos and would paddle around in the warmer waters of the lagoon, feeling the sun's warm rays softly caress their bikini clad bodies. The sea was never cold; it was just like lying in a wonderfully, hot bath. Sometimes they practically had the beach to themselves as the Spanish retired for their siestas mid-afternoon and didn't return until evening. There were few foreigners around aside from themselves, and a couple of Germans. It was a Spanish resort for the Spanish which suited them just fine. At around 7pm they would crack open a bottle of wine on the beach and sit and chat until it was almost dark. They loved watching the sunset as the sky became a wonderful array of breath-taking colours that was postcard perfect. Later, they would return to their hotel and shower, their favourite music filling the room as they rushed around, drinks in hands, trying on dresses. Every night was a fashion show as they swanned around like models on a catwalk, taking photographs of each other as they tried on several outfits, one after the other. They would chatter and laugh before heading to the restaurant for a meal after which followed a pub crawl and a few cocktails. They received plenty of male attention and whilst extremely flattering neither of them were bothered. Mel was obviously loved up, but Shannon was just grateful to be sharing a week's vacation with her friend – she didn't need anything more! In truth, it was the last thing on her mind. One evening was spent on the Catamaran, known as the 'Party Boat' which they boarded at 900pm and passed three hours merrily drinking Sangria and Tinto Verano. They weren't quite brave enough to dive offboard like the crowds of younger revellers but that was mainly due to the hordes of jellyfish they had spotted whilst peering over the edge. Both feared jellyfish and were thankful that the nets on their beach kept them at bay. There was only the occasional sighting of a brown one, which apparently was not dangerous. Another evening, they visited an Argentinean restaurant famed for its fantastic, mouth-watering steaks whilst the sounds of holiday makers participating in Karaoke floated through the dining area, arousing giggles and laughs from all corners. The week passed quickly and before they knew it, they were arriving back on Irish soil more refreshed and positive minded than they had when they left.

They had talked a lot when they were away. Mel had confessed that she was thinking about leaving the apartment, that things were progressing with her relationship and that it had been on her mind for a while. Shannon had been appreciative of her honesty but told her that she knew whatever happened, however their lives veered in different directions, they would always be friends. She admitted that, whilst she would miss her greatly, she totally understood and agreed with her decision. Shannon had also told Mel that she would consider meeting with Steve to hear his explanation and both girls had concluded that there was something bizarre about the whole situation although they had no idea what.

17

When they finally arrived home, they were delighted to find that it had been stocked up with fresh bread, butter and milk and a note from Pete advising them that he would see them in the week ahead. The place had been given a clean, both the kitchen and bathrooms were gleaming and the living room dusted and hoovered. They both had tea and toast with butter and jam and made their separate calls home to advise that they were back on home turf. Shannon was glad to hear from her father that all was progressing well with Gemma's pregnancy and that her dreadful nausea was subsiding. Mel was equally glad that her mother was getting over her sickness and was well on the road to recovery. They were both relieved that there were no messages on the answering machine although Shannon admitted that she was almost slightly disappointed. The saying, 'Out of sight, out of mind' came into her thoughts. When Steve was in London, it was easier to distract herself, but now that he was back, she could not get him out of her mind. Old feelings that she thought she had buried had resurfaced and much as she was trying not to listen to the little voice in her head that wanted to forgive and forget, it was proving so difficult. There was no doubt she still had strong feelings, but she had so many conflicting emotions that she found it hard to think straight. She could not understand the sequence of events that had occurred in the pub before she left and she was almost afraid to find out.

She was glad that she had another couple of days off work so that at least she could get out for a couple of runs, sort out her laundry and see her father and Pete, if he was not too busy.

After a little nightcap with Mel to celebrate the end of their successful vacation together, both retired to their rooms for the night. When morning arrived, they got stuck into the tedious task of unpacking after breakfast before

Mel headed off to see her mum. Shannon hated unpacking. Despite having clothes washed at the hotel laundrette whilst away she felt the need to wash them over again. Sand always seemed to get everywhere. Having completed some of her chores, she jumped in the mini and headed to her Dad's bearing a few little gifts for himself and Gemma. She had no idea what to buy for them, but she found a pair of gorgeous Spanish shells her dad would appreciate. For Gemma, she bought a beautiful little necklace and some duty-free beauty creams. They were delighted to see her and couldn't wait to hear all about the holiday. She had gone a lovely shade of brown, Gemma noted, with envy. No matter how long she stayed in the sun, she always remained milky white. When she was younger, she had taken a few ferocious burnings in her quest for a tan and it really was not worth it. Growing up, her dad had sworn by vinegar as a remedy for sun burn. He used to douse her in it despite her protests. She knew full well that her friends would take the hand and tease her for smelling like a chip shop. Shannon however took the sun well.

'Least I won't have to put on the false stuff for a couple of weeks,' she said.

She found it amusing that despite lying in the sun every day trying to get a little colour, as soon as she set foot in the Green Isle, the rain was lashing down and it was freezing cold. Why bother even trying for a tan when you knew that as soon as you got returned you had to wrap up in a fleece and jeans? She was glad that she had brought a warm cardigan for the flight home because as soon as she had stepped off the plane at Aldergrove airport she was immediately hit by the coldness in the air. She looked over at Gemma, admiring her neat but obvious baby bump. She was in such high spirits and felt that she was over the worst of her morning sickness. After a while, Gerry headed out to the garden to do a little weeding and left the pair of them to chat over coffee. Shannon was starting to feel more relaxed with her; in truth she didn't really see her as a stepmother, more like a friend. She decided to confide her worries over recent activities. As she explained in detail what had happened before she left, Gemma began to look more and more troubled.

'Shannon, are you sure that you can trust this friend of yours? It all sounds crazy,' she stated, calmly.

'I don't know who I can trust anymore,' Shannon answered, appearing somewhat troubled.

'Well, maybe you should air on the side of caution. It might be worth your while to meet Steve, hear his side of the story. To quote, 'there is no smoke without fire,' Gemma said.

'You're probably right, I am just feeling scared. I am petrified of what I will discover but I know that something is not right,' Shannon agreed.

Gerry suddenly appeared in the room, 'What is not right?'

Gemma and Shannon burst out laughing and told him it was nothing for him to worry about before fleeing to the kitchen to commence dinner. There was no point discussing it with Gerry for he would fret and that was something that Shannon desperately wanted to avoid.

It was great to have good old home food again, Shannon thought, tucking into her creamed potatoes, crispy chicken, broccoli and peas with proper butter and HP sauce, followed by apple tart and lashings of whipped cream. Not great for the figure but that was the least of her worries right now. Later, they all sat and watched The Bucket List starring Jack Nicholson and Morgan Freeman, a fantastic film that was both funny and sad whilst portraying a very real and moving storyline. Gemma was feeling particularly hormonal and wept her own buckets at the end of the film much to the amusement of the others. She started giggling, then crying before laughing hysterically again declaring herself an emotional mess. They had a pleasant evening and Shannon was glad she had thrown some things into an overnight bag for she stayed over again. Not that it would have mattered anyway for her old bedroom had not been changed and no doubt she had an old pair of pyjamas lying about in some closet or another. Her room had been left exactly as it was, with belongings from childhood still lining the shelves where they had always been. There were various items of her clothes still hanging in the wardrobes and there were boxes stacked neatly in a corner containing her books and CDs. She really ought to clear it out but that was something she would get around to soon enough. At present, there was too much going on particularly regarding Steve. She just did not know what to do about the situation, but she did know that she would not risk getting hurt by him again. Once was enough!

Later in the week, Steve decided to do some training. It had been a busy couple of weeks and a lot had happened since that night in the bar. He had no regrets about confronting Pete. As far as he was concerned, he was right to approach the group and say what he had said. He was worried about Shannon; she was too trusting. He thought that by now she might have considered the possibility of meeting up, but he had left at least two or three messages on her phone and she had failed to respond. He had heard from Anita that her mother had died and this had disturbed and upset him greatly. He couldn't believe that Shannon had to cope with that on her own just three months after he had abandoned ship. No wonder she didn't want to meet him. He simply had to get through to her. He would tell her his story whether she wanted to hear it or not. He had nothing to lose and everything to gain. Perhaps he would drive out and visit her father, offer his very late condolences. He liked Gerry. They had been friends. They had enjoyed the odd game of golf and always indulged in great discussion and debate on History, Religion and Politics. Sometimes they would hit the pub together for a pint and follow it up later with several more.

Maeve had been a great hostess too, always welcoming and kind. He was devastated that she had lost her life so tragically; she was just too young to go. 'God takes the best' some say but it doesn't mean that it's the best for those left behind to pick up the pieces and start over. Poor Gerry, what was he going to think of him now? Firstly, walking out on his precious daughter and then not even acknowledging the death of his wife. He knew that Gerry had lived for the woman. She was his soul mate and they were the perfect match. Steve had no idea how he was going to make it up to him. He should have been there. And poor, poor Shannon, he thought. At least, he knew about it now, so it was time to address the situation and that he intended to do very soon. It was no wonder that she had come to rely on Pete so much and he would have been waiting in the shadows ready to jump at any opportunity to get closer to her. He recalled how stunned Pete had been to see him in the bar that night. He didn't seem the 'big' man now. He looked scared, like a rabbit caught in headlights, ready to scamper off as fast as he could. That gave him a degree of satisfaction, to see him sit there in his discomfort and squirm. However, he knew that he was a strong adversary and he had to be cautious, very cautious. Circumstances could have been very different had he met him on his own. The fact that he was in company and particularly in Shannon's company would have caused him to behave more rationally. Steve knew that underneath that façade lay a bloke with very serious mental issues that could be inclined towards violence of frightening proportions. To think that Shannon trusted him so implicitly filled him with extreme unease, but he had to proceed in a way that ensured her safety. That was his main priority. Anita also had to be protected for Mc Glynn was evil personified and would do anything to hurt him or anyone close to him. On a much lighter note, his purchase of a new detached property on the leafy outskirts of the city had gone through and he was looking forward to a new start, preferably with the love of his life.

He had fallen in love with the house as soon as he had set foot in the place. It was ideal with four bedrooms, downstairs bathroom, kitchen and utility room and a detached garage which would make perfect storage space. It was all very tastefully decorated and there wasn't much needed doing – it was ready to live in and he was ready to live. There was also a private, south facing garden, not too big and not too small; just the right size for him to maintain. He hadn't forgotten Shannon's love of a good garden and planned on purchasing some nice furniture for it. He could not wait to vacate the bedsit as it was just too small and to find a house that he loved so much and so quickly, which he could afford was a dream come true. He smiled to himself as he pulled on his training gear and started some warm-up stretches after which he adjusted his MP3 player and locking his door, pressed start on his Garmin before setting off with a light jog. He usually ran about three times a week and headed in the direction of Loughmill Forest. There were not many people around, in fact it was quite isolated, but he loved that isolation. He spotted a runner ahead and sprinted past him, U2 filling his ears with 'I still haven't found what I am looking for'. Only he had found what he was looking for, he smiled to himself, but it wasn't a real smile, it was just the irony of it!

He was breaking into a steady pace now and took a sip of water, sometimes slowing down, and then speeding up again. His Garmin displayed his speed and his mileage and having run a few marathons by now, he knew that this was a breeze. He continued through the forest, over soft, muddy ground, up steep hills, singing along sometimes with Bono, although nowhere near as brilliant. He covered seven miles before backtracking over the same route. Two miles into his return journey, he noticed the same runner in the distance, dark baseball hat and sunglasses although there was no sun. He looked fit and athletic, but his pace was dire! When they were a few yards apart both looked up to acknowledge the other before recognition set in and they both stopped and stood face to face, the aggression between them swamping the air around.

'Well, Well, Well, if it isn't you again,' Steve said, mockingly.

'I would say it was a pleasure but then that would be a lie,' Pete replied, with equal hostility.

'So, have you come clean yet?' Steve asked.

'Why should I? She just thinks you were a few sheets to the wind.'

'Yeah, well, far from it; let me tell you. Now are you going to tell her the truth or shall I make it easy for you?' Steve queried, impatiently.

The punch to the lower abdomen came so quickly that Steve immediately stumbled to the ground, winded.

'I have told you before and I will tell you again, go back to where you came from or else …,' he roared, his eyes bulging with so much hatred that Steve's memories of what had happened before came flooding back with a vengeance.

Pete glared at him menacingly before turning on his back and continuing casually on his route. Ten minutes passed before he was knocked off his feet by a blow to the back of the head.

Steve did not scare easily, not anymore. He threw himself on top of Pete and grabbed him in a tight headlock.

'Never ever, do that again. Be a man for once in your life,' he fumed, gripping him tighter.

'Be a man, you say,' Pete scorned. A man, who just happens to have your precious Shannon wrapped around his finger? Yeah, that's right, Stevey boy! Little do you know, eh? She and I are as thick as thieves. We are closer than ever. You're well in the past, mate,' he taunted.

'Yeah? That may well be, but you're going to be the loser here, big time. When she discovers what really happened, she won't give you the time of day, it's only a matter of time,' Steve ridiculed.

'The time of day or the time of night Steve - because I see her in the day and I see her in the night, sometimes all night. Do you understand what I am saying?' he jibed.

'In your dreams, you wish,' Steve roared, feeling his heart beat like a bomb in his chest.

'Oh yes, I have been keeping her warm since you left, so lonely she was after you took off, and so needing to be loved,' he sneered, viciously.

Unable to control his rage, Steve punched him hard on the face, not knowing whether to believe anything that came from his vile, dirty mouth. He hit him again, splitting his lip open, before releasing his grip and cursing at him in rage. 'The truth always comes out in the end McGlynn,' he snorted, leaping back quickly when he noticed Pete searching in his pocket for something. Had he a gun? A knife? How could he have been so careless as to confront him out here in the middle of nowhere? He felt relieved when he saw the set of keys which Pete waved gently from side to side, a cruel smile sitting on his twisted mouth.

'Is that meant to tell me something Pete?' Steve laughed.

'These are my keys, my keys, Pete smiled, but this one is particularly precious,' he sniggered, seductively running his finger softly along it from top to bottom.

This one is Shannon's key, or rather it was Shannon's key, now it is my key to Shannon's, so you see Steve, we are close. I have a key to her house and that's how close we are.'

Steve was dumbfounded but showed no emotion. This was going to be so much more difficult than he had thought.

'You keep that key Pete, caress it all you like for you won't have it long,' he said, before once more ordering him to tell Shannon the truth. With that, he sped off like a leopard, his head spinning with all sorts of thoughts. He was angry, angry at himself for losing his temper and angry at Shannon because she was living in a dream world if she felt this guy was a true friend. He should have just finished him off there and then. If it weren't for the consequences maybe he would have just given him a good beating and threw him in the river. Everything was such a mess! Where would it end? He had never come across such arrogance and deviousness in all his life. What a coincidence too, meeting him like that, in a forest of all places? Life was strange sometimes. He had given him quite a thump, but he deserved it for telling such blatant, sinister lies. If Shannon only knew the half of it, she would end their friendship immediately. God knows what lies he would tell now! Oh, to be a fly in the wall!

Pete was enraged. He had not bargained on another episode so soon; that was for sure. It seemed like Steve was turning up everywhere, like a bad penny. He couldn't believe that he had stood up to him this time. He had backed off so quickly before. When he let himself into his bedsit, he headed straight to the bathroom to assess the damage. He peered in the mirror and noted the bruiser to his eye take shape. He knew it was going to be a belter and he intended on using it to his advantage. His lip was throbbing and swollen. He splashed some water around his face and without hanging around, headed to Shannon's. He would tell her exactly what Steve had done and she would not be happy. She would thank her lucky stars that she was out of that relationship. He realised then that he had not seen her since she had returned from holiday and he missed hugely. And to think that if he hadn't lied about Chloe he could have been there too. That still grated on him. It could have been the perfect opportunity, but he had ruined it with no help from anyone. She was alone in the flat and answered his knock immediately. Normally he would use his key, but he didn't this time. When she opened the door, he was entranced by how beautiful she looked. She always had amazing skin but somehow with her golden glow she looked even prettier if that was humanly possible. He leant towards her and gave her a kiss on the cheek, forgetting all about his own face, battered and bruised. She stood back and looked at him, confusion in her eyes.

'What on earth has happened to you?' she cried.

'Ah, I'll tell you later, how was your holiday?' he wanted to know.

'Later? Later? What has happened? Tell me now,' she ordered him. 'Right now,' she repeated.

'I met Steve, I was in the forest and he came up behind and clobbered me,' he stated, in almost an emotionless manner.

Shannon looked visibly shocked, just the reaction he expected and needed. He knew he looked terrible although by playing it down he would potentially gain more sympathy. She wondered if he was in shock as he seemed quite blasé. He obviously did not want to upset her, but she was extremely perturbed.

'What? He just punched you? What happened? I have never known Steve to be violent in my life.'

'He said that he did not like or understand our friendship and he punched me,' he declared. 'I didn't even see it coming, I didn't think he had it in him,' he added.

'But surely there was more to it than that?' she persisted.

'On the contrary, believe me. I am just as surprised as you. I was out for a run and he launched at me from behind. That ex of yours can pull a fine punch. I had my music on, so I had no warning. Then once I was lying there with my lip cut open, he asked me how I was and told me how nice it was to see me again. Very, very strange,' he said, pulling the blood-soaked tissue from his pocket to place again between his lips.

117

Shannon gasped and quickly handed him a clean tissue, grabbing the used one and throwing it in the bin.

'And he just hit you? Are you sure? What was said? He didn't just belt you for nothing, did he?' Shannon cried, stunned that there had been yet another row but trying to assess if Steve had been provoked or had just belted Pete for no reason.

'Ok, so maybe I told him to leave you alone and that you had been through enough what with him taking off with Anita and your mum dying, and well… before I knew it he had swung for me…maybe he thought I was being hateful but I swear I was trying to protect you. He just seems to think that he can waltz straight back into your life and start all over again like nothing happened, like he was away for a month or two rather than the last two years. For God's sake Shannon, two whole years! Have you forgotten what he did to you? I haven't forgotten!' he finished, looking at her intently, his eyes blazing.

'Okay, okay, I believe you,' Shannon answered, hurrying into the bathroom and returning with a cold flannel. She grabbed some ice-cubes from the fridge and after winding the cloth around them she started to dab gently against his cut lips. She then softly dabbed another cool cloth against his swollen eye for a couple of minutes after which she fetched a couple of diet cokes from the fridge. She still wasn't sure what had really happened. Pete seemed vague and there was no point pursuing it further.

'Where did you see him Pete?' she asked.

'Just on my usual route, around the three, three-and-a-half-mile point where the river widens out,' he answered.

'And was there no-one else around?' she asked.

'Not a sinner,' he replied.

'I am going to call him and give him a piece of my mind, I don't understand what has got into him,' she cried.

'Do no such thing,' Pete urged. 'Seriously, just let it be, he will probably lie his way out of it, please just leave it. It must be hard for him to see you again, but he has only himself to blame. I guess it's just a case of the green-eyed monster rearing its ugly head.'

'That's simply ridiculous and there is no reason to carry on like that,' Shannon replied.

'How was your holiday anyway, Shan?' he asked, keen to switch the topic of conversation away from Steve.

'Really enjoyable, you would have loved it,' she responded, aware that he wasn't in the mood for continuing their current discussion.

'How are you and Chloe getting on? Is it serious? I would love to meet her.'

'Who knows?' he answered. 'I wouldn't buy a hat just yet.'

They were interrupted by the telephone ringing and Shannon leapt up to answer it.

'Hello,' she said.

'Shannon, it's Steve,' Steve said, urgently. 'I need to talk,' he added.

'Steve, I do not know what your game is, but I am sick of it. I have Pete here and you have done quite a job of reorganising his face.'

'Let me explain exactly why,' he pleaded.

'Why should I? It is not a good time, he is here with me now, I will phone you back,' she whispered, glancing across at Pete to gauge a reaction.

There was no reaction though. Pete looked a million miles away.

'Shannon, I have left you dozens of messages and you have never once returned any of my calls,' he complained, sadly.

Shannon reassured him that she would be in touch shortly before hanging up the receiver and returning to the living room where Pete had laid himself across the sofa and closed his eyes. He had heard everything though, but he never let on. It was best to say as little as possible and besides, he was enjoying the attention. She did care about him. It was evident how much she cared, seeing to him now, wiping away the blood from his eye and his mouth, looking out for him. This was what he wanted. This was good. What happened was good. Now she would see him for what he really was. He knew from the way that Shannon was talking that she was going to meet Steve or speak to him and he was seething about that, but for now he had her just where he wanted. There was no doubt there would only be one winner here and it was going to be much harder than he had anticipated, he thought, peering at her from a half-closed eye. Perhaps he would just doze a while and they could talk it through later. No doubt she was not finished with her line of questions, but she wouldn't be pushy, not when she could tell he was in pain and needed some rest. Half an hour passed before he sat up and there she was, sitting beside him on the sofa, her legs curled underneath with a magazine in her hand.

'Fancy coming with me to the cottage?' he suggested, out of the blue.

'What? You mean now?' she asked.

'Yes, why not? Unless you have other plans,' he said.

'No, I'd love to. I better drive though because your eye is almost closed over,' she offered. She didn't really want to go but she felt guilty that he had become embroiled in all this drama.

Mel returned just then and Shannon informed her that she was heading away for the night to Killywillin.

'Would you like to come too, Mel?' Shannon hinted, looking at Pete for approval. Pete agreed immediately although cursed himself for not having left fifteen minutes previous. He liked Mel a lot, but she did not form part of his plan. He would have to put up with it for now though. Mel didn't need any persuasion however and the girls hurriedly threw some clothes into holdalls, grabbed their wash bags before declaring themselves ready and raring to go. Shannon quietly gave Mel a brief update on the latest ruckus that had arisen but told her not to mention it. It was a touchy subject, but she would fill her in later when it was just the two of them. It was a quiet journey to Fermanagh. Shannon drove whilst Pete navigated but thankfully with the new road between Dungannon and Ballygawley, the journey was half as long as six months prior. However, it still felt like forever getting there what with all the bendy country roads. She couldn't go over 30 mph on these lanes, or she would end up in a ditch. When they finally arrived at the cottage it was almost dark. Pete told them to wait in the car so he could switch the lights on and do a quick run around the house, make sure it wasn't too messy. It seemed to take more than a few minutes though and the girls noticing that it was about to teem down decided to run for cover. Pete heard them bolting for the door and quickly ushered them inside, before leading them through to the kitchen and returning to the car to collect their overnight bags. The girls had seen photographs of the cottage before and were taken aback with how Pete was managing to transform it. Pete proudly showed them the master bedroom which he said was theirs for the night and he was on cloud nine that they expressed such admiration for it. Of course, he was particularly interested in Shannon's reaction and she did not disappoint, especially when she entered the ensuite, which to her surprise had his and her marble sinks and a matching double shower. The built-in full-length mirrored wardrobes were identical to the ones that she had purchased a few months ago in Ikea and she teased him about copying her style. He had also picked out a beautiful, canvas painting of an African woman playing the piano and Shannon was mesmerised by it. She loved to paint herself sometimes and appreciated artwork. She felt inspired to purchase a few blank canvasses and paints and get started once more.

'I like your taste Pete,' she giggled knowingly.

'Thought you might,' he smiled, before going to sort the fire. He fetched some wood, sticks and turf from outside and before long had lit a great, roaring fire in the living room. He produced his new wine glasses which he had picked up in the Homebase Sale and some nibbles including seedless olives, cheese and breadsticks and the three of them sat well into the night supping wine, talking and laughing. Shannon had brought her laptop down and displayed a slide show of holiday photographs that she had uploaded the previous day. The place looked idyllic and it made Pete regret more than ever the set of untruths he had concocted regarding his 'fake' girlfriend. He was far from impressed however to see a photograph of Shannon in a Spanish pub performing her usual party trick to an interested audience of foreign men.

'There you go again Shan,' he said sternly, barely managing a smile. He really hated when she did that and she had promised she would stop.

'Ha, ha, I was on holiday, give me a break,' she answered, indignantly with that great gleaming smile of hers.

He loved the pictures of the sunset and said that it looked like a very beautiful and relaxing place and that maybe one day they could all go back.

18

Later that night, Shannon popped to the bathroom but quickly sent a text to Steve.

'Steve, At Killywillin in Pete's cottage. Mel here too, call you in week ahead,' she wrote.

She slipped her mobile into the drawer of the bedside table and switched it to 'silent' before joining the other two who were drunkenly dancing around the living room. It was unlike Mel to drink much but she was obviously letting her hair down after recent worries.

'Better watch yourself Pete, you don't want to bag yourself another black eye,' Shannon said, teasingly as she watched him stumble against the coffee table.

'Yeah well, that prick of an ex of yours better watch himself or I'll leave him with more than a black eye,' Pete yelled, over the music.

Shannon noticed the aggression in his tone but said nothing. Whatever was going on, she was determined to get to the bottom of it. He was probably just very drunk and he had every right to be annoyed after being delivered a hefty shiner like that.

'Let's go for a walk, will we?' he proposed, topping up their glasses as he spoke.

'What? Now? Are you mad Pete? It's as black as your grave out there?' Mel cried.

'So? Ever heard of a torch? he chuckled, come on, it will be fun,' he persisted.

And so the merry trio blindly traipsed down the field towards the river just as a bat emerged from nowhere and the girls screamed with such fright that they raced back to the house where they collapsed on the floor, with tears tripping them as they doubled over, laughing hysterically like a pair of hyenas. Eventually, the girls headed for bed and Shannon checked her mobile and found a reply,

'Glad that you are okay, I am glad Mel is with you,' it read.

Shannon frowned as she re-read it, questioning if Pete was right and Steve really did have a problem with their friendship. She quickly saved the message and set her alarm, she knew that in the morning they would be heading back reasonably early and before they returned, she wanted to have a look around.

When she did awake, she was surprised at how utterly peaceful it was. She could understand Pete's love of the place, but it was so isolated and deserted that she could not imagine living here herself. At least in the city, it was so lit up at night that it almost felt like daytime. No, she could never live somewhere as desolate as this. She threw on her coat and toddled down to the river. It wasn't half as scary in the light of day. She had never seen so much greenery, glorious rolling fields and assorted trees upwards and beyond the river. He had described this scenery to her so often and with such enthusiasm. It was so picturesque. She knew that this was where Pete's parents had met their untimely ends and wondered did this trouble him. Maybe he felt closer to them when he was here. She shuddered thinking about it. It was so quiet that if you had the misfortune of hurting yourself no-one would find you for days. There was little sign of life bar a few sheep grazing here and there and cows lying bunched together not far from the river's edge, so she guessed that there must be someone that came around to tend them. As she sat admiring the river, she wished that she had packed trainers so that she could go for a short jog. She was absorbed completely in her own thoughts and dreams, although the cold air forced her to wrap her coat tighter around her body. She could not get Steve out of her head. Even though it had been two years not a day had gone past when she hadn't thought of him. She heard Pete call her name and she shouted back and waved her hands in the air. As she watched him approach, she noticed that his eye had now turned a shade or two of purple. He looked fresh and well rested despite his drinking well into the early hours of the morning.

'What do you think Shan? It's stunning, isn't it?' he said.

'Yes, it is Pete, it is breathtakingly beautiful. Do you think one day you will settle here?' she enquired, looking at him intently.

'For sure Shan, this is where I grew up. I love it here, it is a different life,' he said.

'When do you think you will come back to stay?'

'That's a good question, it depends on lots of things,' he replied.

'I will miss you so much when you leave the city, but I understand,' she replied hastily.

There was a long pause before she asked,

'Does Chloe like it here?'

'Yes, she does, did............' 'Look, she is not for me, I am going to end it,' he declared.

'But why? You sounded so happy, what happened?'

'Nothing, it is just not working, I can't even be bothered talking about it,' he answered, shaking his head.

'She is a nice girl, attractive but much too serious,' he added.

'That's a pity,' Shannon said, 'I am sorry.'

'Don't be, I'm not,' he responded, before pretending that there was a huge spider crawling on her back to which she immediately screeched and started pulling at her coat to knock it off.

'Just joking,' he laughed, as she ran towards him, knocking him back on the grass, but he held onto her, pulling her to him on the ground. Then he rolled playfully on top of her holding both her arms behind her head. He looked at her then, her hair tossed wildly all over the grass and before she knew it, he was leaning in for a kiss. She stared back at him, she couldn't speak, she saw that something in his eyes again and was suddenly confused. She was so relieved to hear Mel shouting their names and they both sat up quickly, Shannon grabbing a hair band from her pocket to push her hair back off her face.

'Not disturbing anything, am I?' Mel yelled, waving at the pair lying on the ground.

Pete could not believe her timing. If only he hadn't shouted in twenty minutes previous, she would still be in bed. His luck was not in at all. He looked across at Shannon who appeared somewhat edgy, embarrassed even. She looked back at him but quickly averted her eyes and he couldn't really read what was going on just now in that lovely face of hers. They rose to their feet quickly and sauntered towards Mel who announced that coffee was on the brew and ready to be had. Once back in the cottage the conversation having been slightly stilted for a few moments got back on track and they enjoyed their coffees together. Pete gave them a tour of the house except for his study which he insisted was far too messy and cluttered to allow anyone admittance. The girls proclaimed that they didn't care about the mess, but he was having none of it. The study was out of bounds until he had decorated it. He explained that he was decorating one room at a time and they both teased him for choosing the master bedroom as his first project. They both listened to his ideas on the kitchen and living area which needed substantial work. The two rooms looked dark and dusty. He then gave them a guided tour of the surrounding area naming all the trees and flowers and indicating his plans for sprucing up the garden and patio areas. Before long it was time to pack up, and head for home with Pete promising that they would return soon, that it was extra special when the sun was shining and the ideal place to sunbathe and have a barbecue with no-one around to disturb them. When they finally had dropped Pete off at his place and returned home, both girls were totally exhausted; Shannon especially so, as she had driven the whole way there and the entire way back. Pete had offered to do his share, but she politely declined saying that it may not look great if they were stopped by the police.

19

It was three weeks before Shannon finally plucked up the courage to phone Steve and she agreed to meet him. She did not tell anyone for fear of criticism or advice. Mel was staying at her mums and she was glad for she knew that she would try and talk her out of it or insist on tagging along for back up. She did not want to be questioned or deterred in any way. As far as she was concerned, she had to meet him and hear him out, listen to his explanation and hopefully move on with her life. There were so many unanswered questions and he deserved to be heard, even if it was two years too late. She had no idea what to wear but opted for a pair of white trousers and a turquoise shirt. She went minimal on her makeup and tied her dark hair in a loose ponytail. She felt sick to the stomach and her hands which were shaking, felt damp and clammy. When she heard her doorbell chime, she took her time. There was no rush! She applied a little lip gloss and slowly made her way through the hall to the front door where he was waiting. He smiled at her nervously and they both climbed silently into the waiting taxi which brought them, far too quickly she thought, to the Fisherman's Inn. She was dreading sitting opposite him, being in such close proximity, having to look at him straight in the eyes and remain cool and calm. She was afraid of her own emotions, afraid of what she had felt for him and more than anything afraid that her feelings would get the better of her. Once there, she sat in a corner booth and waited anxiously until he fetched drinks from the bar. She had requested a double vodka and diet coke hoping that a strong drink would ease the butterflies in her stomach. He looked amazing, she thought, fit and healthy with rippling muscles which would have made Superman himself green with envy.

'Thank you, Shan, for agreeing finally to meet me,' he said, smiling tenderly at her.

'Did Anita agree with it?' she blurted out, cursing herself for being so blunt and sounding like a woman scorned, which ultimately had been the case, if the truth be told, she thought.

'Anita is fine, she knows all about it, she is behind me every step of the way,' he said easily.

'Really, why does that not surprise me?' she muttered scornfully, raising her eyes to the ceiling.

'Shannon there was never anything between us, not now, not ever,' he confirmed.

'Why did you punch Pete?' she demanded to know.

'What did Pete tell you?' he asked.

'Let's not beat around the bush Steve, there is no point. Just say whatever you want to say and then we can move on,' she said, impatiently.

'I heard about your mother, he said softly now, I did not know. I am so sorry Shannon, I thought the world of her. I was devastated when I heard what happened.'

'Yes well, I appreciate that, it was very hard, it is still very difficult,' she sniffed, trying to stop the tears that were threatening to emerge at any second.

Steve lifted his hand to place it over hers, but she pulled away hastily, glaring at him in the process.

'Now, I want to know first and foremost, why you thumped Pete and left him with a black eye?' she asked.

'I was out for a run. I passed a guy and didn't realise it was Pete until I was making my way back. When I did discover it was him, I stopped and asked him if he had told you the truth about what happened before I left...' he paused.

'Go on,' Shannon urged.

'I told him that if he didn't tell you the truth I would and that was when he punched me in the stomach. I fell to the ground, he totally winded me.'

Shannon's eyes nearly popped out of her head. Sinking her drink, she waved the barman over and ordered another round, aware that all her good intentions of the last month or two were rapidly disintegrating.

'Please go on,' she insisted.

'He fled but I caught him up. He made derogatory comments and that was when I hit him, please believe me Shannon,' he pleaded.

'Hold on a minute, what sort of derogatory comments did he make?'

'He said that you two were close, very, very close. He insinuated that he was your roommate, that he was keeping your bed warm at night. I couldn't take it Shan. He was sneering at me, trying to provoke me in the worst possible way,' he added.

Shannon's shock was plain to see. She didn't know what to believe. If this were true, then it was awful, but it seemed unreal that her friend, her best friend would concoct such outrageous fabrications. She reflected quickly on the incident in the field at Killywillin, her face blushing as she recalled how he had moved in for a smooch. Had Mel not arrived, what would have happened? Would she have returned his kiss? She couldn't be sure as it had been so unexpected.

'Pete told me that you just thumped him for nothing. To be honest I couldn't quite grasp from him exactly what happened, but the evidence is there, he has a black eye, Steve. You cut open his lip too.'

Steve wiped his brow. He was not surprised that Pete had twisted the story, but it was nevertheless deeply frustrating.

'That is a lie Shannon. It was not like that, he hit me first. I promise you. I told him he had to come clean and he pulled the first punch. Then he scarpered but I chased after him and it was only when he started taunting me that I retaliated.'

'Supposing you are telling the truth Steve ….' she started.

'I am telling the truth Shannon, I swear to you and I beg you to just listen to what I have to say,' he pleaded.

'Okay, go ahead,' she answered.

'Why are you seeing me now, Shannon? All these weeks I have been trying to contact you, leaving messages and you never once returned any of my calls?' he asked.

'Steve, I haven't had any messages, one or two perhaps but that's about it. There were several times though that someone phoned and as soon as I answered the line went dead. I wondered if that were you,' she divulged.

'No, if I were going to ring you, I wouldn't hang up, but I did leave several messages. Didn't you get any of them? I waited for you one night for hours in the Red Tiger, but you didn't show, I prayed that you would, but you didn't,' he said.

'I don't know anything about these messages, I never got any of them,' she answered, suddenly realising that Pete had a key to the flat and could easily have deleted them but quickly dismissing that as a possibility. She was beginning to feel very paranoid.

'Why did you walk out on me?' she asked now, fiddling with her glass and unable to look at him. She swiftly took another huge gulp of her drink as she waited for him to speak. And so, Steve started to explain himself as Shannon sat on intently sometimes putting her head in her hands as she attempted to make sense of what he was saying.

'I was out one night in a bar about a week before we split up. I met Pete and....' he started.

'Oh no, Steve, this is getting ridiculous now, he cannot be responsible for everything,' she cried.

'Shannon, you must remember the night, shortly before I left, that I came back from the pub and I was really upset. I had taken a short cut home from the pub. You know how we always walked the long way around when we were coming home from there. Well this time, I was drunk and I set off down the alley by the side of the supermarket, I know I always warned you not to take that route, but I just wanted to get back to you quicker. I missed you. I was stupid, and too drunk to make a sensible decision, otherwise I would never have gone down that way myself. For goodness sake, don't you remember I always pestered you about taking a taking a taxi back or if you were with friends to keep to well-lit places. However, I wasn't so good at heeding my own advice. I was about halfway down the alley. It was dark and it was raining heavily....'

He stopped and took a deep breath. 'Suddenly, there he was. Pete. Of course, I didn't know it was him at that stage. He just appeared from nowhere and before I knew what was happening, he had a knife to my throat and was threatening me.'

Shannon's mouth dropped open in shock and she felt a chill run down her spine as she endeavoured to absorb what Steve was suggesting.

'I thought he was a mugger, I offered him money, but he hollered at me, said it wasn't my money he was after. I thought he was going to kill me and I told him he could have whatever he wanted. He sneered at me; he was wearing dark clothes, a hoodie, a black one and dark blue jeans. Shannon, I swear to you, I would know those eyes anywhere and his voice....... I recognised it straight away.'

I said to him, 'Is that you Pete? It's you, isn't it?'

He was not happy Shannon, he was mad. He sliced my leg and said that he would cut up my face if I didn't get the hell out of your life. He threatened that if I didn't, he would kill you. He made it very apparent Shannon, he wanted my life with you and if he could not have you, nobody would,' he explained, watching her carefully.

The more Shannon heard the paler she became. She looked as if she would pass out. It was so much to absorb.

'He told me that if I told you, and he would know if I had, that he would finish me off. I am sorry Shannon, but this is just the beginning, I'm afraid. Everything I have told you in the last half hour is the truth but there is more to come, more shocking stuff.'

'Oh my God, Steve I think I have heard enough, he really threatened to kill me, are you serious?' she cried, her eyes widening more and more in a mixture of terror and disbelief.

'He did, he's dangerous Shannon, I didn't know what to do,' he replied, looking at her with worry written all over his face.

'But why, why would he do that? Why would he make such threats?'

'Shan, he is obsessed with you, he has been for years. Everyone else could see it, but you,' he whispered.

'Mel has always thought that, she has said so many times, but I didn't believe her, I didn't want to believe her because I didn't feel the same. I just wanted things to stay the same. I am just back from Killywillin Steve, I would have been there on my own with him only Mel just happened to arrive back at the apartment and I invited her along,' she sobbed.

'Where is this place, Killywillin, Shannon?' Steve asked gently.

'It is in the sticks, the absolute back of beyond, in fact do you remember years ago when we stayed at the Five Bridges Hotel, it is actually quite near that. There is a crossroads about five miles South of the hotel, you take a right turn and eventually pass a big, sprawling farm. Then there is a forest which stretches for about a mile, directly after which you take another right onto a very rocky little road about two miles long. Eventually, you come to the cottage which is by a little river. Only for the cottage's vivid red roof you would probably pass it by without noticing. Outside is laid in decking, it is pretty but quite run down looking. I wouldn't last five minutes if I had to stay there alone.'

'Shannon, you have to act ignorant now, pretend you know nothing,' he warned.

'How the hell do you expect me to do that? Tell me Steve, why did you not just go to the police when all this happened? I don't understand. I can see that you would have been scared but surely you didn't have to take such an extreme measure as to just leave the country, leave me.'

'Shannon, you don't know what he is capable of. As I said, there was a lot more to it than that,' he went on.

'Okay, go on,' she urged.

'About a fortnight before I left, I was in the classroom one day. There was a girl called Mandy, she was quite cheeky and outspoken. She was also confident and very intelligent, a straight A student, by far the brightest in her class if not her year. Classes had finished for the day and most pupils had gone home so I was surprised when she came in and asked to speak to me. I was busy, clearing up and doing some marking but she said it wouldn't take long, that she needed advice and as I was her form teacher, she felt that she should come to me. As it turned out, she said she was having trouble at home, her parents were going through a bitter divorce, her younger siblings were running riot all over the place and she was finding it tough to get through her studies. I talked to her and asked her how she felt I could help and she just totally dissolved in tears. She was all over the place. I didn't know what to do and tried to comfort her as best I could; I told her that I could talk to one of her parents and explain that she was struggling. She said that wasn't necessary, that it would only cause more problems and so I suggested a meeting with the school counsellor but again, she declined. Anyway, she told me that she would see how things progressed over the following two weeks and that maybe she could talk it over with me again.'

'I am getting really worried here, Steve. What happened?' Shannon asked.

'What happened was that when she left my classroom, she took herself off to the Principal's office and made an allegation. She must have taken a detour to the toilets on the way and ruffled herself up a little. She said that I had made an inappropriate advance and turned on the waterworks. Naturally, I was immediately summoned to the Principal's office, her parents were informed, the police were called and I was suspended, pending an investigation.'

'Oh my God,' Shannon said. 'Why on earth did you not tell me this?'

'I honestly was devastated. I could not believe it myself. How could I tell you about it? I just wanted it to go away. She was 15 years old Shannon and I was basically being accused of inappropriate behaviour. I couldn't cope,' he said.

'So, what happened next?'

'Well, they called her in, they told her that this was a very serious allegation and did she understand the implications of her words. The police questioned her as well, and I think she must have crumbled under the pressure. She finally confessed that it was untrue and that she didn't know herself why she had done it. There were several indescrepancies in her story, I heard later, but still the whole thing was hard to bear. The school quickly lifted my suspension and asked me to return to duty as it were.'

'Steve, this is just awful. I cannot believe that I had no idea that this was going on. Why did you not tell me?' Shannon wept, clearly distraught.

'I did not want to worry you. I buried my head in the sand. I just did not understand how it had happened. You and I were happy. Things were going well. I did not know how you would react and I could not cope with my own reaction never mind yours.'

'Shannon, it wasn't the girl's fault, I found out later that it was all down to Pete, she had met him at some sort of fitness class and was clearly infatuated. She used to follow him around like a puppy dog apparently and he was undoubtedly as manipulative as he was charming.

Eventually, he found out that she was in my form class and he very cleverly used her to his advantage. I found out from a parent of another girl in the class whom I met after I had been suspended. I was horrified. She told me that she had heard gossip and felt it only right that I should know. Then when I met him in the alleyway and he produced a knife, I knew that this guy would stop at absolutely nothing to get me out of the way. He called me all sorts of names that night, he told me that I was a paedophile and he would broadcast it by whatever means necessary if I didn't leave. He called me the scum of the earth and said that I had to go. I know it was a cowardly way out, but I became scared. I didn't want to go to the Police because I was now known to them and I didn't trust that they would believe me and so I handed in a sick line to work and left.'

Shannon put her head down on the table and wept openly.

'Where does Anita come in to all this?' she mumbled, through her tears. Never in a million years would she have thought that Pete would be capable of these things. Surely something in his personality would have given her cause to have doubts but he had displayed nothing but kindness. How could he have pulled this off? How could she have been so stupid? She felt her stomach churn as she waited patiently for him to continue.

'I met her one day in the park, I was in pieces, I was worried sick, but I could see no solution. I couldn't eat and I couldn't sleep, I felt like my life was in tatters. I was frantic, distraught. Anita came along, out of nowhere, walking her friend's dog and she knew instantly that I was in poor spirits. She sat alongside me and I poured my heart out to her and told her that I had to go, that I had to leave you for your own safety as well as mine. I had never had much time for Anita as you well know but I saw a different side to her that day. She has had her own struggles with abuse from her dad. He drank all the time and beat her and

136

her mother black and blue. She told me to think about it and consider telling you. She asked me if I wanted her to talk to you, but I told her I couldn't risk it. I packed all my stuff when you were at work and organised a flight for later that day. I can honestly say that it was the worst day of my life. A friend of a friend was able to rent me a room and I only had to stay one night in an hotel before I was permitted to move into new accommodation in London. There was no point leaving a note because I would have to tell you what happened and that was too dangerous. It was the hardest thing that I have ever had to do. I headed over there on my own not knowing what lay ahead, the digs near Soho were basic and gloomy and it was a real shock to the system when just a fortnight later Anita arrived on my doorstep. I was probably more relieved than anything when she turned up. I was in such an awful state and had nobody I could confide in or trust. She helped me find a counsellor whom I started seeing on a weekly basis. I registered with a doctor too who put me on a course of antidepressants. I was afraid to leave the house. I had nightmares all the time. Eventually after a month or two I found a job at a local gym and began working out because I felt like such a lightweight, like I had totally let you down, taken the coward's way out. Obviously, I resigned from the teaching job, but I didn't want to go to another school, not at that stage. Anyway, Anita moved in for about a week until she found something suitable for herself. Luckily enough, a flat became available on the ground floor of the neighbouring block and so she was close by. She immediately contacted a recruitment agency and found work temping in the personnel division of one of the banks. We were always only friends. There was never anything more. She knew that I was madly in love with you and after a month or two she met a guy in London. His name is Gregory and they have been together since. He is a good guy, and he is crazy about her. London was alright but I never really settled.

Neither did she! She missed her mum too much and was always worrying that her father would one day go too far. Eventually, Anita's dad did go too far and her mother plucked up the courage to kick him out once and for all. Anita was flying home regularly at that point to check in on her and decided that London was just too far away. One day we were talking and she could see that I was missing you as much as ever and suggested that perhaps enough time had gone by that we could return. We thought that perhaps Pete would be out of the picture by now or maybe he would have met someone or who knows even settled down and married or had a family of his own. Secretly I hoped that he would be stalking someone new or have carried out some criminal act and been taken in by the police. Naturally, we knew that perhaps you might have moved on too and that was what petrified me more than anything. My fear of losing you overtook my fear of him. I had to come home and face the music, be it good or bad. Gregory indicated that if Anita were to move back and sort herself out with work and accommodation that he would follow suit, if that was what she wanted. Of course, they had discussed their future and it was inevitable that they would be together. At the minute he comes over every other weekend and sometimes all of us just get together and hang out. Obviously, because I have been away for so long, most of my friends have either got engaged or are already married so sometimes I just head to Anita's on a Friday or Saturday night and we have a meal and a drink together. I haven't been out doing the pub scene as you might expect because that just isn't me anymore. It's nice of course sometimes but not all the time. I still like a few beers or a few glasses of wine!' That's about it. It's not the same when you're on your own. It's not the same without you!'

'Wow!' Shannon said, wiping away the tears trickling freely down her cheeks.

'Are you okay?' Steve asked softly, taking a tissue from his pocket and passing it to her. 'I know this is a lot to take in, I just hope that you take me at my word and maybe eventually you could find it in your heart to forgive me.'

'What do we do now?' she asked.

'That is what I am trying to figure out. The main thing is that you give no hint that you have seen me. He is as mad as a badger. He cannot get any idea that we are in contact,' he advised.

'Do you think I should confide in Mel?'

'No, absolutely not Shannon, she may be unable to disguise her feelings if she knows the truth and if he senses any difference to the normal, he will become suspicious,' he replied.

'But she is always on at me, she thinks we are the ideal match, she tells me that we should get together and part of me thinks she says the same things to him. I would need to tell someone though, perhaps Gemma?' she stated.

'Gemma, who is Gemma?' he wanted to know.

'My stepmother, my very pregnant stepmother,' she said, smiling.

'Wow, that is fantastic news, when is the baby due?' he enquired.

'Not long now, she is well into her pregnancy,' she told him, looking around as she was interrupted by the cry for last orders. They had both had had enough to drink by now and decided to order a taxi home. Thankfully it arrived promptly as it was starting to rain and they climbed into the back seat and instructed the driver of the address.

After a moment or two of silence Steve turned and looked at her, 'I know that this has been a bombshell and I am sorry that things turned out this way. I am telling you from the bottom of my heart, that it is all true and I just hope that we will be able to get through it. I never stopped loving you and I always will.'

Before she had a chance to reply, the taxi stopped outside her house and after thanking the driver she turned her eyes sadly to him, 'I need time to figure this out,' she said, 'we'll talk again soon,' and with that she patted his hand lightly before stepping out of the cab and with what seemed like the weight of the world on her shoulders trudged up the path towards her front door, not once glancing back.

Once inside she flicked on the lights and peered out the window. The taxi driver had not gone and she realised that Steve was probably waiting to ensure that she was okay. It suddenly crossed her mind that Pete had a key. He could be here. Oh God, she thought. What if he is here and hiding? She felt vulnerable on her own and seeing the taxi still outside, beckoned Steve back over to the front door.

'Please don't go,' she whispered. 'Mel is at her mums and he has a key, I cannot stay here on my own tonight,' she gasped.

Steve leaned towards the taxi driver and whispered something before quickly settling the fare and following Shannon indoors. Together they checked each room thoroughly before settling down with a small glass of wine each. Shannon was in an awful state, she was completely terrified and was struggling to keep it together. So much for playing it cool, she realised. She was trembling all over, panic stricken. She would make up the sofa bed in a while and Steve could sleep there. She didn't know what the future would hold for them but there was no way she was going to rush into anything. She had too much to lose. He was still her one great love and the old chemistry had not dispersed, relentlessly tugging at her heartstrings. It had not diminished one bit but for now they had a lot to sort out. Suddenly she didn't even want to finish her wine and decided to call it a day. Having bid Steve goodnight, she turned in for the night. Sleep did not come easily however, and she tossed and turned all night long until at about 4.00am she was awoken by a noise outside. She could feel the sound of her heart thumping in her chest as she tiptoed to the window and carefully peered out. She saw a shadow but could not make out who or what it belonged to. Was he out there? She wandered aimlessly into the living room where Steve now lay in deep slumber. She took the sofa opposite quietly watching him snooze until eventually, she herself finally nodded off. She was awoken several hours later by a gentle nudge and Steve whispering that he had better go. He kneeled on the floor beside her, gently adjusting her fluffy blanket to keep her snug and warm. He reassured her that he loved her and was so sorry for abandoning her but would never leave her again if she could find it in her heart to forgive him. Shannon felt a strong desire to kiss him but held back. It wasn't the right time. She told him that she needed to process all the recent information but was hopeful that everything would be okay. He seemed satisfied with that and said he would contact her later to check how she was but insisted that they both be extremely careful. When Mel returned home that evening, she found it challenging to hide all these new revelations, but she was too petrified to divulge any details. Everything that Steve said had made sense, and she really wanted to believe him. On the other hand, she found it incredible that Pete had gone to such drastic measures to keep them apart. The whole week, she felt like she was going through the motions, keeping up the pretence that everything was fine when inside her heart was breaking all over again. If Pete was indeed as vicious as Steve had portrayed, then how would she cut her ties with him? And he had a key to the apartment? He could literally come and go whenever he wanted, day or night. How would she retrieve the key without his suspecting something? Was he really in love with her and if so, how had she missed it? True, Mel had hinted that they were perfect for each other and true, sometimes she had noticed him watching her in a way that made her question his intentions, but she had never taken it seriously. And what about the phone calls that Steve said he had made to her and the messages he had left? Why had she not received them? None of it made sense. And of course, there was the incident also in the field in Killywillin. Would he have kissed her had Mel not suddenly appeared outside? She shuddered now as she remembered! It was all very uncomfortable. Was he capable of hurting her? Was she safe? Should she indeed return to her father's place for a while and concoct some sort of reason for doing so? And Steve? Was it possible that he could be lying? Why had he left it so long? Was he not worried about leaving her behind with such a maniac? Was he convinced that she was safe? How could he be? Was he that weak? None of it added up. She did not know what to think anymore and really needed to confide in someone. She decided then and there to contact Gemma. She knew that she could trust her. What about her dad though? Should she tell him? Maybe not! He would panic but how would he feel if something did happen and she had not told him. He would want to protect her. She was his only daughter. Did he deserve to be kept in the dark? She picked up the phone and dialled her stepmother's number. Gemma answered after two rings and Shannon told her that she needed advice and wanted to speak to her alone, preferably as soon as possible and not in the presence of her dad. Gemma agreed and immediately arranged a time when she knew Gerry would be out.

20

It was Saturday morning when Shannon arrived at the family home. Her dad was off out enjoying his weekly game of golf which was always followed by a dinner and a pint or two at the club. That would allow her the space and time to get Gemma's take on the situation. It would be good to get a neutral point of view. After both women had greeted each other with a warm hug Gemma hurried off to boil the kettle and before long the pair had settled themselves in their favourite spot in the garden. Gemma was looking fantastic and feeling great since all her dreadful pregnancy related sickness had practically vanished. She was anxious though as to why Shannon wished to speak to her alone, but the anxiety turned to deep concern when Shannon slowly started to explain the whole troubling situation. She confided the whole chain of events, scarcely taking a breath to pause, from her meeting Steve for the first time in Debenhams to all the subsequent encounters finishing with his explanation for why he had scarpered more than two years earlier. Gemma was aghast. She listened silently, as Shannon discussed her confusion regarding Pete and how they had been such good friends, how he had been there for her 100% in her time of need. She discussed Steve and the dreadful row in the bar followed by the fierce dispute in the forest. She told her about the accusation involving the teenager, the threat on his life and potential threat on hers. Gemma was astounded. She wanted to tell Gerry immediately, but Shannon begged her not to. She ordered Shannon to go back and pack her bags and come and live with them for a while. She thought that it was the only solution and that at least that way she would be better protected. In the meantime, she must think of a way of retrieving her key from him so that he did not have access to the flat. There was also the question of Mel and how she would feel at

Shannon's abrupt decision to return home but between them they decided that the answer to that was to tell her that Gemma really could do with some extra help. Shannon felt sure that Mel would understand, the question was would she understand later, when the truth came out.

After a couple of hours of serious discussion, Shannon left, feeling much better having offloaded her troubles, and promising to return soon with her things. When she pulled up in the car, Mel stepped outside to greet her,

'Hi ya, Pete's just off the phone, he wants you to call him on the mobile.'

'Ok Mel, I'll give him a call shortly. There was something I wanted to talk to you about first. Five minutes later when they were both settled with steaming mugs of coffee Shannon said, 'Remember you told me on holidays that you were thinking you might move out?' she said.

'Yes, sure I do,' Mel answered, hesitantly.

'It's just, well Gemma has been struggling the last while and she asked me today if I would consider moving in for a while, just to help her out for a bit. I know it's all very sudden, but I feel I should do it. I have stayed away for so long, and I want to be there for her. After all, she is carrying my little sister or brother!'

She looked at Mel, who was smiling softly back at her.

'Listen, I don't mind at all, in fact I think it is a great idea much as I will miss you. In truth Tom found us a flat but I didn't know how to tell you. I was waiting for the right moment. You know I think the world of you Shannon, I just wanted to make your life easier, not harder,' she stated.

'You have made my life easier Mel, you have been brilliant and I really appreciate it. I don't know what I would ever have done without you and I will never forget your kindness and patience. It can't have been easy, but I am grateful that you supported me through what was a very dark time. Let's have a drink and celebrate and sure we can do some packing perhaps this weekend and throughout the course of the week ahead,' she suggested.

With that, they opened a bottle of white wine and chatted. They decided that they would spend the next few days boxing their belongings and agreed that it would be easier if they both moved out at the same time. They were startled by the sound of the doorbell to which Mel shouted, 'That's probably Pete.' Shannon felt her spine tingle with pure trepidation and nerves. How would she manage this? She felt chilled to the core at the prospect of seeing him and retaining a sense of normality following Steve's declarations.

The chink of the key in the door followed by his familiar clearing of the throat confirmed that indeed it was him.

'Hello, he shouted, just thought I would pop over for a while,' he said, catching on quickly that something was going on.

'Great news,' Mel roared before Shannon had the opportunity to speak, we are moving out.'

'Moving out, moving out to where? Am I missing something?' he cried.

'No, Mel is moving in with Tom and I am going back to Dad's for a while,' Shannon stated, making her way into the kitchen to fetch a brew and gain her composure. Her hands were shaking. She would have to fake illness or come up with some explanation if he noticed.

'You are going back to your Dads? Are you serious? But sure, I could move in with you if you don't want to be alone?' he hinted, eyebrows raised, in anticipation of an answer.

If he had made such a proposal before Shannon probably would have jumped at the chance but everything had altered.

'Nope, I think it would be a good idea to go to Dad's for a while. I have kept away for long enough, so we are going to find someone **to rent** for a while until I return.'

If Pete was put out by this, he did not show it in any way.

'You will be needing this then,' he declared, throwing the key in the air and catching it again with one hand.

'Of course, it might be handy if I hold on to it, that way I can keep tabs on your **new** tenant, make sure that they are of a reputable nature,' he smirked.

Shannon smiled at him, trying to act normal, but her tongue was in knots, her words stuck in her throat.

'Here you go then, I will give you back your key with great reluctance,' he said, pretending that he was deeply hurt.

'Thanks Pete, you're a star,' Shannon grinned, relieved that she did not have to ask for it. She didn't think that it would have been so easy.

'I got another key cut ages ago so I'll have to get that to you too. 'Can I grab a beer?' he asked cheerfully.

'Of course, since when did you need permission?' Shannon teased, whilst realising that it hadn't been so easy after all.

She was feeling a little peculiar now because he was so normal. She almost expected him to behave differently. Maybe he was telling the truth? Thank God, her power of speech had returned. She just had to make sure she gave nothing away. She needed to think before she spoke, it was vital that she made no mistakes.

'So, what about this new girlfriend of yours?' Mel asked.

'Footloose and fancy free,' he replied. 'I gave her the heave ho, time to go.'

'Is that right? I thought you were really into her,' Mel said, sneaking a peak at Shannon.

Shannon pretended not to notice the sideward glance and pottered around lifting magazines. She knew Mel thought they were a match made in heaven. She only hoped that heaven would not come too soon. If Steve were being honest, she might be up there a lot sooner than she anticipated.

'She was nice for a date or two, but she is not the woman I am after,' he muttered.

'And who is the woman you are after?' Mel probed.

Shannon continued lifting and flicking through mail. She felt awkward and ill at ease with the conversation and had an inkling that Mel thought she was being funny. Not in a nasty way of course but nevertheless, she wished she would drop it.

'When I find her, I'll let you know,' he responded, before taking a good long drink of beer and kicking his shoes off. Shannon observed this action. It was funny that a few months back she would have been encouraging him to kick off his shoes and make himself at home. Now she was wondering was he too at ease. Had she made a massive mistake? Could it be possible that he just wasn't who he seemed? How much did she know about him anyway? And he had other keys? Why? She was startled when he spoke,

'Any calls, Shan?' he asked.

'No, not a word,' she mumbled.

She was finding this all very hard and was more perturbed than ever because there just was no indication of a problem. Everything was just the same.

'So, you haven't seen him?' he asked.

'No, I haven't, nor is it in my plans,' she retorted.

'And this sudden urge to move back to your dads? What brought this on?'

'Well, it just seems like a good idea. Mel has found an apartment with Tom in Stranmillis and I figured I would like to move back, save some money and buy a house perhaps.'

'You've never mentioned this before. I thought you were happy here. Has something changed?' he wanted to know.

'This was never going to be permanent,' she responded quietly. He studied her for a few seconds before Mel came bouncing back into the room and described in detail her new home, and Shannon grateful for the interruption, fetched another beer hoping that Pete would go sooner rather than later. But Pete was quite comfortable and why wouldn't he be? She hoped he didn't plan on staying. He could not stay. If he was as vicious as Steve portrayed that could be dangerous. If only she could confide in Mel, it would be so much easier. She felt guilty. What if he hurt Mel? Her conscience was tormenting her with questions, with ill-fated thoughts and feelings. Her body was betraying her too, causing her to tremble. She needed a drink, something stiff to make her relax so that she could deal with the pure dread consuming her body.

'Staying tonight?' Mel asked, out of the blue.

'Is that an offer?' Pete giggled. 'If there is another of these on offer I just might,' he declared, holding up the beer.

'I'll go get you one, 'Shannon offered, almost tripping over herself to get out of the room. She could kill Mel now but then she couldn't blame her. Mel had no idea of her dilemma and now Pete might be staying over. How could she prevent that without causing suspicion? As it was, Pete didn't stay. To her major relief after his third beer, he said he was making tracks. She hoped that he hadn't observed anything odd about her behaviour. She had done her best to hold it together under difficult circumstances. But Pete was not stupid. He knew something was up, particularly when he had hugged her as he was leaving. He hung around on the street outside for a while observing the apartment, sure that she had or was seeing Steve again. She was cooler than usual; he felt it when he hugged her. She wasn't the same. She had flinched on contact and was quieter. Perhaps she was tired or coming down with something or perhaps Steve had gotten to her and filled her head with dreams and promises of the future. Over his grave, he thought.

21

Throughout the next couple of weeks, as soon as the girls returned from work they got stuck into the packing, commencing with the bedrooms and emptying wardrobes and drawers, to taking down personal pictures and ornaments and wrapping them up in newspaper to minimise and hopefully prevent damage or breakages. It did not take as long as they thought because whoever moved in would still need the basics. Therefore, dishes and saucepans, and some pictures and rugs etc stayed put. Clothes and toiletries were all stashed in suitcases ready for transport to their new abodes. Shannon was hoping that this would be a temporary arrangement for she loved her apartment, but she was feeling a bit nervous about all the allegations and besides, she was looking forward to going 'home' for a while. She didn't want to tell him that Gemma was pregnant. It was a perfect reason but not so ideal if he really was a maniac. She was looking forward to the change, she would be safe there and from her couple of telephone calls to Gemma since, her dad for one was jumping for joy. She sent Steve a text in the interim and told him her plans and he replied that he thought it was a wise decision. He signed off his message with an xo, but she never sent one in return. It was far too soon for that and far too much had happened.

Within a month, Shannon was well settled with her dad and Gemma. She had found a new tenant, a young doctor called Mary who had moved over from England with her boyfriend. Mary had taken a six-month lease which was ideal and Shannon was glad she could potentially move back in again. It would have been awful financially if she had to keep up with the payments on the property. She had insisted on contributing at home even though Gemma had categorically told her that it was not necessary. She was getting along with Gemma swimmingly and spending lots of time with her Dad, going out for walks and visiting people that she had not seen for a long time. Gemma seemed to be growing bigger by the day and they were all really looking forward to the birth of the baby. She was now running about three times a week and could manage five or six miles easily. She had registered for a 10k and was feeling fitter and healthier. Work was also busy and whilst the hours could be long sometimes it allowed less time to fret about everything else.

Steve kept in contact with her, mainly by text and there was a suggestion that they might meet up soon. She had no intention of jumping back in headfirst. She had countless messages from Pete requesting to meet her and she replied that she would do so soon, although the very idea of it scared her massively. She saw Mel regularly and sometimes even more so than when they had shared the flat together. She always felt guilty that she had not confided in her, but it seemed too risky. The less folk knew the better. She would have to tell her eventually though. Sometimes Cara would pop by the house and the more she grew to know her the more she liked her. She was seeing someone but was quite secretive about him and they all suspected it was the guy she had met ages before in the pub but she just giggled when asked and said it was all very new and she didn't want to put a scud on it.

Pete meanwhile was spending his days moping around his bedsit. He missed Shannon desperately. The weeks seemed to be dragging by and since she had moved home, he had not seen her. She said she was flat out between work and helping her dad and step-mum around the house. He had walked by the apartment a few times and knew that there was a new tenant and wondered just how long Shannon intended staying away. He understood leases were normally granted for six months or a year, and the thought of hardly seeing her for that length of time was driving him insane. He knew she was settling in well and appeared happy, but it was not enough for him. He missed being able to pop by when he pleased. His imagination was running riot and he wondered if Steve had wormed his way back into her life again but had no way of finding out. He did not know where he lived otherwise, he would pay a visit and sort him out once and for all. He had returned to the forest multiple times but there had been no sightings of his rival. He had seen Cara quite a bit and even though she was fun, he knew that there was no future in it. They had been for a meal or two and enjoyed an odd flick, and he had been to her cottage on several occasions. He always stayed, as it was so much nicer than his horrible bedsit. He knew that she was far more into him than he her, but he kept her sweet, showering her with compliments and buying her the odd bunch of flowers which usually came from the garage down the road. He was surprised she was a lot different from his initial first impression. Without the layers of war paint and skimpy attire, she was pretty, good company and helped fill the void in his life since Shannon had gone.

Sometimes, she would ask him questions about their relationship and where it was headed but he always fobbed her off telling her that he was having a good time and he wouldn't be with her if he didn't want to be. She also asked him about the girl that he had spoken of in previous times and he told her that he hadn't seen her in a while and would always quickly change the subject. He wished that she would leave Shannon out of it because he could not bear to discuss it, least of all with her. However, alone in his bedsit it was always Shannon who invaded his thoughts and every morning when he woke up it was her face that always came to mind. Sometimes in the heat of the moment he had almost uttered her name but managed to stop himself just in time. That would go down with Cara like a lead balloon. He had to see Shannon, he could not wait any longer; perhaps he would head into town and catch her on her lunch break. Cursing himself for not having thought of it sooner, he pocketed some cash and caught a bus to the city centre. He looked at his watch and saw that it was nearing noon and hoped that he would reach the recruitment agency on time. She always took an early lunch, always had for as long as he remembered. Said the town was less busy at that time whereas if you waited the extra hour it took ages to purchase anything because of the lunchtime queues. It had started to rain as he entered her office and he was greeted at reception by a bubbly, blond girl in her early twenties. Shannon was in the back kitchen when she was advised that someone was asking for her out front. She peeked out the door and when she saw him, she felt a stiff stab of tension. There was no way of avoiding him and as she made her way over, she forced herself to smile as naturally as possible.

'Hi,' she smiled. 'What are you doing here?'

'Just thought I would lure you away for a coffee down the street, my treat,' he replied, cheekily.

'Sounds good, she said, aware that no excuse would suffice. I'll just fetch my coat.'

She ran into the Ladies and shut the door. She looked at herself in the mirror and took some slow, deep breaths before grabbing her mac from the cloakroom and joining him again. He was smiling broadly as he watched her approach, cracking jokes with the young receptionist who was rather shamelessly fluttering her eyelashes at him.

'Some things never change, do they?' she teased, before heading out the door which he had held open for her. She flicked open her umbrella and he quickly took shelter underneath as they started to walk quickly down the street. She was glad that this part of the city was very busy and directed him towards a bustling coffee shop not far from where she worked. They both ordered a Latte and sat down.

'It is so good to see you Shan, I have missed you,' he said, looking her straight in the eyes.

'Yeah, yeah me too,' she replied. She was aware that her face had rouged slightly and her hands unsteady.

'Your hands are shaking,' he said. 'Are you okay?'

'They do that sometimes,' she laughed, 'I am just cold.'

The half hour dragged. He asked her all about her new accommodation and how it was panning out and how long she planned on being away. He asked her about the new tenant and what lease she had signed, if it was for six months or a year. He asked her about Steve and had she seen him or if there had been any contact to which she said that all was quiet on that front and that she was concentrating on herself and getting her life together. He told her about the cottage and described in detail some of the work that he had done. He thought that it was all coming together nicely and he was pleased with the progress. He informed her that he was planning a night out at the weekend and would she come. She said she wasn't sure, that she was trying to steer clear of the partying scene for a while. He asked about Mel and how she was and if they had seen much of each other and Shannon said that she had seen her once or twice. She did not want to tell him that she had seen her more than that in case he wondered why she had not made a similar effort with him. After settling the bill, they headed back out into the rain and bumped straight into Anita. She didn't see them at first but when she did, she darted back nervously to let them pass.

'Hi Shannon,' she said, timidly, her eyes fluttering up towards Pete.

'Hi there,' Shannon replied.

'Ignore her Shan, she is a total waste of space,' Pete hissed, displaying an air of impatience and arrogance as he towered over her small frame, pushing out his chest like a

153

peacock in what Shannon immediately recognised as a method of intimidation.

Anita turned on her heels and walked quickly away but not before Shannon noticed a look on her face, a look revealing unease and fear. Shannon was not surprised at her reaction because Pete's entire body language was extremely menacing.

'Anita', she yelled, chasing after her.

'Is everything going okay with your new recruit?' she asked, warmly.

'Yes, she is doing really well. Be careful Shannon,' she warned, setting off again at a brisk pace.

'What was that all about?' Pete demanded to know, his tone calmer.

'She is a client Pete, my relationship with her is purely business. What is the saying?

'Keep your friends close and your enemies closer.' 'There is no love lost between us, let me assure you, but she is Personnel Manager of a massive, reputable company and any business these days is good business, especially in our economic climate,' she defended, brusquely.

'You are right there,' he laughed, and to her dismay he put his arm over her shoulder and pulled her close. She understood he was doing this for effect, marking his territory, or was he? Nevertheless, he seemed satisfied with her reasoning and escorted her back to the agency but not before begging her to reconsider meeting him at the weekend for a few drinks.

Having said his goodbyes he decided to head for a pint which led to another and another. He did not talk to anyone. He wasn't in the mood. His mind was working overtime. By early evening, he decided that he would walk by Mel's salon and perhaps she would fit him in for a trim. That was his excuse anyway. However, Mel knew instantly that he had had a few and told him that if he called back, she would be finished shortly and she would join him for a beer. The trim could wait for another day. She wasn't much in the mood for a drink, but she felt quite concerned that he had started on the booze so early in the day and wanted to ensure that he was okay. She liked Pete. He had been good to Shannon, to both of them. But Pete had already been on the sauce for God knows how long and conversation came more freely than usual. He told Mel that he had just met Shannon and they had a coffee. He asked if she had seen much of her and was stunned to hear Mel say she had seen her three or four times a week which completely conflicted with what Shannon had told him. He was also shocked that Mel appeared to have no knowledge of the confrontation which had taken place in the forest. Either that or she was a fine actress, he thought. She appeared utterly dismayed and upset as she admitted that it was all news to her and that her friend had not told her any of this. Pete continued to knock the drink back until Mel insisted on ordering him a coffee to sober him up. The coffee was refused!

He confided that they had bumped into Anita and seemed to be getting angrier. Mel mentioned that she had visited the salon and that she seemed annoyed about everything that had happened but that just irked Pete even more. He learnt from Mel that she was employed by a large firm of chartered accountants on Mc Guigan Street and later some on-line browsing revealed all the information he needed to form his plan. Research completed to his satisfaction, he started packing all his things, in large, black bin bags. It was time. Mel had told him that she was sure Shannon had strong feelings for him but that it was going to take time. It took him a few hours to get organised and by the time he finished he was exhausted. The following evening, he drove into town and parked on double yellows, hazard lights switched on. He watched intently as staff from McGuigans started to emerge from the rather grand looking building to make their way home after a day's work. He finally spotted Anita exit accompanied by a female colleague and when they parted company, he followed her, retaining a safe distance behind. As she made her way up the street, he trailed behind, observing her every movement. She continued on foot for some time and disappeared for about 10 minutes taking a shortcut through the Seaway Park. There was only one exit from the park however, so he was able to drive around and wait – traffic was dense, but he made it to the other side just in time to see her disappearing down a side street, her bright yellow overcoat ensuring she was easier recognised. She was wearing headphones and seemed oblivious to anything or anyone around. Not the most sensible thing in the world for her to do, he thought. Finally, she headed through a gate which led to a set of apartments which he knew were relatively upmarket and as far as he heard extremely expensive. She had obviously landed on her feet. He watched as she headed inside, the door held open for her by a young couple who looked no more than their early twenties. He waited until they had moved on before pulling up outside. He gazed at the block until he noticed the lights come on in a corner apartment on the third floor. He identified her petite silhouette clearly as she wandered around. The curtains were open and he had no doubt she was alone. He drove across to the visitor's car park and took the first space available. Then he waited for about twenty minutes until he saw a young professional approach the door and he chased after her, ordering her to wait.

'Hi,' he said, 'I have a friend lives here and she asked me to give her a shout if I were in town, only she is not answering her mobile and her landline is busy. I have come all this way so if it is okay, I will just go on up and rap her door,' he grinned, turning on his most charming smile as he deftly slipped by.

That was so easy, he thought, before sprinting up the three flights of stairs and boldly rapping Anita's door.

She answered straight away and just as quickly tried to slam it shut but was nowhere near quick or strong enough.

'Not so fast, dear,' he said, stepping inside and casually wiping his feet on the wiry doormat in the process.

'How the hell did you find me? Did you follow me?' she demanded, her insides quaking with fear.

'It wasn't rocket science Anita, you led me here all by yourself. Mind you, it would have been quicker had you been driving, I thought we were never going to get home,' he sneered.

'What do you want Pete?'

'Cup of coffee would be nice to start with.' 'White, no sugar,' he commanded, rudely.

'Just get out Pete, or I will call the police,' she shouted.

'I don't think so Anita, get me a coffee like a good girl now,' he ordered.

Anita tottered into the kitchen, wiping her brow. She could feel little droplets of perspiration trickle along her forehead as she wondered what he wanted and how ever was she going to get rid of him?

'There you go,' she murmured, handing him the smallest cup she had, 'now tell me what you want. I have a friend arriving at any minute.'

'How convenient,' he smiled, 'lucky that you must press a buzzer to permit entrance, otherwise I might have to gulp this down in one go. Mind you, that's probably why you have given me a cup this size – an egg cup would do a better job!'

'I'm going to the bathroom,' she responded meekly, turning away.

'Your mobile please,' he snarled.

'What?' she stuttered.

'I want your mobile phone,' he dictated.

She passed it over reluctantly, her knees knocking together as she trembled.

'Okay, off you go, and don't even consider picking up your landline,' he threatened.

When she returned, he ordered her to grab her overnight bag.

'Pack all you need for a few days, you are coming with me,' he barked.

'What do you mean by that? I am not going anywhere. Just tell me what you want,' she gasped in horror.

'You have nothing to fear Anita, so long as you do exactly as I say. There is no time to waste,' he insisted.

'Look Pete, this is impossible. Just tell me what you want from me and I'll do it,' she begged, but her sorry pleas fell on deaf ears. She could tell by his stern, facial expression that this was no joke.

'Just throw a few things together for a few days away. That's what I want,' he smiled.

'Okay, okay,' she muttered, starting towards her room. He followed her and stood by the door watching her every move.

'Where are you taking me?' she sobbed.

'It will all become clear soon,' he answered, returning to the sitting room.

After she had packed, she sat on the bed for a second or two. He was waiting on her and as her eyes darted around the room anxiously, she assessed if there was any way she could escape. Even if she made it to the balcony, she could scream for help but there was no way he would let that happen. She was three floors up and it was simply impossible to flee. He shouted at her to hurry and she did so obediently, begging for divine intervention, for Him to intervene and save her from whatever hell she was about to suffer. As they were leaving, he held the door open for her to pass through first; otherwise she would have bolted and slammed it behind her.

'Do nothing silly, I am warning you,' he reiterated. 'If you do, you will be putting yourself at risk not to mention others and I know you don't want to do that.'

By this stage her heart was in her mouth. She was stunned and shocked that he had reached this new level of insanity. She feared greatly for her safety and was dumbstruck. She opened her mouth to speak but no words escaped. She didn't think she could scream even if she wanted to. Besides, it was growing dark and there was so sign of anyone. She considered again what he wanted from her, what he was going to do, where were they going. He opened the door to the passenger seat before jumping in next to her, assuming the driver's position. He turned the key in the ignition and she was suddenly startled by the sound of Depeche Mode playing at full volume.

'My, you're on edge, aren't you?' he complained. 'I am not going to hurt you. You have no need to fret.'

'You, you do realise that people will be looking for me?' she began.

'Yes, but they won't find you, of that I can be sure,' he patronised, as he drove forward towards the open security gates.

Suddenly, Anita reached for the door handle, but he was faster. He immediately did an emergency stop, flinging her forward in the process. He glared at her angrily as he locked all the doors and scolded,

'Try anything stupid like that again and you will be sorry. I am being very nice to you, but I will get nasty. Do you understand?'

She looked at him, disgusted at his utter vileness. She was scared out of her wits and deeply panicked. What was he going to do to her? As they drove further and further away from her accommodation she peered out the window at the streetlights casting ghostly black shadows of darkness in their paths before all the bright lights of the city vanished. As they sped down the motorway, she felt herself become increasingly sleepy but she was aware of shooting pains in her chest emphasizing her state of sheer panic. How she wished she was anywhere else but here! She must have nodded off at some point because she only woke up when the car jolted to a stop and she felt the effect of the seatbelt as it performed its necessary function. She wondered if she was dreaming at first but soon discovered this was no dream. She had no idea where he had brought her and her initial fear turned to severe apprehension. She had suffered insomnia in recent weeks and felt like she had been dragged through the bushes. She considered if he had drugged her as she could remember next to nothing about the journey.

'Now, we are here,' he revealed. 'Do you like it?'

'Do I like it? You're asking me if I like it. Pete, for God's sake, please, I am begging you, please bring me home,' she implored hysterically.

'I will, of course, all in good time.' 'Come in and I'll show you around,' he smiled, beckoning her to join him. 'You will love it here. It is really peaceful.'

She followed him slowly into the cottage and shuddered as she stepped inside. It looked dismal in places, she thought, glancing cautiously around her as she took in the chilly blackness of the surroundings. There was no way she would love it here.

'Tomorrow, he said, I will have to return to the city, but I will make sure you have everything you need. In the meantime, I will sort dinner.'

'Okay,' she agreed. She had resigned herself to the fact that she was not going anywhere anytime soon. Better to appease him for the moment than get him riled, she decided.

He switched on the television for her and started to prepare a fire, humming to himself as he did so. That finished, he retreated to the kitchen and commenced his food preparations whilst gulping the contents of a large glass of red wine. He offered her one, but she refused. There was no way she was going to touch a single drop of alcohol, but she accepted a glass of coke. It seemed no time before he called her for their meal and she was surprised to see a half decent Chicken Caesar Salad with Garlic Bread. She ate what she could because she knew she had to, but she did not speak a word. When they had finished their grub, he made her a cup of tea and threw more sticks on the fire.

'Are you okay?' he asked her.

'Look, the meal was good and I enjoyed it, but I am hardly okay Pete, I just want to go home, your argument is not with me,' she said quietly.

'No, you are right of course, my argument is not with you, it is with him. He will not back off,' he thundered, storming off into the kitchen and returning a couple of minutes later with another glass of red wine and a coke with ice for her.

'If your argument is with him, then why kidnap me?' she demanded to know.

'It is hardly kidnap,' he replied sharply.

'Of course, it is kidnap,' she said, 'what other word can be used to describe your taking me from my home against my own free will?' she whimpered.

'Think of it as a mini-break, it will be nice, you will enjoy it,' he assured her. Now come on, I will show you your room. There is no point you trying to do a runner either, it is pitch black out there and there is not a house in miles,' he stated.

Anita looked around the room. The bedspread was white and black, a zebra design with two matching towels tossed on top. It was clean and tidy. She noted a few items around that indicated there had been a female present at some stage – a bottle of cleanser and a bright red Revlon lipstick. She racked her brains at who he might have taken here but dared not ask for fear of worsening his mood.

161

'I'll leave you to it,' he said. 'Goodnight, I'll be up early in the morning and we will have breakfast before I go.'

When he shut the door, Anita quickly ran to the window but when she looked out all she could see was the pitch darkness of night. There was no light whatsoever and she could only hear the rustling of the trees swaying in the wind outside. It was creepy. There was no way she would even attempt an escape as knowing her luck she would be attacked by a fox or some wild animal roaming around out there. She wondered how long he was going to keep her captive and fretted that nobody would notice her absence. She lay on the bed staring at the ceiling for what appeared to be hours, she tossed and turned and sobbed her heart out before sleep finally came and she was plunged into an alien world of horrific nightmares. She dreamt that Pete pulled out a gun on her and aimed it straight between her eyes whilst Steve urged him to pull the trigger. More than once, she woke up and her pillow was saturated with tears and she felt like a child again, helpless and deserted. This was much worse though. For all the time she had spent locked behind her bedroom door at her parents' home, she knew that it was for her own safety, but this was much worse. Her mum did not have a key and would not be coming for her, she didn't even know where she was and Gregory would not worry about her, not for a couple of days at least. They did not talk every day like a lot of couples and he would think nothing of her not calling him and when he did call her, he would assume that she was busy. All those fears and night-time terrors that she suffered as a child had resurfaced with full force to haunt her and what was hardest to bear was that she had no idea where she was but there did not seem to be another sinner around. In the morning, still shattered she realised that Pete must have drawn the curtains and placed a blanket over her. She was still dressed but her shoes and socks had been removed and placed neatly at the foot of the bed. She felt sickened that he had been in the room whilst she was asleep. Making her way into the shower she stood underneath the warm water imagining just for a short while that she was back safe and sound in her own pad. Afterwards, she regarded herself in the mirror and started to cry again before splashing cold water over her face. She picked out her old, loose fitting boyfriend jeans and a baggy top from her holdall before running a brush through her wet hair and cleaning her teeth.

She could hear pans clanging in the kitchen and the smell of bacon and eggs wafting its way towards her, but she just felt sick to the stomach. Nevertheless, she tried to eat a little before curling up in the foetal position on the old, battered settee, still feeling crippled by the tiredness caused by her terrible ordeal and the disturbed sleep she had had. A short time passed before Pete followed her through. In his hands were cuffs and she gaped at him in confusion as he roughly shackled her feet together. Surely, he was not about to tie her up like a prisoner but that was exactly what he did.

'Come on Pete, bring me with you, bring me home, please,' she begged repeatedly.

'I will not be gone long. I must go to the city and I'll be back later. Don't try anything silly. There is no point,' he insisted.

With that, he turned on the television, handed her the remote and a couple of DVDs before fetching a plate of ham and cheese sandwiches and two large bottles of water.

'In case you get dehydrated,' he declared, 'I am leaving your hands free in case you need the toilet,' he said, before smiling at her and heading out the door, whistling to himself.

'By the way, in case you are wondering, I have disconnected all the phones so do not overexert yourself by poking around,' he warned, peeping through the door, before locking it behind him.

That was it. He was gone. Anita heard the car roaring off into the distance and then it was silent. She could not believe that this was happening and she could not understand for the life of her why he had taken her, why he had resorted to such drastic, irrational measures. How had she got into this mess and what was she going to do? Would anyone notice that she was missing? She sighed heavily. How long would it be before he returned and what was he going to do with her? That was what scared her most. He was bound to know that if she escaped, she would go straight to the police. She had no idea of her whereabouts. How would anyone know where to find her? And he had disconnected the phones and taken her mobile! She started to scream and wail but there was no-one around to hear. This must be his place, she concluded, wearily. It was obvious he had been doing some work to it. She had noticed a half full skip outside last night and he was clearly trying to get the place in shape. There were no photographs on the wall, just one or two paintings and an ornament or two on the mantelpiece. A damp, musky smell filled the air and there were layers of dust coating the old coffee table and the television. It was gloomy, but it had potential. Within a couple of hours, Pete had reached his bedsit, where he hauled everything into his car boot, three bin bags at a time. Once he had loaded his vehicle, he returned inside and gave the place a quick clean before ringing the landlord and confirming that he had moved out. He agreed that the deposit be kept due to his short notice on vacating the property before driving into the city centre where he headed for Shannon's office. He wanted to find out what was going on and why she had lied to him but when he got there, he was told that she was on annual leave. Raging like a bull, he returned to the old battered Peugeot and drove the two hours back to the cottage. When he arrived, everything was quiet and he found Anita lying on the floor, shivering. Damn it, I forgot to light a fire, he thought grimly. He noticed that she had a cut to her head and it was obvious that she had fallen and possibly hit her face against the hearth. He lifted her up swiftly and lay her across the sofa. He tried to talk to her, but she was mumbling quite incoherently. He quickly unlocked the shackles, wrapped a blanket around her, switched on the heating and made her a hot cup of tea before fetching his first aid kit and tending to her wound.

'Now then,' he said, gently. Let's get you sitting up.'

Slowly, he eased her into a sitting position and bathed her forehead with a warm facecloth whilst coaxing her to take a drink.

'What happened?' he asked.

'Not sure,' she whispered, wishing she could edge away from him without his noticing. 'I went to the bathroom. I must have tripped on the rug and banged my head.' She ate some toast and drank her tea before he led her to bed after which he poured himself a strong whiskey. It was apparent that she had done some snooping, but he was too tired and she was in too much of a state to worry about that for now. He reconnected the telephone line and pressing 141 first, dialled Shannon's mobile number.

'How are you?' he enquired jovially whenever she picked up.

'Good, good,' she replied.

'I called at your office today, but they said you were on leave,' he said.

'Yes, I took a few days off, it has just been hectic recently,' she replied, detecting a mild accusation in his tone. She was very much aware and suspicious of every question he asked and every answer she gave. She was not in the mood for another interrogation after the day he had brought her out for coffee.

'I can tell,' he stated, 'I have hardly heard from you.'

'Look Pete, can I possibly phone you tomorrow? There is someone at the door, I think it might be Mel; she wanted to see me about something,' she declared.

'Okay,' he responded chirpily, although he wondered if she was telling the truth.

He said goodbye and hung up the phone. It seemed likely that Mel would tell her about meeting him and he started to mull over the potential conversation they might now be having.

22

Shannon was far from okay though. Her mind was in turmoil. So much seemed to be happening and she felt like she was on a seesaw emotionally, one wrong move either direction and she would be knocked off balance and fall to the ground. Just when her life took on the semblance of a soap opera, she wasn't sure, but it just seemed to be one thing after another these days. Gemma had gone into labour prematurely and given birth to a little girl but whilst utterly delighted with the news there were still concerns over the baby's health and wellbeing. Both mother and baby appeared to be doing well but everything had happened so suddenly and so fast that they had scarcely had time to take it all in. It had been a complete shock to the system for everyone concerned but particularly Gemma and Gerry who really had not anticipated the events which had unfolded quite unexpectedly and dramatically by any account. There had been no signs of an imminent birth and Shannon and Gemma had headed out for a stroll in one of the local parks, while Gerry remained at home intent on cutting the grass using his new ride-on. Gemma had been telling Shannon about her birthing plans and how she really yearned for a water birth at home. The girls had only gone a mile or two before Gemma said she felt a little strange and the two of them had sat for a while until Gemma insisted she was fine to continue. Rather than continue however, Shannon had recommended that they go back the way they had come just in case and it was clear on the return trek that there was some pain or other irking her. It was in the car that her waters suddenly broke causing Shannon to almost crash, so astounded was she by the sudden whoosh and subsequent cry from her stepmum's mouth. As Gemma started to apologise for the mess to the seats Shannon switched on her hazard lights and whisked her straight to the hospital, phoning her dad on route and advising him to come immediately. Thank God they were only a few miles from the hospital, and they were able to get there minutes later. On arrival at the Midwifery unit, Gemma was swiftly taken to a room where she was examined and subsequently prepped for surgery. She was in theatre even before Gerry arrived and an emergency caesarean section was performed as the baby was premature and obviously there was an increased risk of complications. Gerry had driven as fast as he could and when he darted through the arrival doors of the maternity wing his face was ashen and he looked like he had aged twenty years. The baby had been taken immediately to the NICU (Newborn Intensive Care Unit) which had the necessary medical staff and equipment that were required to deal with the multiple problems faced by premature infants. To all intent and purpose though, things looked okay and it appeared that the baby's lungs, which was the biggest concern, were developing well enough. Gemma had been taken to the recovery suite, she had some haemorrhaging and would be monitored closely until staff were sure she was fit to be discharged. Shannon was hoping that they would get out soon and, in the meantime, she would busy herself preparing the nursery and trying to get things organised to ensure a smooth settling back in period for mother and baby. The last thing on her mind at the minute was Pete and whilst she hoped that she didn't sound too curt when he had called she was certainly not about to tell him about her new little sister, whom they had already decided to call Megan, one of her favourite names. She was beautiful, only four and a half pounds in weight, but God how she loved her already. They all did which was precisely why she had withheld the news from Pete, she could take no risks because if he was even half as brutal as Steve had described, then perhaps no-one was safe. As she opened the door now to greet Mel, she tried to abolish all these horrible thoughts from her mind. Mel was bubbling with excitement over the baby and Shannon showed her a little photo, whilst proudly describing in complete detail the new extension to the family. Of course, it was hard to feel totally elated as the little baby was not out of the woods yet. She had a long way to go and to a certain extent Gemma was in denial over exactly how long recovery would take, even after countless discussions with the hospital staff who had informed her and Gerry that it could take weeks before little Megan would recover sufficiently from such a premature arrival. She filled a couple of glasses of sparkling white wine to the brim and sat with her friend in the conservatory amicably discussing Megan and how delighted they were and how they just couldn't wait for her to be home with them. It wasn't long however once the baby talk had died down until Mel became serious, looking her friend straight in the eyes, and demanding to know about the incident in the forest and why she had not been told. She also wondered why Shannon had told Pete that she had hardly seen her when in fact they had seen each other often. Mel was not confrontational. On the contrary she was of mild manner and a loyal friend. Shannon could tell that she was hurt at being kept in the dark.

'Oh Mel, it is so complicated,' she cried.

'Try me, I'm all ears, I just want to know what is going on Shan,' she encouraged.

And so, Shannon proceeded to divulge the recent events that had occurred, stopping every so often to apologise for not having confided in her earlier. Mel's reaction was one of disbelief and anger. She was deeply upset not so much that she had been kept out of the loop, but that Shannon had been living in total fear, not knowing who to trust any more. The next half an hour, Mel sat in a stupefied silence as she listened to Shannon describe everything that had unfolded in the prior months. She felt indescribable guilt that she had tried so many times to pair them off. Had she got it so wrong? And what about Anita? She had been so devastated when she had left the salon that day and she had been so curt and sharp with that poor girl. She was also annoyed because she had told Pete she had seen lots of Shannon which on reflection would have proved to him that something was amiss. Was that why he had arrived at the salon that day, drunk as a skunk, hardly able to stand? It was all too much for her and she broke down again and again, unable to disguise her anguish, unable to accept that all this time she had tried to push the two of them together when quite evidently Pete was not who she thought he was. Was she that bad a judge of character? Was it true? Or could it be possible that Steve was lying through his teeth, that things had just not gone as he had planned and that Pete perhaps was an innocent party in his warped game. It beggared belief. Mel had been fond of Steve but when he had taken off like that leaving her friend's life in tatters, she figured that she had got him wrong. Now it looked like the tables were turning and she, like Shannon no longer knew who or what to believe.

When Gerry arrived, they were forced to change the subject as all this would have been too much for him to bear. He was in good spirits however and sat with the two girls sipping a glass of wine whilst writing lists of all the things they needed for the baby. He was very impressed with the medical staff at the hospital and praised their skills and care before talking about Gemma and how proud she had made him. When he finally retreated to his beloved garden, Shannon told Mel that she had not told her Dad anything about the whole situation. She also admitted that she had decided not to tell Pete about the new arrival.

'I am worried Mel, I really am, if this is true then I am an awful fool,' she said.

'Look, let's not jump to conclusions too fast Shan, maybe Steve has an ulterior motive,' she suggested.

170

'I know he wants me back Mel but now all communication is via text, if all this is true then it is too risky to be seen together,' she insisted.

'What about Anita? I believe you ran into her the other day?' 'Pete told me you met her,' she said.

'It was awful, she looked perplexed, I felt so sorry for her, if the truth be told. Again, if what Steve said is true then, she was acting out of concern for him; that is why she went to London, to make sure he was okay. Furthermore, Steve said she has a boyfriend, Greg or Gregory I think he said and that they are really happy together.'

'So, there was never anything between them?' Mel asked.

'It would seem so, he says she and Gregg are really solid and it sounds serious, he is going to move over here shortly so I would say that's a strong signal that they are committed.'

'Oh gosh we were calling her every name in the book. It looks like we were wrong about her. This is terrible. Funny enough, when she came to the salon that day, she was very unsettled, particularly after I told her about your mum, she was so shaken up, so troubled looking,' Mel said.

'Where did it come from, that story Mel?' Shannon asked.

'What story?' Mel said.

'That Anita had followed him to London and that they were together.'

They both stared at each other for they could remember exactly what they were doing when the awful truth had emerged. Mel had persuaded Shannon to go out for a drink. Shannon had lived in her dressing gown for days on end, drowning in her own self-pity, not eating or sleeping, just existing. She finally agreed to make an effort and the two of them headed to the local at the end of the road. Pete had joined them for a beer and they had been talking about Steve. That's when Pete, seemingly very hesitant, told her softly that he believed he had not gone to London alone, that Anita Dolan was with him and that they were

171

living together as a couple. When they asked him how he had discovered that, he replied that he had heard it from Anita's sister in law whom he had met in town one day. He said that he had not wanted to tell her, but he thought that it would be cruel to keep it back. Now they wondered if Anita even had a sister in law! Shannon suspected that was another lie for she had heard no names of any siblings – just talk of her mum and dad. Could that have been another lie? She would check with Steve if Anita had any other family later but hoped against hope that she did, otherwise it would appear that she had been betrayed in yet another horrible way. Was their whole friendship built on lies? Of course, after Pete had divulged this information, Shannon had been totally distraught and ran home broken hearted to her mum's and Maeve had been brilliant. She just knew exactly what to do. She had not offered advice, but she had listened to her daughter and held her in her arms as she wept uncontrollably, unable to take in that within a short space of time her whole life seemed to have fallen apart. Shannon recalled now how upset her mother had been, as from the very first moment she had met Steve she reckoned that he was the one for her daughter. He was gentle and kind, but he was firm too and he had a calming effect on Shannon, something which she needed from time to time. As much as she loved her daughter, she knew that she needed someone strong to keep her in check and she believed Steve was the one to do that. Now Shannon wondered what the truth was, but she tended to be more swayed by what Steve was telling her and if Pete was as crazy as it seemed, then God only knows what he would do next.

'It does not look good for Pete because I do not see how or why Steve could concoct such a story but to the same degree he has been such a wonderful friend, could he really be capable of all of these things?' she asked now.

'I don't know, I just cannot believe it but on the off chance that it is true then we need to proceed with caution.'

'Another minor point is that Steve said he phoned the house several times and often left messages, which I never received,' Shan pointed out.

'Well, I never picked up any or obviously I would have told you right away,' Mel stated, solemnly.

Later, after debating the issue for several hours, Mel left in a rather sombre mood and Shannon ran a hot bath before dialling Pete's number. She had been quite short on the phone before and she did not want him to pick up on it and jump to the wrong conclusions. They were probably the right conclusions, she thought but it was best let him think that everything was fine. However, she recognised the need to be prudent. There was no answer from his landline and when she tried his mobile, she could not connect and so she left a quick message advising him that she would see him soon. Next, she phoned Steve and arranged to meet him the following week out of town. He suggested a picnic on the beach if the weather held out and she agreed. It seemed more of a romantic setting in a sense, but it was likely that they would not be spotted there, she figured. Steve was delighted to hear from her, and whilst he knew that he was a long way from sorting out their relationship he was pleased that at least they could be friends for now. Who knew what the future would hold or what would happen, but this was a start. When the call ended, he phoned Anita straight away to update her but there was no answer and he decided to try again later. He knew that she always went to bed at about 10pm and she was quite religious about it. She insisted that she needed a full eight hours sleep otherwise she simply couldn't cope. However, when he phoned later, there was still no reply. She must have gone out, he thought. Such a shame he had missed her because she would be happy to learn that

Shannon had contacted him and to hear that he finally had a date to move into the new house. He had only found out earlier that day when the Estate Agent had called and he was ecstatic that things were going to plan. He had forgotten to tell Shannon about the house, but she had a lot going on and seemed busy. She was overjoyed that she had a little baby sister although it seemed that mother and baby although doing well, were still in hospital. The baby would be in the Special Care Unit for a few weeks yet, but the medical staff were excellent and apparently good progress was being made.

Two days later, he had a slightly panicked call from Gregory who informed him that he could not reach Anita and that it had now been a few days since they had spoken. He wanted to know if Steve had been speaking to her himself. Steve explained how he had phoned a couple of times unsuccessfully and had no answers to the messages he had left. When Steve called her mobile number again it went straight to voice mail. He decided to phone her offices and was promptly informed that she had not shown into work at all nor had she made any contact by phone in the last few days. They told him that if he heard anything to let them know as soon as possible as they were also concerned. Feeling more anxious than ever, he decided to drive to the complex where she lived but when he buzzed up to the flat there was no response. It was all very odd and he could feel the muscles in his body tighten with anxiety. He waited until he noticed a young man exit the building and quickly pushed past him. He raced to the third floor, three steps at a time where he started to hammer the door. He sounded the bell and shouted her name loudly but there was no answer. He then banged her neighbour's door but was told that he had not seen or heard her in several days. He rushed out to the car park and immediately clocked her silver BMW. But where was she? If she had not taken her car and was not in work, where could she possibly have gone? He phoned Gregory and explained that there was no sign of her but that her car was in the parking bay and Gregory was as baffled as he was. Next, he phoned Shannon and told her that he could not get in touch with her and that he was going out of his mind with worry. He asked Shannon if he should kick the door down, but she told him to ring her brother, that maybe one of her family had a key.

'Shannon, Anita does not have a brother, she is an only child. She does not see her father at all, unless she has gone to see her mother…,' he cried.

'Are you sure? I mean, I thought she had a brother,' she said. 'Pete told me after you left for London that he had been talking to Anita's sister in law and she was the one who told him about you two going off together.'

'Oh, my goodness, this is getting worse! Do you believe me now? That is total bullshit. Anita has no family other than her mother.'

'You don't think that he has taken Anita, do you Shannon?' he bumbled.

'No, no, he wouldn't do that, would he?' she nervously whispered back.

'I don't know anymore,' he said.

'What are we going to do Steve?' she asked.

'I'm not sure, I need to call at her mums and see if I can find out anything. I'll call you later,' he said, climbing back into his car again.

Twenty minutes later and with some careless driving involved, he arrived outside Anita's mum's house. May Dolan was surprised to see him and immediately offered him a cup of tea which he politely declined saying that he simply had to talk to her. Without taking a seat, he hurriedly explained that he had not seen or been in contact with Anita. He expressed concern over the presence of the BMW in the car park but stated that she was evidently not at home nor had she attended work for a few days.

Unfortunately, however, Anita's mum had not seen or heard from her, but she did have a spare key and they decided to head back to the complex and gain access. They both jumped back into the car and sped to the apartment and with breakneck speed raced upstairs once more. When they entered the room and called her name, it was no surprise to be met by silence. They wandered from room to room calling her name, but she was not there and nothing appeared to have been disturbed. All her clothes were still neatly hanging in the wardrobe and there was a half-finished cup of coffee on the table. Steve noted the Nescafe on the kitchen counter but said nothing. Anita drank tea or water. Who had been here? Her mum padded around, opening cupboards and closets, searching for any clue that might reveal her daughter's current whereabouts.

'She takes her holdall wherever she goes but I cannot find it,' she declared.

'Okay,' Steve replied. 'Maybe she decided to get away for a few days, perhaps she just needed time on her own.'

'Perhaps, but I don't see why,' May replied, looking puzzled.

Aware that he was wasting time, they locked up and Steve dropped May home, doing his best to reassure her that she was probably fine and had gone off to get her head cleared. Secretly though, he knew that this was improbable and felt deeply troubled and he knew that her mum, despite putting on a brave face was equally apprehensive as to her only daughter's disappearance. It was not like Anita to vanish without a trace. He phoned Greg again and told him that the flat was undisturbed but that her holdall was missing. He also mentioned the half empty coffee cup but confessed to simply clutching at straws. Maybe she was planning a surprise visit to England. Greg was about to hit the big 40 and there was a possibility that she had decided to surprise him. Perhaps she had taken a taxi to the airport which would explain the presence of her BMW still parked

176

outside. They reluctantly agreed to give it one more day without panicking unnecessarily and when he phoned Shannon later, he advised her what he had done and to be extremely cautious just in case. Shannon felt ill at ease. She was missing Gemma as a confidant the last week or so and wouldn't have wanted to burden her anyway. Even if she wanted to talk to her it would have been virtually impossible as if she wasn't surrounded by medical staff in the hospital, her father or Cara were never far away. Cara had surprised her regarding the baby. She always insisted that she didn't want children, but Shannon felt that perhaps she had changed her mind.

23

Shannon thought right. Cara could not pass a shop without buying something for the little one and yet again had gone into town to buy some cute little clothes for her niece. She had been to the hospital to see her on several occasions already and it had really stirred up some maternal feelings in her that she had not known she possessed. She had never felt a great desire to be a mum; she always considered that Gemma had more motherly instincts than her. Even when they were younger, Gemma had always played with dolls, washing them and changing their clothes, doing their hair in various styles whereas she had been more the tomboy of the two. She liked climbing trees, playing football, going on her scooter and bicycle, mainly anything outdoors. She didn't like the thoughts of being pregnant, putting on weight and especially going through labour. However, since Megan's birth she had felt such an overpowering sense of love that she wondered if perhaps she was softening to the notion of parenthood. Once inside Debenhams she purchased some gorgeous baby grows before spending a fortune in Mother Care on bibs and little trousers and tops. With her shopping expedition finished, she headed for a full facial and it was so relaxing she could have just fallen asleep there and then. She was in good form. She and Peter were going great and despite not having seen him for a good few days now, he constantly texted with assurances that he could not wait to see her again. She was extremely attracted to him, he was so handsome although somewhat moody but then again, she could be moody herself. He never spoke of the girl whom he'd mentioned when they had first met; she had tried to broach the subject countless times, but it never went down altogether well. She spent many a time dwelling on what he had professed in the pub, that he was in love with someone and that there seemed to be some sort of love triangle going on. She recalled his mention of her ex returning and his anger about it and she remembered Gemma warning her off him. But she didn't want to be left on the shelf and she was intrigued by him. There was a coolness that he gave off which made her want him even more. He could also be attentive and caring. She did not know much about him though. He didn't like talking about himself or his family. He never invited her to his place either and she didn't understand that. She knew he lived in a bedsit and that he had a place in the country. He always seemed to have money and was generous with it. She wondered if he had inherited a wad of cash for he never seemed to work. As she was driving home, she took a detour and pulled up outside the bedsit. Normally she would not dream of letting anyone see her without her make up but as he was always saying he preferred her 'au natural' she decided that she would stop by and say hello. She was surprised by how unkempt the place looked. There were weeds in the garden and rubbish strewn outside. She knew that there were four bedsits within the house but wasn't sure which was his. She examined the names of the residents on the door, but his name was missing. She buzzed up to the first and to the second but had no joy. When she tried the third there was no answer at all and when she tried the fourth, she finally got a response.

'Hang on and I'll come down,' said the guy through the intercom.

A minute or so later, a lanky built, middle aged man appeared who explained that he had just moved in. He said that he believed that the prior tenant was named Pete but that he had gone. Cara felt numbed. Had he really moved out and not told her? Surely, he wouldn't do that. Thinking that there must be some logical explanation she immediately called him on the mobile. When he answered, she didn't say hello but launched straight in with the questions.

'Pete, it's me, where are you?' she demanded to know.

'I'm at home,' he said.

'Pete, I am at your home and they tell me you have gone, so, where are you?' she roared.

'Cara, calm down, since when did you become my private detective anyway?' he yelled back, annoyed with her obvious anger at him.

'Pete, just tell me where you are? Why did you move out? Did something happen? Why did you not tell me?' she asked, impatiently.

'Look here, I just got fed up, it was poky and dirty, so I decided to come down to the cottage for a couple of days,' he replied.

'So, you just moved out of the bedsit and back home to the cottage where you grew up?' she shouted.

'Never mind, does it matter?' he shouted.

'Yeah, it matters, of course it matters. It's miles away. Are you with her?' she screeched.

'With whom?' he shouted, starting to feel harassed.

'That girl, the one whom you declared your undying love? That's who!' she screamed.

'I am not having this conversation,' he roared, slamming the phone down.

Cara was livid. She immediately phoned back but was directed straight to voice mail which really infuriated her. Who the hell did he think she was? She left a message for him which she totally regretted afterwards.

Sobbing, she leapt back in the car and drove to Gemma's. When she arrived, Shannon was there alone. Gerry had returned to the hospital to see Gemma and the baby. When Shannon opened the door, she was met by a sobbing and distraught young woman who without her make up looked so much younger and more vulnerable than she had ever imagined.

'My goodness Cara, are you okay?' 'What on earth has happened?' she asked.

'Long story, long story, any wine in the house?' Cara stammered, clearly very upset.

'Yes, I'll go fetch a glass and you can tell me all about it,' she suggested.

Shannon returned promptly with two glasses of Chardonnay and set them down on the table. She placed the bottle of Chardonnay in an ice bucket anticipating that it would disappear fast.

In between sobbing Cara outlined what had happened, how she had a row with her boyfriend, that he had moved back home to the country, which was over a two-hour drive away. She also confided that she was sure he was not on his own.

Shannon tried her best to console her, but words were no use. Cara wailed about being badly treated and that he had been the best thing that had happened in ages.

'Maybe something has happened Cara, it is not good to have these conversations by phone. I'm sure there is a perfectly good explanation and when you meet him it will all become clear,' she commented, whilst wishing that she could heed her own advice.

'What is his name anyway?' she wanted to know.

'His name is Pete, vanishing Pete, I feel like I am going out with a magician, a ghost even, one minute he is there and the next he is gone.'

'What is he like?' she asked.

'He is gorgeous Shannon, really fit and handsome, caring too but he can be distant and sometimes a little moody,' she replied.

'Where did you meet him?' Shannon quizzed.

'I met him in a bar, actually we met in a taxi first, he was on his way to meet someone but was denied admittance to some haunt in town because he wasn't suitably dressed. Anyway, he ended up in the same bar as me. He was not in the best of spirits, seemed keener on knocking back some spirits though. I was out with Gemma that night; she was not overly impressed with him. Thought he was a bit strange, weird even.'

'Why was that?' Shannon enquired.

'She just thought that I was wasting my time. He kept talking about this other woman.

'Why bother with someone like that?' she asked me.

'Ah, I see,' Shannon asked. 'This is the same guy you spoke of a couple of months back, isn't it?'

'Yip, same one, no fool like an old fool,' Cara sighed.

The two girls sat up talking until near midnight when Gerry arrived back, Gemma trailing behind, smiling as usual but looking tired, nonetheless.

'I brought Gem back, had to drag her out of there by the heels, didn't I love?' Gerry said, leaning in for a kiss.

Cara rushed to her sister, squeezing her tight and Shannon was close behind. She was delighted to see her too and was surprised that she was beginning to form a very close connection there. Initially, she had found it difficult to understand how her father had moved on so rapidly, but she appreciated that her father had to get on with his life too. He was still a young man and she loved him with all her heart, but she knew that he loved Gemma just as he had loved her mother. He still talked of her mother, and Gemma seemed quite happy with that which pleased Shannon. She did not want to feel that the subject of her mother would be out of bounds, a closed topic that could not be openly discussed as that would have been uncomfortable!

After a mug of hot chocolate, Gerry persuaded Gemma to have an early night. She was exhausted and needed a good night's sleep. The baby was in good hands and they would leave first thing in the morning for the hospital, hopefully bright and breezy. It was virtually impossible to get any shut eye there amidst the continual hive of activity between maternity staff and anxious parents scurrying around the wards.

After Gemma had gone upstairs, the others sat chatting amicably, Cara spilling the beans on her rocky love life and Gerry advising her not to jump to any fast conclusions.

24

Miles away in the back of beyond, Anita was anxiously flicking between news channels hoping and praying for a report on a missing female, her! She had no idea what day it was and had no notion of dates or times. She slept when she could and rarely spoke. It seemed like months since he had kidnapped her, but she knew that it was only days. She had not taken her thyroid medication and she was out. Normally, she ordered a repeat prescription, but she knew that even if she had access to a computer, he would not allow her to fetch it. He would insist on picking it up himself and then she would be on her own for hours again. It had been a couple of days now without her thyroxine and the old familiar tiredness was starting to invade her body once more. She was feeling lethargic and could hardly keep her eyes open. The skin on her hands was becoming dry and itchy with little open cracks that were painful. Her scalp was becoming progressively dry and flaky and felt tender to touch. She had given up on asking him when he was bringing her home as he just became increasingly more agitated. She had heard him on the phone earlier and knew that something was playing on his mind. He was cross and appeared unsettled and she knew that it was best to say nothing than ask what was bothering him. Suddenly, the music was switched on drowning out the sound of the TV. She was sick to death of Depeche Mode and The Jam playing at full volume! She peeped out through the glass double doors leading to the kitchen and watched as he took out two glasses. She went to the toilet and when she returned, he had switched the television off and switched the music down a notch or two. He handed her a glass of diet coke which she accepted. She had a suspicion that there was vodka in hers and she supped slowly.

'So, you are a popular woman,' he said. 'Lots of folk looking for you, apparently.'

'Can I see my phone?' she asked.

'Yes, if you wish,' he smiled, handing it over.

She looked through her messages and counted numerous missed calls, mainly from Steve, Greg and her mum.

'Can I just phone to say that I am okay?' she stuttered.

'Over my dead body, pet,' he answered, seizing it from her, before tossing it in the smouldering flames.

'Why are you doing this?' she whimpered.

'He was not meant to come back, it is his fault,' he bellowed.

'But he loved her, he still loves her. She loves you, not in the way you want but she is fond of you, of that I have no doubt,' she declared.

The sharp slap to her face came out of the blue and she fell back, stunned.

'Don't dare say anything like that again, do you hear?' he yelled.

This is it, she thought. She felt so weak, but she didn't care anymore. Slowly, she stood to her feet and trudged to her bedroom. She was his captive here. She should have kept quiet. He was truly a psychopath. She could hear him now outside the room talking and swearing to himself; like he was having a conversation with someone. He was asking questions and answering them. She looked out the bedroom window and wondered if she dared make a bid for freedom. He was obviously not going to let her go. Maybe she should go back in there and apologise, get him drunk and then make a run for it. She had no choice, she had to do something. She wondered where he kept his torch and cursed herself for not having thought of it before. When she entered the kitchen, he was pacing back and forth. He didn't notice her at first, not until she started to speak and then he stopped and looked up. His thick eyebrows were arched together in a deep frown like he was running lots of things round in his head and she had perhaps interrupted his train of thought. She said how sorry she was, that she had been thoughtless and had spoken out of turn. He appeared satisfied with her apology and offered her a nightcap which she politely accepted insisting that she fetch it for him. She knew that he was already quite drunk and poured him a strong whiskey. He watched as she opened a bottle of vodka and poured a double measure into a tall glass before adding diet coke. Humming gently, she told him she was just going to fetch her specks from the next room and as she lifted them off the small coffee table, she reached for her other glass of coke which she had been sipping earlier. Then, peeking into the kitchen to check what he was doing she raced to the bathroom and poured the one containing vodka down the plughole before hiding the glass beneath her bed. Having done that, she returned to the kitchen with her coke. Thankfully he had changed the music and whilst she didn't recognise it, it was somewhat easier on the ear. She hoped that because he had seen her pouring the vodka that he would relax for all she needed was one opportunity to try and escape the hell hole which had become her confinement.

'Why did you two come home? Could you not just have stayed put?' he suddenly moaned, appearing calm for a moment.

'Our families are here, we missed them. I missed my mum so much and Steve, he missed.........,' she hesitated.

'He missed who?' he screamed, his calmness vanishing in an instant.

'He just, he didn't like it over there,' she hastily responded, kicking herself for putting her foot in it.

'I have loved her all my life, all I ever wanted was her, she is everything to me, everything,' he groaned.

'I know that Pete, I believe you and what is for you will not go by you, so my dad used to say,' she uttered.

'Fat lot of good that did him, I know all about your dad,' he scoffed.

'Have another drink,' she insisted, pouring more whiskey into his glass. She could tell that he was sinking it fast and she only hoped that he would continue as he had started and hopefully pass out soon. He was ranting and raving like a lunatic and his speech was quite slurred. She had mixed the whiskey with water initially but the more he drank the less water she used. He didn't seem to notice, however. If he had noticed, there would be serious repercussions, of that she was positive. He continued to talk nonsense as she just sat quietly observing his erratic behaviour. He was rambling, talking about Shannon and the things that they had done together, talking about her mum's death and how she had fallen apart and how he had been the one to help her pick up the pieces. He talked about Steve and how he just was not good enough for her. She needed a real man. He did not fit the bill, he never had and never would. He talked about his parents and how reserved and snobby they were, how he always felt that he was not good enough, that he had not lived up to their expectations but thankfully he did not have to anymore. That problem had long since been dealt with. He was sneering, she noticed, and she could see the spit squirt from his mouth, his face contorted like he had been through the horror of a facelift gone terribly wrong. He was foaming at the mouth, drooling like a baby, an oversized giant of a baby that was psychologically more damaged than anyone she had ever met in her whole life. She was afraid now. It was dangerous to speak as he was working himself up into such a rage that she was worried he would lash out yet again. He jumped to his feet suddenly and grabbed the whiskey bottle and she could tell that he was totally inebriated. He had probably been drinking since morning. He was unsteady and when he tripped over, he fell to the ground with a heavy thud. As he lay there on the hard floor, he grumbled and bleated for a few moments and then passed out. An eerie silence filled

187

the room. This was her chance. She waited a few moments. She stood over him, but he did not stir and then she flew into action. She raced to the drawer in the kitchen and quickly retrieved his shackles. She bound his feet and fled out the back door. It was dark and spooky. She felt like she was playing a part in a thriller movie and she was the main character, a sort of cat and mouse flick. She was the mouse, scuttling away to hide and escape her predator. She consoled herself that whatever animals were out there, none could be worse than him for he was the greatest beast she had ever had the misfortune of knowing. This was a risk she simply had to take. She knew time was limited but figured it best to flee than remain where she was. If only she could reach a telephone booth, she could phone the police and all would be fine. Damn it, she only had enough money for a 20 second phone call. This was not good. She wondered should she go back in and hunt for loose change but decided it was now or never, best to try and get away whilst he was comatose. She wouldn't find a telephone kiosk out here anyway.

As she closed the door quietly behind her and set off quickly down the lane, she felt wrought with tension, her fear causing her to quiver uncontrollably from head to foot. She had to get a grip on things and fast, she could do this, she had to do this!

The sound of an owl hooting almost lifted her off her feet, but she quickly overcame her fright and picked herself up again. God knows how long it would be before he came looking for her. If luck was on her side, she might have a few hours. She debated over whether she should stick to the main road or possibly trek over the endless fields. Maybe she would find a house out there but what was the likelihood of that? Hadn't he told her that there was nowhere within miles? Was that the truth or just another dark threat? She wished that she had her mobile phone but figured it was burnt to smithereens by now. The moon was out, casting some welcome light along the way and she thanked the good god for it otherwise she would have been as a blind man without his guide dog. As it was, it provided a faint ray of hope. She had never come across anywhere as deserted in her life. Her eye was still stinging from the ferocious whack he had planted earlier. She was sure she did not look a pretty sight what with the other eye already disfigured from the bang to the hearth just a few days before. That was the least of her worries though. However, it certainly impacted on her vision which was struggling in the dim moonlight. Her heart was thumping rapidly in her chest; how she detested the dark ever since she was little. She had always preferred to sleep with her door ajar and insisted lights were kept on. It was only when her parents were rowing that the door was locked on her mother's insistence. Unfortunately, rows were a frequent visitor to their increasingly unhappy home. She always looked under her bed and checked her wardrobes to make sure no-one was hiding inside. Her dad had made her watch horror movies as a child, often she had tried to leave the room, but he did not let her. Her fear made him laugh and she often sat crouched in a corner, hands covering her eyes as she tried to block out the sights and sounds of horrific films that were certainly aimed at the adult market and not for a child of 6 or 7 years old. Her imagination was getting the better of her now. The moon though welcome was casting dark, creepy shadows and even the trees appeared menacing standing tall and dark, swaying gently in the breeze. She did not know when things had started to go so wrong with her parents. It had once been a happy home but then her dad had been involved in an accident at work and that was the catalyst. Time off work led to boredom and depression which in turn led to the bottle. She would never forget the first time he hit her mother. It was over the simplest of things. She had overcooked his steak, murdered it, he had said at the time. Her mother had looked at him and laughed telling him that he could cook his own steak next time if he wanted but he didn't appreciate her comment and been quick to raise the back of his hand and deal her a stinging blow. Of course, immediately afterwards he had been overcome with remorse and vowed he would never do it again and her mother being the angel she was had forgiven him and blamed herself for provoking him. But that had been the first of many times until one evening he went too far and his fist landed her head first against the Aga, leaving her face battered black and blue. She had needed stitches then and when asked what had happened, she had told the truth which led to his being arrested and put behind bars for a while. The time apart had given her mother enough time to believe that she would be better off without him but he always managed to persuade her otherwise and she continually took him back. Like most women who are victims of domestic violence her mum thought he would change but he never did. He didn't want to change. Yes, Anita knew all about violence and combined with drink and medication, her father was truly a lost cause. She often remembered the Japanese proverb she had discovered as a child 'First the man takes a drink; then the drink takes a drink; then the drink takes the man.' She had not understood it then, but she sure as hell understood it now.

Pete was certainly drinking copious amounts of alcohol. She scarcely touched it, she had once heard it referred to as 'the devil's vomit' and believed that's exactly what it was. She was not teetotal and enjoyed the odd glass of wine, but she never overindulged and certainly never touched spirits. She had witnessed first-hand the destruction and devastation it caused to her own family and now she was witnessing it all over again with Pete. With the amount of booze he was consuming she was sure that he was capable of anything and she knew that if he caught up with her, he would probably kill her. He was ruthless. If she said what he wanted to hear then that was fine but if she slipped up and said the wrong thing then God only knows what the consequences would be. She recalled meeting Steve in the park all those years before and how appalled she had been when he told her everything that had happened. She knew what Pete could do, what he had done, she also knew that he was completely obsessed with Shannon and that ultimately if he couldn't have her, he would ensure that no-one would. It was a terrifying, awful predicament. Had he taken her as a warning to Steve? Was this about frightening him? Showing him that he would stop at no lengths to get what he wanted? Showing him that if he could do this to his friend, he could also do it to Shannon. Her feet were getting sore from the lane's rough, stony surface and she wished that she had trainers rather than flimsy slip on shoes. She was sure she had walked a few miles by now and could feel blisters developing on her feet. There was no question of going barefoot, she had to tolerate it. If folk could do Lough Derg for three days barefoot surely, she could do this. They did not have to do Lough Derg in the dark however and she silently promised herself that she would do the pilgrimage if He brought her out of this, safe and sound. She could hear the long, overgrown grass quiver in the wind and she felt jumpy and nervous. As soon as he came to, he would come hunting his prey, her, and so she decided that she would be best to venture into the fields. She only hoped that there would be no animals around. She did not want to think of the creatures roaming these terrains at night for there were bound to be foxes or even mice or rats. She shrieked loudly when she felt something touch her hair. What was it? Her heart was racing. There could be bats. She hated bats. They could get entangled in her hair and feeling around in her pocket, she found a bobble and fixed it tightly in a ponytail. She was wearing her glasses, but they were of little help. She dandered in amongst the trees and felt around with her hands. There was barbed wire, behind which lay green fields and she carefully climbed over. However, as she did so, she tumbled and fell head first, losing a shoe in the process. Now she was on one side of the wire and the shoe on the other. She tried to recover it, but she just could not see and was forced to leave it behind. Damn it, he would probably find it in the morning, she thought, although her conscious mocked her that she was being perhaps too optimistic. Barefooted now she gathered pace and moved quickly and silently away from the beaten road. The grass was softer on her feet and she moved as fast as her legs could carry her. She was exhausted and thirsty; she had taken a bottle of water with her, but she had to make it last. Maybe she would make some headway when dawn arrived. If she could just manage to keep walking, she would do so for it was best to gain as much distance as possible.

25

Back in the city Cara had arrived home the morning after the night before. She had sat up to all hours with Shannon hoping against hope for a call to her mobile. She checked her landline but there were no messages on it either. She regretted her row with Pete and really wanted to make amends. She phoned his mobile but there was no answer. He must be angry with me, she thought. She felt possessed with insecurities and misery as she recalled their recent times together. She had no idea what he was doing or who he was with and it was opening a whole set of emotions which were buried deep in her past. She opened her laptop and logged in before fetching her camera to upload her most recent photographs. There were ones of Gemma and Gerry and the new baby and of Shannon and her, laughing and enjoying a drink. There were a couple of nice ones of herself and Pete as well, fooling around in front of the camera. She really wanted to see Pete and tell him that Gemma had had her baby. In fact, she had intended asking him if he would like to come to the hospital with her to see them. She did not want to scare him off though. When the photos appeared in front of her on the screen, she smiled. They were delightful. She decided that she would send him an email and attach some pictures. She thought that he would like that and she suggested that they meet up and perhaps visit the new arrival together. She knew that he logged in most days to the internet so hopefully by evening she would get a reply.

Pete, however, was not so good. He woke up on the kitchen floor feeling groggy and ill. He had the hangover from hell. At first, he was not sure where he was, he wiped his eyes and got up to go to the bathroom. Then he heard the noisy jingle of his shackles and stared at his feet in horror. He laughed aloud, before bumming his way over to

193

the study where he retrieved his spare key and opened the lock. He screamed Anita's name, but knew himself that she would be long gone by now. He consoled himself though that the possibility of her escaping was extremely remote. He could just about manage to get to the main road and he had lived here most of his life. There was little chance that Anita would succeed. He was angry though. He could not believe that she had tied his feet and left him there. He took a swig of his whiskey and went to the toilet after which he grabbed a banana from the fruit bowl and quickly stuffed it in his mouth. He had recalled Shannon talking about bananas reducing the horror of hangovers. She had explained that heavy drinking depleted the body of potassium and as bananas were high in potassium, they replaced that what you lost whilst drinking. They were also high in B6, a vitamin shown to reduce hangover symptoms and a natural remedy against heartburn and nausea. Whether or not they did help the symptoms of a hangover he wasn't sure, but they weren't going to do him any harm, so that was good enough as far as he was concerned.

Grabbing the bottle of whiskey, he set off on his bike to look for Anita. Every so often he took a swig of drink, he was confident that he would find her. However, there was no sign of her at all and finally he returned to the cottage in a furious mood. He kicked the door open and marched around the house, searching every room. He looked in the fire and found the charred remains of the mobile and praised himself for removing that problem when he did. There was no chance it would work now anyway. He checked her room but everything she had was still there. He would have to go out again and was raging at this inconvenience. She truly was a force to be reckoned with, a complete pain in the neck. He was getting fed up with her. He decided to check on the internet and see if there was any news, if she had been reported missing or if the police had been notified. There was nothing though, so no news was good news. Time was of the essence though. He logged in to his emails and as he waited for his messages to come through, he took another gulp of whiskey. Up popped Cara's name and he frowned as he read her message. Then he opened the attachments and started to look at her photographs. He yawned widely as they appeared on slide show format. The wee baby was okay. A baby was a baby after all, they all looked the same! Typical family pictures! Cara looked quite nice. She was not his normal type, but she was easy company. She was obviously sorry for her prior behaviour and so she should be, he thought, deciding that he would reply later when he had found Anita. Cara was in every picture, her and Gemma, her and the baby, the three of them together. Wait a minute? Who was that? he thought, staring at a photograph of a middle-aged man. But, that must be Gemma's husband. He looked very familiar. He flicked to the last photograph and immediately his eyes widened in unimaginable dismay. It was Shannon! How could this be? He flicked back to the prior pictures and identified the familiar gentleman. Gerry? Oh God! This could not be. What would Shannon think if she was shown these? He was maddened and enraged as he organised the pieces in the jigsaw together. It was mind-boggling. He stormed back into the kitchen, a stream of expletives oozing from his mouth, as he started to trash the place. He was seething. Now he had problems! Suddenly it occurred to him that she might have forwarded the pictures to Gemma and if Gemma happened to show them to Shannon, he would be really snookered.

'Bitch,' he roared, lifting a bottle and flinging it at the mirror, smashing it into hundreds of little pieces. He lifted books and ornaments and anything he could find and hurled them around. He put his boot in the door, all the while cursing and swearing like a man possessed.

'Damn, damn, damn,' he roared aloud. 'This is complicated. They are all bloody related and she didn't even have the decency to tell me about the baby. Something is going on. What the hell am I going to do now? I will bloody well sort this out once and for all. I will kill every last one of them.'

He sat on the sofa rubbing his head trying to figure out what was going on and what he was going to do. Obviously, Cara was Gemma's sister and Gemma was Shannon's step-mum, Gerry's wife. But it was blatant that none of them knew about him yet otherwise Cara would have said. It would not be long before they put two and two together. He was running out of time. He had to think fast. But what would he do? He had to ensure that Cara did not show them the photos. 'Damn it,' he yelled. 'This is bad, this is really bad.' He reached for the phone and dialled Cara's number. He could imagine her rushing around looking for it, she was so disorganised and never could find anything. However, after ten rings when he was almost about to despair she suddenly picked up.

'Hi,' Cara answered, grinning widely, as she recognised the Caller ID.

'Hi there,' he said, 'I thought maybe you had gone out,' he stated, immediately adopting a warm, soft tone.

'No, couldn't find the phone, it was down the side of the sofa,' she answered, laughing.

'Just got your email, I loved your photographs, you looked great and they just made me miss you more,' he lied.

'So, you're not angry with me then?' she wanted to know.

'How could I stay angry with you?' he replied, softly. 'I was actually thinking that you might want to come away with me for a few days, spend some quality time together. What do you say?' he asked.

'Well, yeah, when are you thinking?' she responded, delighted that he had called.

'How about now?' he asked.

'Now? What about my work?' she giggled, thinking how keen he sounded.

'Could you not just take a few days off? I miss you so much and I could pick you up in a couple of hours,' he suggested.

Cara was already getting excited. She did not want to turn down his offer, especially as he was making such a huge effort. Work was important but matters of the heart were much more so, in her opinion. Besides, she had some leave owing to her and with a little reshuffling of appointments; she would be good to go.

'Where are we going to go?' she demanded to know.

She was already anticipating a spa in a nice hotel, sitting around in fluffy white dressing gowns, enjoying a spell in the hot tub, having massages and facials with beautiful meals and bubbly perhaps in the evening, not to mention what would follow afterwards behind the closed doors of their sumptuous bedroom.

'My surprise,' he commented.

'Okay then,' she shrieked.

'See you in two hours. Be ready! Looking forward to it! Bye,' he finished, quickly hanging up and scowling around at the state of the house.

He did not know what he was doing but felt sure that everything would fall into place.

He set about lifting what visible shards of glass he could see. It took longer than he expected. It was surprising how much damage he had done in so little time. He would never get rid of all the little fragments, but he would gather what he could and hope that Cara didn't notice. He really needed to find Anita but the main priority for now was Cara. Anita would wait, he hoped. As soon as the house was in satisfactory order, he set off in the car, gulping from his large bottle of water. He wouldn't need to be stopped by the police as he was way over the limit. He proceeded very slowly along the lane, scanning the fields around for any sightings of Anita but it was like she had vanished into thin air. He tried to recall what she had been wearing the night before, but his mind was blank, and besides there was no colour other than green in the smooth velvet meadows around. He did not anticipate she would venture into the forest and that was what he hoped. If she was brave enough to go that way, then he was on borrowed time but if she took the other option, that was fine. That would be funny, he thought to himself smugly.

A few hours later, Cara was sat alongside him, nattering away ninety to the dozen, as usual. He wondered did she ever take a breather. She was relentless plus ever so touchy feely. It was hard to concentrate on the road at times. She was dressed in a pretty green maxi dress which emphasized the colour of her eyes, but he was sure she had put on a few pounds. He brought up the subject of the photographs and she babbled away telling him all about the baby and how she was still in hospital and she talked about Gemma and Gerry as well. She failed to mention Shannon but that was fine as it was the clearest signal so far that she was totally oblivious of his connection with her. She would find out soon enough, he thought. She kept asking him where they were headed but he insisted she would find out soon enough and when, two hours later they arrived at the cottage, she looked at him as if he had horns growing out of his head.
'Where are we?' she demanded to know.
'At the cottage, my cottage,' he replied.
Of course, she had heard him talk of the cottage and despite her bitter disappointment that she had not been whisked off to a luxury hotel; she tried to act like she was pleased. He took her in and showed her around and then proceeded to pour a drink for them both. Whilst Cara changed into something more comfortable, he went

outside and glanced around. Where was Anita? Would she show up? It did not seem likely! He stood outdoors for a few minutes until he heard Cara shouting at him. He had no idea what he was going to do next. All he could do was wait. She came up behind him suddenly and wrapped her arms tightly around his waist. As he turned towards her and kissed her, he tried to forget for a moment or two all his other troubles. He released her hold of him gently and proceeded to the kitchen to fetch a bottle of wine. She had other things on her mind though and quickly dragged him into his bedroom. She was a passionate woman, he thought, and he was not complaining. But it was what it was. Sex! She went on and on about making love, but he didn't love her. He merely took what was on offer. Afterwards, they enjoyed several tipples and he thought that it was quite nice to have a distraction. It was nice to spend time with a woman who appreciated him even if it was not the one he so desperately desired. It was late when they drunkenly returned to bed and repeated their earlier performance. When she was fast asleep, he remembered he hadn't locked the room where Anita had stayed – had she gone in there? Probably not, he imagined for if she had seen her belongings, she would have had yet another childish tantrum. He couldn't find the key so quickly ran around and bundled all traces of Anita into a nearby wardrobe. Satisfied that everything was hidden, he had a drink before silently climbing in beside her and falling asleep.

26

When dawn broke, Pete jumped out of bed, eager to commence his hunt. He was glad that he had remembered to set his alarm for he would never have awoken. He pulled some clothes on, shovelled some Weetabix in his mouth and set off after he had written a quick note to Cara to let her know he would be back soon. He didn't think that she would surface before mid-day which gave him ample time to do what he had to. He trundled along slowly, scanning the sides of the lane but again, it was mission impossible. There were so many trees and the grass on the verges was so overgrown that it would take hours, maybe even days to do the thorough search that was required. After about three hours, he returned to the cottage, feeling deflated and annoyed. As he had suspected Cara was still in bed and he left her there to slumber and went out to patio area. It was beautiful to sit in the silence feeling the warmth of the sun on his face. After a while, he decided to head to the nearest town for some groceries as supplies were running very low. Cara would not be impressed if she did not have milk for her coffee and he needed to keep things as normal as possible until circumstances dictated otherwise. He grabbed his bank card and keys and took off with the intention of doing a quick shop and returning as quickly as possible. The nearest town was a half hour drive as he knew all the shortcuts so he would be gone an hour and a half at most.

Cara heard the car leave and immediately leapt out of bed. She padded into the kitchen and drank a pint of water before searching for a bite to eat. She found a little bread and raspberry jam and poured herself a black coffee before heading outside to the sun. It was a beautiful day and she realised that Pete had obviously sat out earlier, for the remnants of his breakfast remained on the picnic table.

Carrying her coffee and a little blanket she had found in the kitchen, she wandered down to the bottom of the field, attracted by the gushing sounds of the river. She perched herself on the grassy bank and sipped her drink, gazing at the barren landscape which seemed to go on forever. She must have conked out briefly because when she woke up, she felt slightly disorientated and a little dizzy, hardly surprising given the boozy shenanigans last night, she thought. Her ears pricked up at an eerie sound and she sat silently, her body stiffening in anticipation. She wiped her eyes and looked around. It was so quiet that it was no wonder she had nodded off. She heard the sound again, it was like a very low wail. She sat up straight, the hairs on her arms standing taut. Where was it coming from? She jumped to her feet, peering around, listening carefully. She heard the sound again, a low whimper. She called out and there came a faint reply, so faint that she could scarcely hear. It sounded like it was coming from the other side of the river. She knew Pete had gone off somewhere and she needed to investigate but how would she get to the other side. The river seemed shallow enough and she decided she would try and wade across. She was unsure of its depth but the waters were still and looked safe. She hastily made her way along the narrow path looking the safest passage over. Shortly she came across an area that appeared her best option and throwing off her trainers, she rolled up her pyjama bottoms to her knees and carefully manoeuvred through the water. She called out again and again and was answered by the quiet, muffled sounds of someone who sounded in distress. Then she spotted a flicker of colour, a very small shade of blue amidst the greenery. She raced forwards conscious that the moans were growing ever louder and after a minute or two stumbled upon a weak, highly distraught woman in great pain, and suffering from dehydration.

'Oh my God, are you okay?' she whispered.

'Yes,' the woman whimpered, but it was obvious to Cara that she was not okay. She was pale and hurt with nasty bruising to her face and eyes. Her clothes were dirty and she was not wearing socks or shoes, her poor feet were red and badly cut. Her hair was tangled with twigs poking out from everywhere, but it was the look in her eyes that Cara found most disturbing. They were glazed and bloodshot and she looked so frightened and unkempt that Cara felt unnerved.

'What in God's name are you doing out here?' she asked.

'Took me, he did, dangerous....' the woman groaned, but she was very difficult to understand.

'Okay, okay, I will go and get help,' Cara said, trying to soothe her. Quickly tearing off her cardigan which she had thrown over her pyjamas, she wrapped it carefully around the young woman. She assured her that she would seek help and return as quickly as she could. The young woman was babbling, talking incoherently and begging her to stay but Cara was in no position to carry her and rushed off back along the verge, across the river and bang into an impatient Pete who had just arrived back having been delayed for much longer than he had anticipated. Normally he could drive the ten miles to the nearest town in twenty-five minutes but today every blasted farmer seemed to be out on his tractor and it took an age to return.

'Quick, quick, there is a woman, she needs help,' she cried, anxiously.

Pete couldn't believe his luck. It had to be Anita and led by a gasping and overexcited Cara, he rushed to the spot where the female was lying.

As soon as Anita saw him, she started to wail even louder.

'Look, there she is, she is not good,' Cara advised him.

'Are you okay? Look, I have found help, we will look after you, please do not worry,' Cara continued, trying to reassure her.

With that, Pete scooped a hysterical Anita into his arms, but she started to wriggle like crazy. She flapped her arms and tried to speak to Cara but Pete was having none of it.

'Don't worry, everything is going to be just fine,' he said softly, looking across at Cara and smiling tenderly.

Anita started to gasp for air, her eyes rolling back and forth rapidly, terror etched across her torn face so clearly it sent Cara into a full-scale panic.

'Quickly Pete, quickly…. She does not look well, she needs a doctor, medical attention now, 'she screamed.

'She will be okay, come on, let's get her back to the cottage,' he replied, ever so calmly.

He strode along purposefully and as soon as they reached the cottage, he lay her down on the settee before ordering Cara to fetch some water and a warm blanket. Cara obediently did as she was asked and then fetched the poor girl a mug of tea and some biscuits which she declined.

'What happened to you?' she asked. 'Are you okay?' What is your name and what on earth were you doing out there all alone? You need to eat something please,' she persisted.

Anita did not reply. She was not in a fit state and still possessed a deeply agitated look. She was safe now, but she was trembling. Why was she so petrified? It hardly made sense!

Pete cast his eye frequently on his guest, he didn't think she looked capable of taking off again. Still he didn't want to turn his back on her for a second.

'Leave her be now Cara, stop asking her questions, can't you see the state she is in?' he commented curtly.

'Okay, okay Pete,' she replied, looking at Anita sympathetically.

'Why don't you go take a bath?' he suggested.

'I don't want a bath,' she answered back.

'I think you should have a bath Cara. I will see to the girl and find out who she is,' he commanded.'

Anita looked from one to the other. What was their relationship? Who was she? She clearly had no idea who this man was otherwise she would not be staying with him here. She could never have imagined that she would have ended up back in the cottage. She had obviously gone full circle. It was quite simply a catastrophe, one that she did not see herself escaping from unscathed. She felt like she was living a nightmare. Where was it going to finish? He was bound to kill her. He might kill both of them. She wondered if this girl had a phone and prayed she did, for it seemed like their only chance to be free. She felt so cold and weak now, her head hurt so bad and her feet felt on fire, it seemed no one was looking for her. She hoped that Shannon was okay because as much as she knew Pete was crazy, now she had witnessed it first hand. He would go to any lengths to get the result he so desperately craved. She wished that he would take a bath himself if only so that she could confide in Cara, but he was sat next to her and had no intention of leaving the two of them alone. At least he was here though which meant that Shannon was safe – safe for the moment at least!!

27

Shannon did feel safe. There was no place she felt more secure than at home. She had been spending lots of time in the family garden with her dad. They had planted some more vegetables and had dug up an area in the back corner for a flower bed. They had pulled up weeds and trimmed the hedges. It was a beautiful day and she was dressed casually in shorts and a light vest top. The skies were blue, there were no clouds and the sun was blazing down. The sound of Dolly Parton was filtering outside from the kitchen. She didn't normally listen to country music, but Dolly was one of the great exceptions. Her dad had brought her to a concert in Dublin once when she was a teenager and from then she had purchased every CD the country singer had ever released. The baby was doing well and it seemed likely that she would be discharged within another few weeks. She really was a miracle. It so easily could have been a different story. The baby had been lucky and it did not seem as though there would be any serious implications from her premature entrance to the world. It was no longer necessary for Gemma to stay overnight at the hospital, but she spent most of her days there. In the evenings, she would express some breast milk before she left, to ensure the baby had enough feeds throughout the night, and in the mornings, she would return first thing and feed little Megan herself. She was putting on weight gradually but despite still being quite small she was in fact thriving. Shannon walked into the kitchen and poured herself and her dad a small glass of wine, a reward for their hard graft and they sat down together to enjoy it and survey the garden which was starting to look so much tidier. It weighed heavily on Shannon's mind that Anita was still missing. She had not yet confided in her father about what had happened because he would re-act badly especially if he thought there was a potential risk or threat to her. He was so happy at the minute and she did not want to be the one to burst his bubble especially if Steve happened to be lying, which by now she very much doubted. She felt sure that he was being completely honest, but she was confused and upset about things in general. She blamed herself for relying on Pete so much and felt responsible for failing to notice what could only be described as an unhealthy and potentially dangerous obsession. As she sat with her dad, they both supped their wine slowly and then set about preparing a meal. Gerry thought his daughter seemed preoccupied but was reluctant to pry concluding that if she wanted to talk, she would in her own time. Gemma would be arriving back shortly and perhaps she could talk to her. In the meantime, he needed to get on with preparing his wife a meal, she needed something healthy and hearty after all the terrible hospital meals she had been consuming day in and day out. There was only so much hospital food that a body could tolerate. There was nothing like a home cooked meal; roast chicken, potatoes and steamed vegetables coated with gravy to satisfy the appetite. Shannon loved the gravy. Nobody made gravy like her mother and when she asked her mum how she made it she would reply that nobody made it like her mother. As far as she had figured out, her mother would use a little red wine and some chilli powder but somehow Shannon's gravy never tasted quite the same.

As Gemma was breast feeding it was vital to continue eating proper, decent food, just as in pregnancy. The dinner was almost ready when they heard the car come to halt on the drive outside. Gemma stepped out, still looking on the pale side but nevertheless beaming from ear to ear as she inhaled the delicious aromas drifting out to meet her. She was so glad that Shannon was staying with them, she had been a tower of strength in these last couple of weeks and a Godsend to have around. She also was such a support to her dad and not having to worry about him was a weight off her shoulders as she focussed her attention on the baby. After saying hello and kissing her husband, she went off for a shower and emerged several minutes later just as dinner was being served. They all tucked in enthusiastically and afterwards over a coffee, Gemma produced her laptop and started to upload recent photographs of the baby. That task complete, she logged into her email account and found one from Cara, sent earlier in the day.

'Oh, look at these photos Cara has forwarded,' she said, smiling to the others.

Shannon and Gerry came over behind her and when Shannon discovered the ones of Pete, she let out a deep cry of despair which caused the others to look at her in a curious and confused manner. Shannon had her hand over her mouth, as she stared speechless at the screen. Suddenly she felt lightheaded, the walls were closing in on her, everything was spinning and as she took a step backward, she collapsed in a heap to the ground. Moments later she came to, her face having assumed a deathly white colour causing Gerry to realise that something terrible was wrong.

'What is it darling? You were out cold,' he whispered, wiping her brow with a lukewarm cloth and helping her to her feet.

She looked at the pair of them, large, salty tears pouring down her cheeks as she wept uncontrollably.

'The guy in the photograph with Cara. That's Pete?' she stammered, in between the heavy sobs which were racking her body.

'Pete, Pete, your Pete is Cara's boyfriend,' Gemma stuttered, reality sinking in fast as she tried to comprehend the seriousness of what she was being told.

Shannon nodded. She was aghast; she shakily stood up and started walking around in circles, talking to herself.

'Shannon, sit down, sit now,' Gerry shouted.

207

Shannon slumped back down on the sofa gaping at the pair of them. She could see the fear and anxiety in every corner of her dad's face. She could see Gemma starting to pace. She knew what this meant. She knew the danger. Oh God. What would they do?' Shannon quickly gave Gerry a short, babbled recap of everything that had happened – she would explain to him in more detail later.

'Where is Cara, where is she?' Gerry cried. He was extremely upset but knew that he had to be the source of calm and reason amidst the storm of confusion going on right now.

'She has gone away with Pete.' Gemma said, her eyes watering. 'They had a disagreement and she forwarded these photos thinking it might butter him up a little. Next thing, he phoned her and said he really missed her and asked if they could go away for a sort of mini break. Cara was really excited, said she hoped that he had booked a nice hotel somewhere,' Gemma replied, looking worried.

'You have to ring her right now, I'll explain shortly, ring her and see if she is okay,' she ordered.

As Gemma went off to call her sister, Shannon called Steve on his mobile and asked that he drive straight to her father's house. Steve advised that it would take an hour as he was on the other side of town, having just collected Gregg from the airport.

'Just get here as soon as you can,' she commanded him, before hanging up and rushing to find Gemma.

'Did you get her?' 'Is she okay?' she yelled at Gemma.

Gemma looked puzzled.

'It was ringing and she picked up alright, she said hello, and then the line went dead.' 'Please tell me, Shannon, what is going on? Has more happened?'

'Gemma, we think that perhaps Pete has taken Anita. She has disappeared and no-one can get in contact with her. Not Steve, not her partner and even her workplace have no idea where she is. It is not looking good. We are almost sure he has her. But now it looks like he has Cara too. I only hope that he cares something for her and that she comes to no harm.'

Suddenly it all became too much for Gemma as she realised the full gravity of Pete's dark obsession. Gerry was listening on baffled, begging for more detail but Shannon instructed Gemma to explain everything, as she nervously waited for Steve to arrive with Gregory.

It seemed forever before they heard the screech of a car outside and the two men came bounding in wanting to know any news.

'What is it, Shan? Have you heard something?' Steve asked, looking greatly alarmed.

Shannon looked from him to Greg before showing him the photos on the laptop.

'Cara has been seeing Pete for ages. None of us had a clue that it was the same Pete. They had a row, she forwarded him an email containing these images and now it seems she has gone off with him for a few days. We cannot reach her. He has undoubtedly worked out the connection. It is inevitable. Just this minute, Gemma tried to phone her but as soon as Cara answered, the line went dead. He must have cut her off or taken the phone away. Cara was here a few days ago after they argued. She was in an awful state because she said that he had left the city and returned to his parent's old cottage. Of course, I had no idea of any of this. He didn't mention it to me. Anyhow, she told me all about him but of course I didn't know it was him. She was really annoyed because he didn't tell her he had moved. It all seems very last minute. When she finally managed to confront him he slammed the phone down. Afterwards she arrived here and was very upset and annoyed about it. She told me that he had told her from the offset that he was in love with someone else but that it was complicated and that her ex had come back on the scene,' she verified, breaking down all over again.

'Obsessed with,' Gemma cried. 'He is totally obsessed with you. He even invented a fake girlfriend to try and make you jealous. I think her name was Zoe,' she said.

'Chloe?' Shannon sobbed hysterically.

'Yes, it was Chloe, he invented her to try and make you jealous, he told us that night at the bar, the night he was denied admittance to the Red Tiger and ended up in the same pub as us,' Gemma said.

'The Red Tiger, did you say?' Steve asked. 'He must have come looking me. I left a message for you asking you to meet me there.'

'I never got it,' Shan screeched.

'He was so angry that night, and I felt really uneasy in his company,' Gemma added.

'Do you have any idea at all where he might be, where he might have taken her?' Steve asked.

'He's at the cottage. It's a cert. He must have taken Anita as a warning to you Steve and now he has the photos Cara has sent through and has gone back to fetch her under the pretence of a romantic few days. We can only assume that he has seen the photographs and panicked. But I don't understand why he would take Cara. He has been doing a lot of work down there the last few months, spending days at a time, decorating maybe. He even told me Chloe was with him at one point,' Shannon said.

'So, perhaps he has both girls now in the cottage,' Greg shrieked. 'We have to go immediately.'

'Yes, I'll get my coat,' Shannon cried, rushing off to the downstairs cloakroom.

'You are not going anywhere,' Gerry shouted.

'No, your father is right, Greg and I will head there now,' Steve said.

'I am going,' Shannon argued, 'there is no way I am staying here, maybe I can talk him round.'

'He told me that if he could not have you, no-one would,' Steve said. 'It is best you stay put, where you are safe.'

'I am going and that is final,' she stressed, already half way through the back door headed for the car.

'If you are going, I am going too,' Gerry said, looking at Gemma for agreement, before grabbing his overcoat. Gemma sadly nodded her approval and urged them to keep her in the loop. Seconds later, the four of them were speeding out the drive watched by a distraught Gemma, who just couldn't believe what was unfolding.

28

Cara had heard her mobile ring and rushed to answer it but just as she said hello, Pete had seized it from her grip.

'Hey,' she yelled. 'Give me my phone, right now.'

'It is probably work,' he stated. 'You're on a break.'

'No, it was Gemma,' she cried. 'Now give me my phone so I can talk to my sister, something might be wrong with the baby,' she shouted.

Pete just laughed and tossed the phone in the air before catching it again, cackling aloud. He removed the Sim Card and handed her the phone.

'What are you doing, Pete?' she screamed. 'That is not funny.'

'You are on a break with me, you do not need a phone,' he smirked.

Cara was raging with him and tried to fight him for it but there was no use. He was much too powerful.

Anita regarded the pair, she felt fragile but a little better than before.

'Least he didn't break it,' she said. 'He threw mine in the fire.'

'Shut your mouth Anita,' Pete hollered, casting her a warning glance.

'What is the point?' she replied, uncaring.

'You threw her mobile in the fire,' Cara accused. 'Why would you do such a thing?'

'He kidnapped me, that is why……….' Anita started.

'Didn't I tell you to shut your mouth?' Pete bellowed, his eyes bulging in anger.

'That is why I was in the fields alone, look at my eyes, how do you think I got these two bruisers?' she continued, defiantly.

'One more word and I will punch the lips off your face,' he screamed with rage.

'Wouldn't be the first time, would it Pete?' she yelled back.

'What do you mean Pete? What is she talking about?' Cara roared. There was something very wrong going on, but she had no idea what. Anita had hardly said a word up to this point, so she was surprised at the girl's sudden outburst.

'I will tell you this Cara, your Pete is not who you think he is, far from it in fact,' Anita said.

'This is your last chance,' Pete spat, becoming more and more enraged each time Anita opened her mouth. But Anita couldn't help herself, what was the worst he would do? He was probably going to do it anyway. She felt a bit braver and she needed Cara to fully realise who and what she was dealing with.

'You see Pete here is so obsessed with Shannon that............' she stopped, as she felt the full force of his fist smash in her face. Blood started to trickle from her mouth and nose as she fell heavily to the ground, smashing against the old, wooden coffee table.

'What the hell are you doing Pete?' Cara balled, rushing to bend over Anita who appeared to have knocked herself unconscious in the fall. She looked up at him in dismay and terror. 'Quickly, do something, she is out cold, what is wrong with you?' she screamed.

Pete stood impassively surveying the scene. He did not reply.

'Pete, can you hear me? What have you done?' Cara howled, standing up to face him. 'You need to call an ambulance. She is out cold. Do it, do it now.'

She was petrified – Anita most definitely had suffered a head injury and she knew she needed to stabilise her head and neck. She roared at Pete to bring her a clean, damp cloth but he just stood there sneering, completely detached from what was going on. She rushed past him to the bathroom where she fetched a towel and began to dab lightly at the bloody, open wound, which was looking ghastly. At the very least stitches were needed but given the other injuries sustained, Cara was sure she needed treatment at hospital.

'Pete, phone an ambulance now, she needs help,' she shrieked.

'No, she just needs rest, she will come around,' he barked back at her.

'Pete, does she look like she is coming around. She is going to die. Pete, what are you playing at?' Where is the phone?' she screamed, jumping up and running around frantically searching for the landline.

'If she dies, she dies,' he taunted.

'What? Are you serious? You bastard, you can't play God with peoples lives,' she wailed, her whole insides whirling around. She was feeling sick and was retching. She was not good with blood. She held her stomach as she threw up all over the floor. The look on Pete's face told her he was far from impressed, but she didn't care one bit what he thought. She could only see the pure venom and hatred in his eyes as he stood there impassively, an evil smirk stretched across his puffed-up, irate face.

'Go and wash your face and your teeth and come back here and clean up this mess,' he growled. He was totally different; she did not know this man at all. He was a monster!

Running past an unconscious Anita, lying out cold beside the fireplace, Cara covered her with a blanket and quickly grabbed her handbag. Once in the bathroom she locked the door and splashed cold water all over her face. She was clueless at to what was unfolding here but had a terrible feeling that she needed to get as far away as possible. The girl needed help and it was evident that none would come unless she took action. She scanned the bathroom taking note of the window and realised she had no hope of squeezing her size 12 figure through it. She reached for a small bottle of hairspray she spotted on a shelf and leaving the taps running she closed the bathroom door behind her and tiptoed to the front door which she gently opened. Closing it as quietly as she could, she crept round to the side of the house. She could hear the television from inside and standing on tiptoe again, peeked through the window to see if Pete was still there and what he was doing. He was standing with his left hand on his hips in the kitchen and she was sure she could see the silver glint of a knife in the other hand. Her first inclination had been to flee but now she felt that it would be better to hide and wait. He would anticipate, she thought, that she would head off down the most obvious way, so she had to go for the alternative option. She sneaked off in the other direction and slipped into the cover of the trees. She could see the lights of the cottage clearly and it seemed no time before his dark, stocky figure appeared at the door looking frantically up and down, over and across, searching for her. She felt like her heart was going to stop, the fear like none she had ever known. She was afraid to breathe, afraid to move one inch, in case she was discovered. He was roaring like a caged animal and she could make out the clear gleam of a large knife held tightly in his fist. She had a second mobile in her handbag, she called it her emergency phone, but it was for business. She was petrified that it might ring but would use it as soon as she could. She watched as he jumped into his car and roared off down the lane. She hoped that he would crash and kill or injure himself such was her own panic. Once out of sight she flew back into the house and grabbed her coat. She looked in on Anita who was lying still on the floor but there was no movement and no sound and she had no choice but to leave her there and flee down the field towards the river. It was not quite dark, but another half an hour and it would be black. She quickly reached the river and crossed it barefoot in the same spot as earlier before slipping on her shoes again and darting up the fields. She was not fit and felt breathless. It was only a matter of minutes before he would come looking. She felt about in her bag for its inner pocket and unzipped it, taking out her phone and flicking it open. The signal was low, but she had plenty of charge. She called Gemma and waited with bated breath for her to pick up. When she did eventually answer, Gemma could hardly speak for crying.

'Oh, thank God Cara, where are you? Are you okay?' her sister screamed, the joy in her voice evident to hear.

'Oh Gemma, it is a nightmare. Stop crying and listen carefully. I have escaped but I'm far from safe. I am in the back end of beyond and he's on my tail. Seriously, he is already looking. I can't breathe Gemma. I I I am so scared, he is mad, totally mad, he has a knife and he has this girl, she is in really poor shape, she might even be dead,' she stuttered.

'Okay Cara, just try and keep calm. Have you any idea where you are?'

'No, I don't, I thought he was taking me to a spa or somewhere luxurious and he brought me here, I have just crossed a river and am heading up through fields…oh God Gemma, please get help, please.'

'Did he bring you to his cottage Cara?' Gemma asked.

'Yes, he did. How do you know about the cottage?' she demanded suddenly.

'Long story, don't worry about that now. Help is on its way, but I don't know how long it is going to be, a couple of hours at least. You need to find cover and hide.'

'Okay, okay, this Anita, I don't know if she will make it. I had to leave her there, but she is out cold.'

'Okay Cara,' Gemma stuttered, 'Stay out of sight, I love you.'

'I love you too sis,' Cara sobbed.

As soon as Gemma put the phone down, she promptly rang Shannon, her voice barely audible. She immediately explained the situation pausing every few seconds to take a deep breath. In between sobs she repeated her conversation with her sister to an astonished and extremely distraught Shannon who had put the call on loudspeaker for the other three to hear. The guys were dumbstruck, Greg looked like he had been hit by a ton of bricks, his colour had drained from his face and he looked ready to faint. Steve seemed to have lost the power of speech and quickly stepped his foot on the accelerator. Gerry remained silent. He was sick with worry and finding it hard to focus. Gemma had given him more information at home, and he couldn't understand how things had got so out of hand. He only hoped that they got there on time. It seemed like Anita was at death's door and they all felt a degree of responsibility. It appeared that Pete had gone to search for Cara now meaning that Anita was just lying injured or dead on her own, and if he did find Cara it was hard to imagine a positive outcome.

'It is time to call the Police,' Steve whispered. 'Greg, can you take over at the wheel for a while.'

Gregg nodded but Shannon knew he was in no fit state to drive and she quickly offered to take Steve's place.

Steve was transferred to CID and quickly relayed the situation. He gave them Pete's name and offered up a silent prayer as they informed him they would do some checks and phone back as soon as possible.

When they did call back, they advised him that they had found a Raymond, Peter Mc Glynn who had a cottage at Killywillin, they had history with him and would to there without delay. Steve warned the officer that he was armed with a knife, that there was one woman who was unconscious and another who trying to flee. He did not want to think that Anita could be dead and he felt nothing but pure dread absorb every fibre of his being. Poor, poor Anita! She was so good and kind and he could not imagine his life without her in it. He did not even want to think about how Greg was feeling right now because they were looking forward to a bright future together. How had he got her involved in this? He blamed himself. When Shannon's phone started to ring, she passed it to Steve, who seeing Mel's name appear, quickly informed her that Shannon would phone back as soon as she could, that if she rang Gemma, she would explain everything. He then dialled Gemma's number and advised her that they were at least half an hour away and that the police had been contacted. Gemma punched Cara's number into the phone and told her to keep on the move, keep strong and that the police were on their way. Cara's limbs were by now aching, she felt as if she had run a marathon and yet she knew that she had only walked a couple of miles, although admittedly most of it was uphill. She did not feel overly inspired by the rows of fields in front of her and apart from anything else she felt extremely unwell. She needed to get into a woodier area to avoid being spotted although darkness was now closing in. She had covered a fair bit of ground but felt like she was on an endless journey. It was quite amazing how absolutely isolated this place was. It was like being in the middle of a desert except there was no camel nearby to give her a ride. She remembered that Anita had said that she had gone full circle and was terrified that she would do the same and end up back at square one. She had no sense of direction at the best of times but every time now that she veered left or right, she looked around her to see if anything looked remotely familiar. She wondered if he was still looking for her or had he returned in his car to the cottage and perhaps followed on foot the route she was taking now. The thought paralysed her.

29

Pete had returned. He had realised after a mile of driving that she must have hidden from him. Not such a silly little tart after all, he fumed. He needed to hurry. He raced around the cottage opening doors, wardrobes, looking under beds, he jumped over Anita as he rechecked the bathroom, but it was in vain. She was gone. He leant over Anita and cursed under his breath at her. She was breathing but it was faint. He picked her up and carried her though to his study and locked the door, then he bolted the main door behind him and stomped off out of the house. He would fetch Cara right away, wherever the wee cow was, and bring her back here and then he would deal with them both. He scanned the area around the house with his torch and headed for the river, confident that he would find her. She wouldn't get far. She did not exercise so a mile or two out here in the dark would be difficult, particularly since she had gained weight recently. She was in no way fit. He really had to sort this out and then he would be free to get it together with Shannon, show her how good a life they could have here, make an honest woman of her once and for all. Once across the river, he began climbing the hills. He was well used to it, he did it frequently as a lad and it did not take a flinch out of him. He thought he heard a car but was convinced his mind was playing tricks on him. So much for a peaceful, country life, he thought. The sound of the car was the police driving quietly along the little road leading to the cottage. The two officers parked at the bottom of the lane in a little rough lay-by. Using torches to guide their paths they moved quietly towards the isolated cottage. It was deadly quiet apart from the blaring sound of the television which had not been switched off. Further help was on route and as they snuck their way cautiously towards the front door, they navigated their way through the darkening night. Seeing the door was bolted, they kicked it in and rushed inside. A car, which they assumed was McGlynn's was parked by the front door and there were no outward signs of a disturbance. Everything was quiet other than the voice of a Sky News Reporter updating viewers on the latest trouble in Syria where a civil war had broken out and thousands of refugees were fleeing the country. Officer Black crossed through to the living room, taking note immediately of the blood seeped into the mat by the fireplace. There were also splashes of blood on the hearth and on a blanket lying on the floor. There was no sign of a body, however. Officer Casey followed closely behind, scrutinising the scene whilst listening intently for any potential danger or imminent threat. As Black pushed open the double doors leading to the kitchen and living area, he was overcome by the rank smell of vomit sprayed all over the tiled floor. There were also fragments of glass scattered around and it was obvious that something had happened here tonight.

'No sign of anyone here, let's check everywhere else,' Officer Black ordered.

'All rooms clear Sir, apart from this one,' he declared, examining the locked solid wood door of the study.

He headed outdoors and peered through the window, but it was dark inside. Lifting his torch, he aimed it around the room quickly spotting the petite figure of a badly injured female lying sprawled on her back on the floor.

'Okay, got a young woman here, looks in bad shape,' he yelled, smashing a portion of the glass to allow him access to work the lock.

'Needs an ambulance right away,' he called again.

'Right on it,' his colleague shouted back.

The policeman reached Anita quickly and then it was all systems go. He detected a faint pulse, but she was in a very bad state and he only hoped she was not as hurt as she looked. It was clear however that she needed to be taken to hospital without delay if there was to be any hope of

220

survival. As for Mc Glynn, there was no sign of him. He was well known to the police, but they had hoped that he had got back on the straight and narrow after earlier exploits in his youth and early twenties. No-one really knew for sure exactly when he had gone off the rails, but it was widely believed locally that he had been a bit of a wild child and caused his parents all sorts of trouble. He had been involved in an array of petty crimes including shoplifting, burglary, disturbing the peace and being a nuisance in general. It was rumoured that he was heavy into drink and drugs. When his parents had died, the circumstances had been bizarre. It was reported at the time that Mrs McGlynn had fallen into the river and her husband had tried to reach her but there had been a lot of rain that Autumn and the river had been high with a fast-moving current. Pete senior had attempted to save his wife but was also carried away by the current. The Coroner had recorded the deaths as accidental - drowning, but many local villagers questioned it and wondered if somehow the wayward son had been involved. He had a lot to gain from their deaths financially. Mr and Mrs McGlynn did not throw their money around easily, but they were extremely comfortable and led a good but simple lifestyle. Pete saw himself as a failure in his own eyes and those of his parents and it was a well-known fact that he was not particularly close to them. They were lovely, gracious people and did their absolute best for their son, but it was rumoured he treated them with contempt even more so in their old age. The strange thing was that on the day his parents died, he too had been at the river but stressed that he could not get to them on time. There was much speculation among locals as to what had happened and whether Pete was telling the truth. The story told was that his mother had tripped over a small pothole and plunged headfirst into the cold waters. Although folk pointed the finger of suspicion towards Pete, there was not enough evidence to suggest that he had been responsible in any way. At the wake and subsequent funeral, he appeared emotionless. It was as if he was either deeply traumatised or just did not care. He discussed plans for his parents' cottage and how he intended to renovate and extend – he described it as his project and somehow that did not go down too well with the local folk given his parents had just passed away so tragically. Although the river had burst its banks, Pete was known for being extremely fit and athletic and the country folk wondered did he do everything he could to prevent their deaths, but there was no evidence of foul play so Pete could never be charged with anything. Now it seemed that perhaps all was not as it seemed for there was one girl in a terrible condition and another out there somewhere, scared witless and trying to get away from him. The ambulance arrived quickly on the scene and Anita was gently lifted onto a stretcher and taken away. It had come quietly with no lights or sirens flashing as the driver had been warned to switch them off in case Mc Glynn was alerted.

The other policemen had arrived too and after doing a thorough check of the house they set off in pairs, one pair back down the lane and the other for the river to try and rescue Cara. Cara had moved to the edge of a field by this stage, it was black now but with the help of her mobile phone light she found somewhere smooth to lie down and covered her body with her long black coat. She was feeling deadbeat both physically and mentally and whilst she had not moved as far or as quickly as she would have liked she realised that it might be safer to stay put and wait for help. The grass felt damp beneath her and it was becoming very cold. She was lying there half an hour when she spotted a bobbing flicker of light, her first instinct was to cry out, but she immediately realised it could well be Pete. All she could do was stay still and quietly weep but her breathing was deep and shallow. It was now pitch black and she was really spooked. She texted Gemma again before switching her mobile to silent mode so that when she replied there would be no sound. This was unnerving, she thought. She was so, so scared. She didn't understand what was going on and only hoped that the police would find her before he did. She continued watching the light, which was probably a torch. It was not far off. She curled up in a ball, she could not recall in her lifetime being as utterly shaken as she was now. She wondered how Anita was doing. She could be dead, she thought grimly. He had whacked her hard and seemed unbothered about her state of unconsciousness. Had she fallen on the carpet it would not have been as bad but the fact that she had slammed her head against the sharp-edged corner of the coffee table was horrifying. She realised that she had made the biggest mistake of her life in ever pursuing him. Now he was pursuing her, but not in a way that she had ever anticipated. She knew Shannon was somehow involved as her name had been mentioned a couple of times, but she was too far gone to make the connection other than there was some link she would discover when this was all over.

30

Meanwhile, Pete was hopping mad, he was sweating grossly like a pig, all sorts of expletives rolling off his tongue. Things were getting out of hand. Cara seemed to have disappeared into thin air. It was like searching for a needle in a haystack. She had just vanished. He sat down on the damp, dewy grass and racked his brain trying to work out what she might have done. He did not believe that she would have used the main lane as he would have found her quickly that way. Perhaps she would just get lost and do a full circle as Anita had. That would be the best outcome. He was glad he had ditched her mobile and consoled himself that at least she had no means of communication on her. He was safe enough for now, he reckoned. He would find Cara and escort her back to the house and then he would decide what the hell he was going to do with the pair of them. He thought of Shannon and hoped that she appreciated the lengths that he had gone to for the sake of their relationship. She better not have rekindled her relationship with Steve, he thought.

Little did he know that Steve, Greg, Gerry and Shannon had just passed the Five Bridges Hotel when they were met by an ambulance coming from the opposite direction, sirens blazing as it skipped a set of red lights and moved swiftly past them. The four of them looked at each other but dared not speak aloud their thoughts. Each knew what the other was thinking. Ten minutes later, as they approached the deep, dense forest that Shannon had previously described to Steve, a police car overtook at high speed. Shannon pressed her foot to the accelerator and tried to keep up. After minutes of small, bendy roads which were extremely difficult to negotiate, it disappeared but she had tailed it long enough to know she was on the right path. There were so many twists and turns that she would never have found this place in the daytime never mind at night but after several more minutes she noticed the police car had come to a halt ahead. Shannon quickly stepped on the brake, but the police knew they were there. A cop jumped out and put his hand in the air. He raced over to the driver's window and ordered them to turn around, that the road ahead was closed.

'We have a situation here,' he stated, firmly.

'Yes Officer, that is why we are here too,' Shannon explained.

'This is no place for any of you. Now go,' he instructed, before catching a message on his radio and promptly running off down the road. They watched as he spoke with the other officer and then the pair of them sprinted into the distance.

'What now?' Shannon asked.

'We follow,' Steve replied.

'Let's just proceed with this, we can keep behind,' Greg said.

Gerry agreed.

'Okay, everyone, we better switch mobiles to silent mode and get our torches ready,' Steve said.

Shannon glanced at her phone and found three messages all from Gemma and then quickly clicked it to the silent setting.

'Right guys, Cara is still hiding in the fields somewhere near the river and Pete has gone after her,' she whispered.

All four continued silently down the lane, treading carefully to avoid potholes. It wasn't long until they noticed the vibrant red roof of the cottage and as they stood staring, they were suddenly grappled from behind by two burly officers.

'What the hell are you doing?' one of them said. 'I thought I ordered you back the way you came.'

'Let me explain,' Steve said. 'The girl who is missing is in the fields somewhere beyond the river.' 'McGlynn is searching for her now and she is terrified, she thinks he will kill her.'

'It is me he wants,' Shannon sobbed, starting to blurt out the whole sorry story.

'Okay, okay, you come with us now,' the officer interrupted, 'but you understand this could be a very dangerous situation and we must be very careful and very hasty. You must listen very carefully and do exactly as we say. There is no time to waste,' he declared.

The six of them moved further up the lane towards the cottage, which was still lit up but quiet now, as the television had been switched off. Upon entering the door, the smell of sick almost knocked them out and Shannon started to retch. They slowly entered the living room and gasped at the sight of the dark red blood splashes staining the carpet and fireplace. Gregg's face was a ghostly white colour as he took in the scene. He slumped on the sofa, praying that someone would tell him where and how Anita was. A policeman following behind instructed them to return to the kitchen area and not to touch anything. He explained that Anita had been rushed away in an ambulance and that they were unsure if she was going to make it, in which case they had a crime scene, a murder enquiry on their hands. He was interrupted by his radio to advise that the two officers who had gone in the direction of the river had still no trace of their target. He informed them that he was on his way to join the pursuit.

'But I need to go too, Officer,' Shannon stated.

'Out of the question Madam, it is far too risky.'

'But he might kill her,' she protested.

'He might kill you Madam,' came the reply.

'He will talk to me, I know that, and I promise I won't hold you back,' she persisted. 'Besides I have been here before, I will be able to lead you to where we should be heading,' she begged.

'In that case I am coming too,' Steve said.

226

'And me,' Gerry repeated.

After some debate Steve, Shannon and the officer set off leaving Gregg, Gerry and the remaining policeman to wait behind.

Upon reaching the water, Shannon explained the path and they managed to wade through the river quickly before proceeding their ascent at a steady pace. After a good fifteen minutes of uphill running, they slowed their pace, all the time scanning and listening for any sight or sound which would alert them to the whereabouts of Cara or Pete. Shannon could not believe what was happening. She hoped that he would give himself up and that above all no one else got hurt. She wondered how he would react to her showing up and did not anticipate that it was going to be easy. Pete had not budged in twenty minutes, but he slowly stood up and aimed his torch all around the field. There was nothing unusual however and he decided that he would retrace his steps and make sure that he had not missed something or more importantly someone. He knew the place inside out so felt sure that if she were hiding, he would find her.

'Cara, where are you?' he shouted.

'Cara, time to come out and play,

Come on Cara bara, make my day,

Come on Cara Cara, what do you say?'

He started to whistle as he walked along singing all sorts of silly songs before launching into the Jaws theme tune.

'Come on Cara, you can come out now,

Silly cow

Oh, come on Cara bara

I'll bring you home tomorra'.

It was the evil laugh Cara heard. He was close, too close, dangerously close. He had obviously retrieved his steps. She was ridiculously frightened and her cheeks were drenched with sweat and tears. When she heard him singing, she realised that he had totally flipped. God knows what he would do to her when he found her.

She could not help herself. She was so hysterical that a deep cry of despair escaped her throat followed by an intake of breath so sharp and so heavy that she immediately panicked. Her heart was racing and could feel stabbing pains deep in her chest as she struggled to breathe. The sudden flash of the torch in her face blinded her and she immediately jumped up but was sent sprawling to the ground by an unexpected blow to the head. Help had not arrived. Hell had grabbed her with no warning and no mercy. This was it!!

'What are you going to do with me?' she squeaked.

He did not respond. He started humming the Jaws sound track again and she blanched, so overcome by dread that no words would follow. It was as if he was someone else. His eyes were wild and glazed over and he had a look of madness.

Continuing to hum, he took out his knife and calmly wiped the blade on his top.

'This gets so dusty if you do not look after it. But you know, it does what it is meant to,' he said softly. 'There is actually no safe place to stab someone. I could go for the heart; you would lose all your blood in about a minute. If I stab you just in the right place, say for example, your leg – if I score an artery, well you would likely die, out here you would die and then no one would find you, no human anyway…there are plenty of animals though.'

'Please don't hurt me,' she begged.

'I bought this a few years ago, saw it in a shop and thought,' Wow, this might come in handy sometime….' he cackled. That same horrible cackle she had heard before. Funny how she hadn't really noticed it previously or was it that she was so caught up in the throes of romance that she had subconsciously chosen to ignore it. It was deadly sinister.

'The police are on the way,' she mumbled.

'Is that right?' he smiled, sarcastically, still polishing the knife like it was a piece of fine glass.

God, how she hated that smirk. Was it always there too? Was that another thing she had chosen to ignore?

'Yes, they are on the way,' she stuttered.

'Well, well, well, is the cortege on its way too to pick you up?' he cackled again.

Cara screwed up her face, before looking at him gravely.

'Why are you doing this? Why are you saying things like that?' she wailed.

'What?' 'You're the one saying that the cops are on the way,' he roared.

'The p p police... they are going to be here any minute,' she wept.

'My, but you have a fine imagination my girl, did you find a phone out here, did you? Was there a phone box in the middle of one of the fields?' he mocked.

'I have two phones,' she declared.

'What?' 'What do you mean?' he screeched.

'My work phone, I've always had two, you took one, but I still have the other,' she said, immediately recognising her mistake.

'Now you have made me cross Cara, I am not nice when I am cross, I tend to find it difficult somewhat to control myself and you have upset me now,' he spat.

His face was so close she could feel his stale breath on her face, and it reeked of whiskey. Normally she would have been fine with him so close but not anymore. She backed away slowly. She felt repulsed.

'There's nowhere for you to go Cara,' he growled.

'Just let me go, if you have an ounce of compassion in your body, let me go now,' she sobbed.

'I think we've got past the compassion phase,' he retorted, grabbing her bag and pulling out her mobile. He immediately read her messages, received and sent, before hurling the phone on the ground, and standing on it. He looked at her now and frowned. 'You have put me in an awkward position, you see initially I thought you were a bit of a tart, all caked in make up with your tight, provocative clothes. But given your persistence, I agreed to see you again and you proved me wrong. You were far more intelligent than I gave you credit for and tonight you used your head. But now your time is running out,' he stated sharply.

Cara immediately shifted her position and attempted to stand but she was knocked to the ground as swiftly as before. It was then she noticed the gleam of the knife protruding again from his coat pocket and her face became wracked with fear. Fear, so clear to see on her face, that he detected it immediately and following the direction of her eyes quickly flicked it out again and held the blade menacingly to her throat.

'Now Cara, dearest Cara, do not try that again, do not move one centimetre or you might find yourself at the gates of heaven sooner than you think.'

Cara could not speak, never mind reply. She only had to look into his eyes to know that he meant every single word. She was completely paralysed with terror. She could feel the blade against her skin, and she almost wanted him to finish her off, to stop the panic which was rising in every core of her being. She did not know what to do, whether to try and reason with him or be quiet, but she decided to keep her lips tightly sealed. It seemed the safer option for now. Besides, she was desperately trying not to vomit again as she knew how he had reacted earlier and there could well be consequences this time if she didn't manage to control it. His eyes were so glazed, expressionless, as if he was in another world. He looked so cold and detached. She wondered if he had smoked something. She knew he enjoyed the odd joint. Perhaps this would explain his reactions. Maybe he needed help. Maybe he had taken something stronger and was on a trip. There had to be an explanation for his crazy behaviour.

'All this time and only now I really know who you are?' he snarled.

She looked at him but still she said nothing.

'Gemma's sister, Gemma, Shannon's stepmother,' he shouted.

Cara looked at him blankly. She couldn't work out what Shannon had to do with this. Did he know her? How was that possible? Her mind started to twist and turn as she tried to comprehend what he was saying. She looked at him blankly, tears flowing freely down her cheeks.

'Can you imagine what it was like, to discover that connection?' he yelled, pointing his finger at her accusingly.

She stared back at him, her eyes like saucers, the knife still held firmly in place. One wrong move, one wrong word and she was a goner.

'All these years, it was Shannon, always Shannon,' he murmured.

It was as if for a second he was far away, and his face softened for a moment as he allowed her image to take over his imagination.

Cara could not believe what she was hearing but desperately tried not to show any reaction to his words. It could prove fatal. Surprisingly, he released his hold on the knife and began pacing once more, up and down. Cara knew it was pointless to run. Maybe the police were near now. But what if they weren't? Could she take the risk? She spotted his torch and sneaked it behind her back. He was ranting and raving again now, talking in riddles that were impossible to understand. She decided to take her chance and leg it. She started to scream as loud as she could muster, piercing, blood-curdling screams which she prayed someone would hear. She had only managed a few yards before she felt her legs collapse beneath her as the full force of his foot sent her headfirst into the soggy earth.

That was followed by a searing pain in the back of her leg which she quickly knew was a stab wound. She looked up at him, stunned and confused, barely able to speak such was the pain. As blood started to gush from the wound, she dropped the torch before collapsing on the ground in fits of sobs, terror and total frustration.

'Pete, please don't. I.. I am pregnant, do you hear? I am pregnant, Pete, I have been feeling so sick, I don't know how it happened," she gasped.

He stared at her and stumbled backwards, a look of sheer dismay spreading all over his face. Suddenly a shout from the distance stole his attention and he swung around, his eyes darting crazily from Cara across the black landscape.

'Pete, Pete, can you hear me?' a voice called from the darkness.

He looked up. Had he heard right? He listened again. His mind was in turmoil.

She's pregnant, how could she be pregnant? Was it his? Who was calling his name?

'Pete, Pete, are you there?' He looked up, wondering if his mind was playing tricks on him. It sounded like Shannon. Was it her? Had she come?

'Shannon?' he roared. 'Shannon, is that you?'

He was confused, he stared at Cara lying on the ground, dazed and bleeding and then seized the torch back and shone it into the distance. What was going on? Had he gone mad altogether? Was he hearing voices in his head?

'Pete, Pete,' the voice shouted again.

No, his mind was not deceiving him. The voice was faint, but it sounded so much like her. He lifted the knife and wiped it clean before carefully inserting it in his coat pocket. Cara moaned quietly. She was watching him but knew there was nothing she could do. Her leg was aching, and she tried to curb the bleeding by wrapping her coat over the wound. She had to be quiet or she felt sure he would finish her off completely. If Shannon was here, then she would not be alone. Help must be near at hand! He was muttering as he looked around and scanned the countryside. He started to retrace his steps hoping to hear the voice again and suddenly he could see the outline of a person approach. He made his way slowly towards the figure, his heart bursting with both joy and trepidation. She had come. She was here. This was as unexpected as it was delightful.

'Pete, is that you?' came the voice again, confirming without doubt that it was indeed her.

'Yes, Shannon, it is me,' he said.

'Pete, are you okay?' she whispered.

As he approached her, he just wanted to pick her up in his arms and hold on to her forever, but he knew that all was not right. They were close now, both shining the light of their torches at one another. He wanted to run to her, but he could tell she was nervous and frightened.

'Pete, come with me. It is time to sort this out. Come back to the cottage and we will have a drink and discuss things.'

'There is nothing to discuss Shannon. All this was for you. Did you not know how much I loved you?' he asked now.

'No Pete, I had no idea,' she said softly, running her hands through her dark hair, which was blowing softly over her face.

She looked so vulnerable and beautiful standing there that he just wanted to weep. But he was angry too and frustrated.

'Steve was never good enough for you. He was a thorn in my side,' he shouted. 'I had to get him out of the picture.'

'You and I, we are good together, we can have a good life, we can get married, have kids, live here at the cottage. I have been working so hard to make it a home for us,' he said, but his voice was tinged with anger.

'The cottage is wonderful Pete, truly it is. Let's just get back there and then we can talk,' she whispered.

Suddenly his mood changed again.

'Did you come with the police?' he shouted.

'No, I did not, I came in the car,' she replied, knowing that she had deliberately misinterpreted his question.

'You're lying to me Shannon. Why are you lying to me?' he barked.

'I am not lying. Why would I lie to you?' she demanded.

'I don't know, you have lied to me a lot recently. You did not even tell me about the baby?' he accused.

Suddenly, a loud wail floated through the air and Shannon jumped back in alarm.

'What was that?' she asked.

'Probably a wild animal,' he suggested coldly.

The wail came again and there was no doubt that it came from a person, a person who sounded deeply anguished.

Shannon started to run towards the direction it came from, but Pete was on her in a flash and wrestled her to the ground. Then he pinned her hands behind her back and knelt over her.

'I am sorry about that Shannon, I didn't mean to hurt you...we can have it all, you and I, we can be happy. I love you, I always have,' he smiled. 'We belong together,' he whispered gently, holding her face in both his hands.

'I know we can Pete,' she agreed, smiling at him.

He stood up then and looked down on her tenderly. She did not budge, nor did she take her eyes away from his. She knew that to glance around would immediately alert him to the fact that they were not alone out here. She sensed that the wailing had come from Cara and that she was hurt and petrified, but she kept her eyes fixed firmly on Pete, the man she had considered her best friend.

'Shannon, I have been in love with you for as long as I can remember. Ever since those days when we were young and carefree. You had so much spirit and passion about you, you just sucked me in with your joie de vivre and when I look at you it feels like nothing else in the world matters.'

'Pete, I love you as well. You're my friend,' she said.

'Friend? I don't want to be your friend,' he yelled, his face forming a deep scowl.

'Well, I want to be your friend,' she said softly, looking him straight in the eyes.

'What about Steve? Have you seen him?' he barked.

'Why bring him into this?' It's not about him,' she whispered.

'You have seen him, haven't you? He has wormed his way back in, hasn't he? Where is he? Is he here? Have you brought that bastard here?' he roared.

He did a 360° turn, his eyes roving wildly across the fields. He stared at her accusingly, his hand reaching into his pocket and producing the knife, which was still slightly smeared with blood, Cara's blood.

'Where are you McCartan, you prick? Show your face you coward,' he roared into the nothingness.

There was no reply, no sound, nothing......

'Come on McCartan, you think you are going to be with her?'

He pounced on Shannon again and dragged her to her feet. He put the knife to her back, one arm gripped around her neck, all the while doing 360° turns.

'If I can't have her nobody will, do you hear me Mc Cartan?' he hollered.

'What are you doing Pete? Let me go,' Shannon cried. She was trying to stay calm, but it was exceptionally difficult with a blade held against her spine.

'Look into my eyes Pete, look at me, if you ever loved me why would you do this?' she sobbed.

He swung her around to face him and he saw the look of pure terror in her eyes. He dropped the knife to his side and looked at her angelic face and murmured,

'It is because I love you so much that I am doing this. All I want is the best for you,' he said.

But then a noise not far away seized his attention. He marched swiftly towards the spot where he had left Cara, but she was no longer there, just flattened grass from where she had been. He realised that help had indeed arrived which was further confirmed by the sound of a helicopter whirring overhead no doubt trying to pinpoint a safe place to land. He sensed a lot of activity around and quickly pushed Shannon to the ground before bolting as fast as he could from the scene. He could hear shouting from behind but did not look back. He just kept sprinting. He needed to get away. No doubt search teams would be deposited into this area quickly, so he had to get as far away as possible. There were not enough men to find him as things stood but that was a problem they could easily cope with. He knew the area better than anyone so that was an advantage and he also knew that he could easily run for miles, but it was important to not overdo it. He could not burn himself out too soon, particularly as he had no fluid in his body. The fact that he had been heavily drinking would not help.

He could hear the helicopter coming in to land and sooner rather than later this area would be swamped with police. It could not end like this. He knew the helicopter would take Cara away and then it would be him and them. They would shoot if necessary or perhaps use a taser gun. He could not be caught.

31

He would spend the rest of his life behind bars for murder, attempted murder. He was not sure if Anita had survived or not. He knew that there had always been suspicion hanging over him as regards his parents but without evidence the nosy people of the village had to accept he was innocent. As he was running, he recalled the day that his parents had died. He had been pottering around in the shed all morning with an old record player he had found in a charity shop. He had been taking it apart hoping to get it up and running again. It had been raining torrentially and had been doing so for several days and he could not comprehend his parents' logic when they popped their heads around the door of the hut and said they were going down to have a look at the river. Both had raincoats on and welly boots. The banks of the river had burst and they were anxious as the water was starting to flood the field. All the crops that his dad had spent years growing were about to be destroyed. Much worse than that, however, was that with the rate the water was flowing into the field there was every possibility it could reach the cottage and cause irreparable damage. That had always been a huge worry for them even when they had first purchased the property. However, the previous owners had assured them that the likelihood of the river bursting its banks was low and they had proceeded with the sale, despite their worries. After about fifteen minutes, Pete was heading into the main house to get something when he heard his dad shouting frantically. Knowing that they had headed off down the field, he raced outside to see what was happening. He glimpsed the back of his dad wading through the river but there was no sign of his mum. He had sprinted towards them in time to see his mum being hurled along by the fast-moving waters. It looked like she had fallen in, and the weight of her welly boots would not have assisted her chances of getting out. Before he could blink, his dad had jumped in after her, but the current seized hold of him too. It was still pouring down and highly dangerous, but Pete did not help. He could have saved his mum or at least made a good attempt. He might have been able to catch her and haul her out, but he didn't even try. He just watched as she was carried further and further down river. At one point, his father managed to grab hold of some rushes by the river verge, but the water was quick to reclaim him. Pete would never forget the expression of helplessness on his face but still he stared on impassively. He may not have been able to help his mum, but he could have got to his dad on time. His mum suffered from ill health, but his father was strong and athletic. It just proved how strong the current was that day that his dad couldn't make it out. They had never wanted him anyway. It was his belief that they had lost the child they really wanted, the little girl who was born five years before him. Her name was Ella and after years and years of trying for a baby, their dreams finally came true when she arrived, but their happiness was not to last and little Ella had died when she was just nine months old. It was a cot death, which was unexplained and unexpected. He did not know for a long time that he had a sister. His parents had never got over her and he always felt insignificant. As he walked away from the river, he wondered had they ever loved him. He felt like he was always second best, playing second fiddle to a ghost. He had simply returned to the shed and hunted for a stylis for the record player, he drank a few beers and then ventured back to the river but there was no sign of parent. They were long gone, swallowed up by the vicious torrents of the river that they had loved so much. His father's welly boots were bobbing around, in the muddy, marshy waters and his mother's blue raincoat caught up in the spikey rushes. He had phoned the police and waited. Emergency services came quickly and after some time retrieved the bodies some distance away.

His parents were placed in body bags and taken away as he was interrogated by police as to what had taken place. Next his mind drifted to what Cara had said. Was it possible that she was pregnant? They had been careful but sometimes accidents did happen. Was she just saying that so he would show her mercy or was it true? He had always imagined himself as a father but not this way, not with this woman. He stepped up his pace now, his heartrate beating fast in his chest, his underarms and back saturated with sweat. It took him another fifteen minutes before he reached his old tree hut, the one he had built when he was a child. It had taken him months to put it together, but it was well worth it for the peace and quiet it allowed him when he was younger. He had called it his 'hide out.'

It was strange how solid it still looked despite the years and the weather conditions that it had endured. He stopped and looked around him, in a few hours it would be dawn and he had to ensure that he got as far away as possible during these last hours of darkness. He immediately retrieved what he was looking for, his spare torch, a little key, and a shovel. He moved away from the hut towards another tree which stood on its own, its leaves shaking gently in the wind and he started to dig. It did not take him long to find his safe, covered in dirt and mud. He inserted the key and quickly flicked it open, fetching his passport and wads of cash and then he re buried the safe. He raced back to the hut again and found his change of clothes, a pair of blue jeans and a sweatshirt. He praised himself for having buried the money. He had found it after his parents had died under the mattress of their bed. The amount was substantial and he had not wanted to draw attention to himself by banking it. And so, he had hidden it here, for a rainy day. Finally, he retrieved his old mountain bike which was not the most modern in the world but if it could take the weight of his legs for a little while, then it would be worth it. He had pumped the tyres a few weeks previous and fixed the lights, so he was good to go. He then finished off a bottle of vodka that he had left there at a different time, he had no mixer, so he drank it straight to try and calm his nerves before mounting the old bike and speeding off across the fields. He would return to the road soon enough, but he would have to cycle on the grass for a while first and take the old disused route back to the cottage. He would pack a small case and be on his way. He would cross the border and disappear for a while until things settled down, that was his plan, his only option. He had waited for Shannon for years; he could wait a few more.

Meanwhile a helicopter had landed, and Cara had been lifted inside on a stretcher. She received first aid and her wound was dressed but it was felt that she should be checked over as a precaution. She was pale and sobbing as she informed Shannon that she was sure she was pregnant. She said that she could not understand how it had happened because she was religious about taking her pill, but it seemed that perhaps she had missed one or been sick and the tablet had not worked. She had done a test before she had come down here and it was positive. Much as she did not want a baby, certainly not at this period of time in her life and certainly not now with the man who had just threatened to kill her, she was very conscious that it was not the baby's fault and needed to ensure that everything was okay. Gregory and Gerry decided to accompany her to the hospital both anxious to make sure she was okay and if Anita, who was already there, had survived her ordeal. Shannon looked desolate and kept apologising to Cara and crying that it was all her fault, but Cara told her not to be daft, that Pete was just plain crazy.

As the helicopter lifted off the ground, Steve and Shannon remained behind, both crushed at what had just taken place. They decided to return to the cottage as they had to pick up the car in order to get to the hospital and see what was happening there. It took about twenty minutes for them to get back and on arrival they were shown the study. Shannon was informed by the police that she should prepare herself before she stepped inside. There she was met by a scene that shocked her to the core. Photographs of her lined the room, comprising a sort of shrine. She was stunned that the walls were covered from top to bottom with images of her. She noticed several of her personal belongings which she thought she had mislaid. There was a jewellery box, a few books, some of her favourite CDs and DVDs – there were items of her clothing neatly stacked on the shelves including a pair of jeans, a few tops and even some underwear. She did not know what this meant but it seemed possible that Pete might have been devising a plan for her to live here, with or without her consent. Had he planned to kidnap her as he had done Anita? She was wiped out now, deeply traumatised by the night's events. Steve was especially attentive and very concerned for her emotional wellbeing. It had been a lot for her to take in. When her mobile rang, he answered it and explained to Gemma what had happened. He informed her gently that Anita had been rushed to hospital and that Cara had been taken to the same one for treatment and that Gerry and Gregory had gone with her. He did not mention anything about Cara's pregnancy – that was up to Cara. They had all been shocked by her revelation but there was so much going on presently that they had not managed to absorb it completely yet. They had yet to hear word on Anita but were leaving immediately to go to the hospital and urged her to pray that everything would be alright. He reassured her that as soon as they knew anything, they would let her know straight away. A few minutes later, an exhausted Shannon and Steve left the cottage, escorted by the police to their car. When they arrived at the hospital, they were advised that Anita was in surgery and led to the waiting room where the others including Cara were waiting. Cara had been examined and hospital staff seemed satisfied that she was fit to be discharged. They had confirmed her pregnancy and carried out a scan. A heartbeat had been detected and whilst everything appeared fine, she was advised because of the trauma she had suffered that she should rest and not return to work for at least a month. It was hours before they were informed by the surgeon operating on Anita that the surgery had progressed well and they were hopeful. She was sedated and it would be later that day before they would be able to assess her condition properly. She had suffered facial cuts from her fall which were superficial, but the main worry was that she had developed a blood clot in her brain which they had had to remove. They appeared confident that she would pull through. The psychological damage would probably take longer to fix. In the meantime, it would be necessary to remain vigilant and monitor her regularly. The next twenty fours would be critical.

Four weeks later, the whole clan of them had assembled for Steve and Shannon's housewarming party. They had seen no point in wasting any more time. Instead, after talking things over repeatedly they decided to try and rebuild the damage. Everything was back on track, except that there was no sign of Pete. Shannon and Steve were keen to move forwards and enjoy living together once more in Steve's new property. Anita, who was now on the mend, arrived arm in arm with Gregory. He had moved permanently over to Ireland whilst she was still in hospital and was there to support her through her recovery. She still suffered recurrent nightmares and was seeing a counsellor to help her talk through what she had experienced during her kidnap ordeal but all in all she was progressing steadily and was quite open about what had gone on during those few awful days and nights. Little baby Megan was doing great and Gerry and Gemma were very much the proud parents. Gemma had taken to motherhood like a duck to water and was displaying maternal feelings she never knew she had. She only hoped that Cara would eventually come to terms with her own pregnancy. She was struggling both with who the father of her unborn baby was but also the fact that she would be going it alone. Shannon and Gemma had developed a fabulous bond and were the best of friends. Mel was still the ever-supportive friend to Shannon even though they were both so busy that it took weeks of organising for them to meet up together. However, they both knew that the other was only a phone call away and despite not seeing each other so much, they knew that they were friends for life. It was funny how Mel had always believed Pete to be head over heels for Shannon, but Shannon had always dismissed it as nonsense. Mel had felt thoroughly guilty afterwards about trying to push them together, but Shannon told her to forget it because neither of them could ever have known what lay ahead or what his plans were. Mel's love life was going swimmingly well, she was completely loved up with Tom and he had proposed to her on her birthday with a beautiful, white diamond solitaire. The wedding would take place in the Autumn, with Shannon as chief bridesmaid.

The police had issued a warrant for the arrest of Pete McGlynn. He was wanted for abduction and kidnap, assault, false imprisonment and two counts of attempted murder. It seemed however that he had fled the country and whilst everyone was devastated that he had escaped, they hoped now that they would be left in peace.

243

However, it was hard to find total peace when they did not know where he was. Shannon still found it crazy that she had been so badly fooled. He had wrecked her relationship with Steve and committed so many atrocities that she wondered would she ever fully trust anyone again. She hated him for he had committed the ultimate betrayal. As they all sat around the table toasting each others health and happiness, she wondered briefly what he was doing now. The answer to that question came two months later courtesy of the local police force. They had found a body. The badly decomposed remains had been discovered by a husband and wife out for a walk one evening. It was only with the use of DNA that the body was able to be identified. It seemed that the pike in the Fermanagh rivers were not fussy about what they dined on.

When the phone call came Shannon sank to the floor and wept. A mixture of emotions ran through her. Sadness that he had gone but then he had never been who she thought he was, relief that now she could look over her shoulder without fretting that she was being watched, anger that she had been betrayed by someone she truly loved like a brother, dismayed that his body had been reduced to nothing. However, the overriding emotion was relief that she no longer would have to worry about herself or those close to her. She could move on now safely. She insisted on going to the funeral – she had to go. She needed closure. There was only a scattering of mourners. Who knew if they were mourners or if they just attended based on some sort of warped curiosity? After the short service, she linked arms with Steve, and they walked slowly behind the coffin towards the burial plot. As the coffin was lowered into the ground Shannon heard a deep gasp. She turned around to see a tearful and pregnant Cara standing beside Anita, both being supported by Richard. It seemed they all had the same idea. They were all seeking their own kind of closure.

Printed in Great Britain
by Amazon